We clink bottles again. I lean back on the hood of the car and look at the clear sky above us. The stars are brighter in Mattoon than anywhere else in the world.

"You probably won't get many nights like this in Champaign," I say. "And I doubt the campus cops are as big pushovers as Lt. Grierson."

"That's probably true," Jessica says, leaning back next to me. "It does seem a little easier to escape here."

What Jessica's escaping from, I have no idea.

I glance over at her, and for a moment I want to say the things I haven't told anyone. About how I'm feeling about college. About how I'm afraid to leave my friends. I want to tell her how I am king here, and there I would be just another faceless nobody. I want to tell her that college seems to have ruined my brother and I'm afraid it will ruin me.

But I don't. I look at the stars and say, "Yep." And then Amy pukes again, and this night fades into the rest of them.

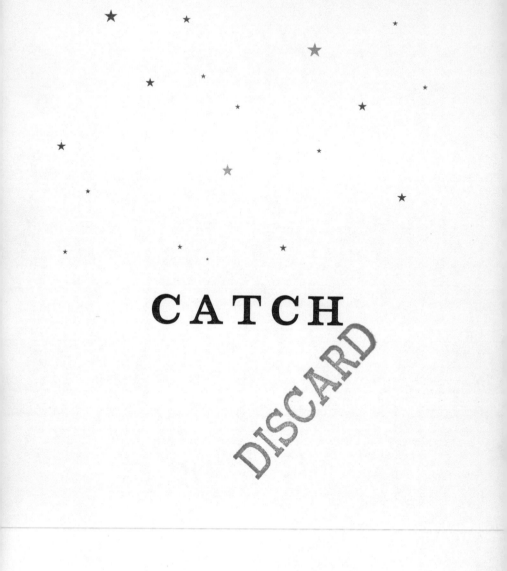

CATCH

CATCH

A NOVEL BY

WILL LEITCH

razOr
bill

Catch

RAZORBILL

Published by the Penguin Group
Penguin Young Readers Group
345 Hudson Street, New York, New York 10014, U.S.A.
Penguin Group (USA) Inc., 375 Hudson Street, New York, New York 10014, U.S.A.
Penguin Group (Canada), 90 Eglinton Avenue, Suite 700, Toronto, Ontario,
Canada M4P 2Y3 (a division of Pearson Penguin Canada Inc.)
Penguin Books Ltd, 80 Strand, London WC2R 0RL, England
Penguin Ireland, 25 St Stephen's Green, Dublin 2, Ireland
(a division of Penguin Books Ltd)
Penguin Group (Australia), 250 Camberwell Road, Camberwell,
Victoria 3124, Australia (a division of Pearson Australia Group Pty Ltd)
Penguin Books India Pvt Ltd, 11 Community Centre, Panchsheel Park,
New Delhi - 110 017, India
Penguin Group (NZ), Cnr Airborne and Rosedale Roads, Albany, Auckland 1310,
New Zealand (a division of Pearson New Zealand Ltd)
Penguin Books (South Africa) (Pty) Ltd, 24 Sturdee Avenue, Rosebank,
Johannesburg 2196, South Africa

Penguin Books Ltd, Registered Offices: 80 Strand, London WC2R 0RL, England

10 9 8 7 6 5 4 3 2

Interior design by Christopher Grassi

Library of Congress Cataloging-in-Publication Data

Leitch, Will.
  Catch / by Will Leitch.
    p. cm.
  Summary: Teenager Tim Temples must decide if he wants to leave his comfortable life
in a small town and go to college.
  ISBN 1-59514-069-7
  I. Title.
  PZ7.L537215Cat 2005
  [Fic]—dc22

                                                                    2005008146
Printed in the United States of America

To Bryan, Sally, and Jill, and to Mattoon,
which will always run through my veins

CATCH

CATCH

GRADUATION

1.

I am sitting here, in the dumb graduation gown, which covers a pair of boxer shorts I got from Millikin University's baseball camp and a T-shirt with a picture of Eric Cartman on it. This is supposed to be the most important day of my life, and, save for a thin black sheet of rayon that's making my arms itch, I'm clothed in something that my mom would yell at me for wearing at the breakfast table. You'll never convince me this day is all that important; high school is so easy. This is no great achievement; I'd have to be a complete moron not to actually graduate. Only the burnouts, druggies, and ditzy cheerleaders too stupid to use birth control don't graduate from high school. All you really have to do is show up, and you don't even have to do that all that often.

Nevertheless, Jessica is standing up there, wearing her valedictorian ribbons, looking kind of cute in a goody-goody, "This book is three days overdue" type of way, trying to convince us that this whole charade *matters*. God bless her.

Jessica grew up just down the road from us, and since my mom felt sorry when Jessica's mom died, we hung out a lot when we were kids. I'd say the odds are excellent that the only times she ever got in trouble were my fault. Once when we were hanging out by the creek and I talked her into licking a frog I'd captured. It crapped in her mouth, and she ran home crying. We both got in trouble for that one.

As we got older, Jessica's interests (books, studying, unicorns) diverged from mine (breasts, baseball, breasts), so we didn't see each other much anymore, though we were in some of same honors classes. But she still lives down the road, and we're still friendly—still say howdy when we pass each other in the halls, even though we have nothing in particular to offer each other. Mom's all excited that Jessica will be at college with me this fall. I can't imagine why. At that big campus in Champaign, she'll become just another face, one that nods when I pass the library on the way to the gym.

Jessica is invested in a future that I want to avoid. She really *believes* that straight A's and hard work will rocket her right to the top. It's nice. It's sweet. It's idiotic.

And now she's telling us all about it.

"Graduates of Mattoon High School class of 2005, what we're doing now is irrelevant; it's just prologue to the real story, the lives we'll make for ourselves out there

4

in the real world. Look at the person in front of you. In fifteen years, you'll be lucky to remember their name. We have so much to learn and so much to see. It's an incredible journey."

This is very easy for Jessica to say, considering the person sitting in front of her is not Staci Stallings, who has hiked up her gown so far that I can see her purple thong—with a tiny cloth rose attached—at the top of her thigh. Staci knows I'm sitting behind her. Staci is not thinking about the future and the real world. She's thinking about what we did last month, at Sydney McKenzie's party, in the back of my Blazer. She's thinking we're going to do it again tonight. I'm thinking the same thing. There's your incredible journey, Jessica: a night with Staci Stallings. . . .

"We can no longer plunge ahead recklessly into the moment. We must think about where it's all going to lead."

Staci turns and smiles, her glossy lips curling into a wicked grin.

I love ya, Jessica, you're sweet . . . but I'm going to have to go with Staci on this one.

2.

The last five minutes of Jessica's speech, which runs about ten minutes too long anyway, are lost on me. They could have been in pig Latin, as far as I know. Wasn't paying the least bit attention.

The Horsemen have a hand buzzer. As usual, Jeff's the one who starts it.

I can't come up with a better way to put this: The Horsemen are my posse. LeBron James has a posse; Jay-Z has a posse; heck, I bet even Jeff Probst has a posse; The Four Horsemen are mine: Andy, Shad, Denny, and Jeff. Where I go, they're with me. They have my back. Andy and Shad are actually kind of dim; all they really care about are their trucks and the start of hunting season. (Shad seriously wears that hideous orange hunting cap when we go out drinking.) They're meaty guys, real thick around the neck, but they're only intimidating to look at; in reality they're total pushovers. Denny—the only sucker other than me who's going to go to college, at Lake Land Community, here in Mattoon—wears glasses, is the scorekeeper for the MHS baseball team, and has been dating the same girl, Kristen, since junior high. I have no idea why he hangs out with us, or why we hang out with him, but we do. Maybe it's because he helps keep Jeff in check. Jeff is our troublemaker, the smart mouth who's always getting us into fights with guys from Charleston.

Sometimes his jokes go a little far. I mean, it's one thing to spray a fire extinguisher into nerdy William Dooley's locker; it's another thing all together to do it while Dooley was locked inside.

This latest joke's a great one, though. Jeff, who was oddly quiet through most of Jessica's speech, has now started goosing everyone in the row ahead of us with his hand buzzer. Fat Henry Chinski, with his acne-ravaged face, actually *squealed* a second ago, causing us all to break into a chorus of *oink-oink-oinks*. Jessica could be screaming about how she's going to assassinate the president, and none of the 2005 class of Mattoon High School would notice. Denny's grimacing, half embarrassed; Principal Cadigan is trying to figure out what is going on; and most of the audience is in hysterics. Even Jessica noticed; I just saw her, flustered, read from the wrong page of her endless speech, forcing her to stop, apologize, and start again. She catches my eye, and I give her a "Hey, whaddya gonna do? It's Jeff" shrug. To my surprise, she tries to hide a grin.

3.

"From all of us here at Mattoon High School, we say congratulations, graduates!"

Everybody throws their hats in their air. Jeff chucks his straight up too. In the roof of his cap, he has taped an old Discman he didn't want anymore. It plummets to the earth, smacking Chinski on the forehead. He yelps and falls over. Everybody laughs. Nice shot.

We all stand around as they play the processional music, but none of us line up and exit like we're supposed to. Jeff hands me a flask—"Let's get this party started early," he says—and I slug back some Southern Comfort, which is nasty, honestly.

No one wants to stay here long. My parents are hosting a party back at the house tonight. Everyone marvels at how cool my parents are, and I have to say, they are. I'm allowed to bring back anyone who wants to come. The parents will be grilling and chaperoning, with five kegs and a bunch of tents set up in the field behind the backyard. We can all drink and stay up all night, as long as we promise not to drive home and that there will be no drugs, which is fine, since pot just makes me want to go to sleep. It's going to be a blast.

And speaking of the parents, here they come. I think there might be a race to see who can come over and make me hug them first. Not surprisingly, Mom wins. Also not surprising: she's crying. My mother is so strange. As an emergency room nurse, she can see some guy with his guts hanging out of his ear and not blink an eye. But if Lily and Holden break up on *As the World Turns*, she's a puddle of goo. The black mascara that's running all over her face makes her kind of look like Zorro.

"Oh, Tim, it was beautiful, I'm so proud of you, this is so special, what a wonderful day, my little boy all grown up, you look so handsome, Bryan, doesn't he look so handsome?"

My dad, as usual, is wearing his leather St. Louis Cardinals jacket, over an ugly suit jacket he hates wearing. He shakes my hand, mutters, "Congratulations," and then comes the usual joke: "Jesus, Tim, look what you've done to your mother."

Dad can never go anywhere in town without other fathers slapping him on the back and treating him like he's some sort of god. His picture is everywhere: he's the best baseball player this county ever saw. The only person ever to approach any of his hitting records was my brother, Doug. Who, come to think of it, isn't here.

Dad seems to be reading my mind. "Doug got caught up with some stuff in Champaign," he says. "He'll be at the party." Mom has gathered herself into some sense of composure and is, typically, asking about Jessica.

"Wasn't that the best speech? I cried through the whole thing," she says.

"Yeah, Mom." I nod. "It was awesome. Really touching."

Mom spies her daughter substitute and waves her over. Jessica approaches with her father. Mr. Danner is an economics professor at Eastern Illinois University in Charleston, and he always walks hunched over and nervous, as if he's being chased. He's about a foot shorter than my father, and Dad, playing along, likes to put him in playful headlocks and call him "Herb," even though his name is Charles. I don't think Charles likes this much. I don't think he likes any of us that much. But hey. We're bigger than he is.

Jessica looks like she's being lit up from all directions and floating across the gymnasium floor. She hugs me. She squeezes harder than I knew she could.

"Tim! Isn't this so *great?!* What did you think of the speech?"

Staci's thong enters my brain. "It was great." *Purple.* "Inspirational." *With a rose.* "You must have worked a long time on that." *Staci has a tongue ring.*

"I bet she works a long time on a lot of things." I turn, and it's Jeff, of course. Jeff is never as witty as he thinks he is. "Isn't that right, Mr. Danner?" he says. Jessica's dad

9

looks uncomfortable; he's is the only dad on earth some punk kid could say something like that around. My dad, on the other hand, pops Jeff on the back of the head.

Jessica, surprisingly, is unfazed. "Jessica, it was a lovely speech," my mother says. "Charles, you must be very proud." Mr. Danner stands there and shuffles, bringing his head up ever so slightly before looking back down at his feet. He must have gotten the crap beaten out of him all the time in high school.

"So." Mom turns to Jessica and places her hands on her shoulders. "Will we see you at our little gathering tonight?"

Without thinking, I interject, "Mom, I don't think this is Jessica's type of party." Mom has been wanting me to marry Jessica since we were four. It's very annoying.

Jessica gives me a lopsided smile. "Don't be so sure, Temples," she says. "I might surprise you."

Jeff starts to say something, but my dad hits him again.

4.

I love bonfires. Something about a bonfire makes you feel like a party is teetering on the edge of chaos, like one slipup here or there could send the whole bash careering dangerously out of control. Last year, at a party at Keith Ames's place in Greenup, the Horsemen threw full containers of Off! into the raging flame. The aerosol can exploded and flew through the window of Keith's parents' shed. He was pretty pissed about that.

In the glow of my own bonfire, I absentmindedly throw cold hot dogs at Andy and Shad while finishing off my third cup of beer. I drink fast and with purpose; the Temples men's disposition allows them to handle lots of alcohol without getting too drunk. It's just starting to grow dark, and everything is under control—so far.

I walk inside to grab some cheese. A group of parents is sitting around a huge card table, playing poker. Mom is the dutiful host, scurrying around the room, fooling herself into thinking she has some control over fifty high school kids in the backyard doing keg stands. Dad is at his spot at the head of the table, as always, holding court.

"I remember playing with Ozzie Smith in Walla Walla," he starts. I groan. I have heard this story so often that I can probably tell it better than Dad. So here it is: Dad was drafted out of high school by the San Diego Padres in 1978, where he signed a then-substantial $10,000 bonus. He drifted around the minors for a few years but never came close to the major leagues. He blames this on a "lingering groin injury."

"Ozzie was a little guy, couldn't hit much back then, but man, he was so goddamned fast," Dad says. Everyone has put their cards down and is staring in rapture. Everybody here reveres Ozzie Smith and the Cardinals, almost as much as they do my dad. When the apostles told the story of the birth of Christ, listeners must have looked at them the same way everyone's looking at Dad right now. "We were playing a scrimmage, and he put a bunt down the third base line. I jumped out of my crouch and just *pounced* on the ball. I thought I had the chance to get him. I fired it to first—and the bastard was already standing on second base." He pauses dramatically as everyone gasps.

If this story were true, not only would Ozzie Smith be in the Hall of Fame, he would also have won about twenty Olympic medals. "Right then, the bigs seemed real far away," Dad says. "Thankfully, after the groin finished me off, my girl Sally was still waiting for me back here." Everyone looks at my mom, and she gives the same distracted "yep, that's me" look she's been giving during that story for eighteen years. Yet she always smiles through it, and so do I.

The phone rings. Mom answers, and before she even says hello, her face brightens. "Tim, it's *Jessica*." I smile in the same placating way everyone smiles for their mom and take the phone.

"Hi, Tim. I'm sorry, I didn't mean to take you away from your party. I just wanted to tell your mom I couldn't make it tonight."

"That's all right. Thanks for calling."

"Aren't you excited? Graduation! We're gonna be at college so soon."

"Yeah. It'll be—"

I hear the engine rumbling from half a mile away. The car is a souped-up 1967 Camaro that I used to help Dad put together when I was about thirteen. It is the coolest car that has ever been even imagined by humankind. The backseat on that thing has probably seen more bras than Colin Farrell.

The party has arrived.

"Listen, Jessica, I gotta go." I hang up the phone. Doug is here.

5.

Everyone considers me some big-shot baseball player, and I'm good, don't get me wrong. I was the third all-conference Temples, and I can catch anything you can throw at me. But I never set any records, and nobody offered me any scholarships to play in college like they did for Doug.

Here is how my baseball career ended. We were playing Rantoul, a team we would usually destroy, in the sectional finals. We were up 6–5 in the bottom of the seventh. Josh Cross, our submarining closer, struck out the first two guys and walked the next. Their best hitter, some huge dumb buck farmer, smashed Josh's first pitch right down the third base line, past the diving Roger Dylan, whom I'd just motioned to play closer to the line (a command he ignored). Our left fielder picked up the ball, dropped it, picked it up, dropped it again. The runner on first flew past third and scored. Dumb Buck Farmer screamed into third around the time Dylan cut off the throw from left. The farmer rounded home, though his coach waved his arms for him to stop. He barreled down the line toward me. I caught the ball in plenty of time. He lowered his shoulder and plowed into me with a force I'd never felt before. It felt like my ribs were in one of those card-shuffling machines you see at riverboat casinos. All went black.

I opened my eyes. I saw Dumb Buck's foot hit home plate. Next to the plate: the ball. He'd knocked it loose. He was safe. Season, career, Temples legacy . . . over.

Doug never had a moment like that. Doug was the best at everything. Doug led us to the state finals, just like my dad. Doug would have held on to that ball.

6.

He pulls onto our front lawn, revs the engine a couple of times for good measure, and sits there, idling, for an unusually long time. A rap song is blaring; the grass shakes. We stand there, waiting, like when the rock band is a few minutes late coming onstage. Finally the engine shuts off, the rap song ends, and Doug steps out.

Two endless lines of pickup trucks parked the required three feet from each other lead up to our house, and Doug glides between them like a man preparing to be knighted.

The University of Illinois baseball season just ended, and I haven't seen Doug in a few months. He has grown a beard and is wearing a pair of aviator sunglasses. The last vestiges of sunlight pour over him; he is king.

He has a backpack slung over his shoulder as he walks slowly up to me. I cannot see his eyes behind the sunglasses. He's a few inches taller than me, always has been. He takes something out of his backpack: a CD. It's the 50 Cent record. I've never really liked rap, but suddenly, man, do I ever.

14

"Hey, way to go, dipshit. It's your big day. Got you a present." He hands me the CD and takes the full beer out of my hand. He downs it in two swigs. Jeff is standing next to me. Doug swipes his beer too and takes another big gulp.

My dad. "Hello, son. Took you long enough."

"Had a lot to take care of in Champaign," Doug grunts. "I can't stay. Just wanted to congratulate squirt here on actually not screwing up."

I laugh.

"Nice party," Doug says. "Keep the tail out of my room, would you?"

He comes over and kisses my mom and whispers something in her ear. She frowns quickly, then straightens herself. She hugs him and says, "All right, well, try to make it back for dinner tomorrow. We're having spareribs." He hands her the backpack, and she takes it inside.

He walks to me and pops me on the shoulder without saying a word. He then gets back in the Camaro, slams it into first, and spins out, leaving a considerable divot in the lawn.

I turn around, and Andy and Shad are both standing there with a beer in each hand. They talk over each other: "Uh, got you a beer, man." "Want another one, man?"

7.

I'm on about beer eight now, and even I'm starting to feel it. Mom has long since gone to bed, where she has locked up everybody's car keys, and all the tents have been set up. Dad and a few straggler parents are still playing poker.

15

Dad has cleaned everybody out, like he always does. I don't know why they bother playing with him.

Andy and Shad, predictably, have already passed out. It is amazing to me that such thick guys always punk out so early at parties. Denny and Kristen are making out in their tent. Jeff is standing next to me, smoking a cigarette. It's a smart place to stand. This is the time of the party when girls start swarming.

"So, you ready to get in some trouble this summer?" Jeff asks.

The Horsemen all work at the Kraft plant at the edge of town. After working nights after school for years, this summer they've been promoted to the day shift. Because I'm a Temples, I got the day shift too. It's a sweet gig of hauling boxes from the plant to the trucks out back, which means a ton of money and lots of late nights like this one. Ordinarily, when Jeff says the word *trouble*, it makes me nervous that one of us is going to end up in jail. But he's dead-on this time; I am definitely ready to get in some trouble.

He offers me a drag off his cigarette. I inhale and start gagging. I'm obviously drunker than I thought; I temporarily forgot that cigarettes make me sick. Jeff laughs the way he laughs, like the human race is his little petri dish with which to experiment in sinister ways.

"So, this is graduation," Jeff says. "Seems like the same old shit to me. Bunch of bombed idiots trying to find someone to lay."

"Yeah."

"How's that beer commercial go? 'It doesn't get any better than this.'"

I click his beer can with my own. "Cheers to that, dude."

8.

It doesn't take her long to find me. I'm chugging another beer, walking through the wreckage of the party, when I hear her call from a couple of tents over.

"Hey, Tim . . . you still have that hand buzzer?"

Staci. I walk over to her tent while guzzling the rest of my beer. I crouch down to peer inside the tent. My knees crack. Catching is a bitch on your knees.

She's lying there, wearing a black push-up bra. She has a tattoo of some indecipherable Chinese lettering on the inside of her upper thigh. And she's still wearing the thong, which is still purple and still has that little rose.

"I never asked you what that tattoo meant," I say.

"Why don't you come in here and take a closer look? I'll tell you all about it."

Like I said: Who needs college? I can continue my education right here.

JUNE

1.

Some people can't handle mornings. To these people, the act of waking up is an affront, an egregious bother, an impossible hassle. The look they give you when you try to rouse them is similar to the one they'd give you if you, say, pissed in their coffee. It doesn't even matter what time it is. If you didn't make them get up, they'd just lie there all day. No sleep is enough. I don't understand these people. Sleep is boring. Sleep is something I do because I have to, not because I want to. There's so much to do out there; sleep is *nothing*. Sleep is the absence of life. If all you want to do is sleep, man, you're wasting it all away.

So, as usual, I'm the first one up this morning, making coffee for Mom, Dad, and Doug. Doug's the worst at waking. One time, when we were kids, he actually hid under the bed so he could sleep longer. Mom called every neighbor she knew until, after she'd taken the day off of work, convinced he'd been abducted by some radical Mormons, the dog started licking his face. He got grounded right good that time.

Making coffee is immensely satisfying to me, because I don't drink it. The gratitude on people's faces when you hand them their morning coffee warms me; you're the guy with the syringe and tourniquet for the heroin addict. They *need* it. You're automatically on everybody's good side—which is where I like to be.

Mom's the first one up. She always looks like a mole rat before she has her coffee; she squints like you're on the other side of the room, even if you're standing right in front of her.

"*Thank* you, Tim."

"You're welcome, Mom. I spiked it with some Captain Morgan for you, as usual."

"Very funny."

Dad comes in next. My father's the only person I know who puts on Oakley sunglasses to read the paper. Then again, he doesn't actually read it. He just flips through the sports page, checking the Cardinals box score, scanning for sports scandals. He loves it when athletes get busted for something. There's a good one this morning. "Stupid Leonard Large got another DUI the other night," Dad cackles. "That's his third one this year. Hey, Leo . . . you're a *millionaire!* Hire a driver!" I hand him his coffee. "Thanks, Tim," he says. "So, you ready for your first day?"

I'm starting at the Kraft plant today. Doug, who seems to be living with us again, though no one has really explained

22

to me why, is working with Dad at the city parks department. They need the help. At the end of the summer, Mattoon is hosting its twentieth annual Bagelfest celebration.

Yep, twenty years ago this August, Lender's Bagels, those rubbery microwavable bagels, likely to be the lone survivors of a nuclear holocaust, moved their production plant to Mattoon. It was the largest infusion of jobs our sleepy burg had ever seen, so the mayor declared Mattoon the Bagel Capital of the World and started a yearly festival called Bagelfest. Once a year, the entire town heads to the square—more like a cul-de-sac, actually—and eats free bagels while riding bagel-themed rides, watching the Bagelfest parade, and voting on the Little Miss Bagelfest contest. One year my father was the grand marshal of the parade. He tossed bagels into the crowd, pegging Jessica's dad on the side of the head with one.

This year's Bagelfest is a very big deal. The grand marshal of the parade, all the way back from Hollywood, is Jacob Kuhns, the biggest star our town has ever produced. He was a few years ahead of Doug in high school and moved to Los Angeles to become an actor. He made a bunch of commercials, and his big break came this year, when he played a corpse on *CSI* (my mom screeched when we saw him; he had a big bullet hole in his head. Like every other woman in town, she thinks he's the hottest man alive). He's coming back for the biggest Bagelfest ever. The parks department is stretched to its breaking point, so Doug is helping Dad out. Though right now, he's refusing to unlock his door.

"Doug, get up! It's eight thirty!"

Dad pounds on the door repeatedly, but there's still no response. Mom looks down and shakes her head. "He's sure as hell not going to make me look like an idiot on his first day on the job, that's for damn sure," my dad growls. "Get your ass *up!*" More pounding. This is a lot more morning activity than anyone is used to. I'm glad I made the coffee.

Finally Doug opens the door and stumbles out. I've barely seen him in the week that he has been home, and he looks terrible. His hair is shooting out in all directions, his eyes seem implanted in his cheeks somewhere, and his face has pillow creases on it. There's some dried drool caked into his weedy beard. He looks like the burnouts at the high school who spend their lunch hours smoking joints in the parking lot. "I'm up, I'm up, quit yelling, Christ," he mumbles. "Where's the coffee?"

2.

I arrive at the plant fifteen minutes early and am greeted by Chuck, who's going to be my supervisor. He's a disgustingly fat man, with his gut practically tucked into his shoes. (My dad refers to this affliction as "dunlap," as in, "His belly dunlap over his belt.") He has the same look a lot of adults in Mattoon have when they see me, like I'm some sort of rock star blessing them with my presence. Not that I'm arguing; it's an instant calling card. People fall all over me whenever I walk into a room, and I don't have to do a damn thing.

"Tim Temples, how ya doin', my boy?" He slaps me on the back and puts his arm around me, even though I've never met him. "You ready to get to work? Ain't nothin' more challenging here than facing those Rantoul boys. We're glad to have ya!" He's wearing a tan shirt, and even though the workday hasn't started yet, he already has large pit stains. His tie barely makes it down to mid-stomach.

"So, how's your dad doin'?" he says. "I haven't heard from him in a while. I called him the other night but haven't heard back yet."

Wonder why *that* is.

"So, kiddo, we're gonna put ya to work right good. Just sit tight, and I'll take ya over to meet Larry. You'll be workin' with him." Then he waddles off.

I mill around Chuck's office for a bit. It's covered in pictures of him with various Mattoon luminaries, including the mayor, Jacob Kuhns, and both my father and my brother. I'm in the picture too, though I'm about eleven and wearing an oversized catcher's mask. (The picture is signed in my dad's handwriting: *Keep swinging for the fences, Chuck!*) He has a row of bowling trophies prominently displayed. I pick one up. It says: CHUCK LEWIS. FIFTH PLACE. KRAFT. 1994. Behind it is a picture of his two fat children. They look like they freebase batter.

He has a St. Louis Cardinals calendar on his wall, from 1999, with pictures of Fernando Tatis and Willie McGee. A ticket stub from that season—a wholly unmemorable one in Cardinals history—is thumbtacked over Willie's face. That's sacrilege, as far as I'm concerned.

I really hope I don't have to spend much time with Chuck.

From behind me, an irritated female voice: "What are you doing in here? Who are you?"

I turn around and see her.

3.

She's smoking a cigarette, which, against every male instinct I have, is the first thing I notice. She's wearing a black tank top and tight black jeans that she must have crowbarred herself into. She has long black wavy hair that is almost certainly not her real color. Her face is round and looks slightly weathered.

She is, more than anything . . . *flush*. She is round and shapely. She is almost covered in clothing, but it seems like her flesh is everywhere, taunting me. Her neck looks so soft. Her breasts rise and fall out of her tank top as she breathes; my brother once described a girl like this as "looking like she's got a bear in there." Her *feet* are luscious, and I can't even see them. She looks tired but, let's face it, *hot*.

Man, could I do some damage to this girl.

I must have been thinking this for a beat too long because her face is getting harsher. "You're at my desk. Move."

I snap out of my trance and go into the mock humility/charm/effusiveness that I always use when I first meet a girl. You'd be surprised how well it works.

26

"Oh, excuse me, ma'am, I'm sorry, I didn't mean to be a bother," I say, with a slight grin. I have a very nice smile.

"Well, you *are* a bother, and don't call me ma'am, Christ, I'm not your fucking grandmother," she barks. She's still holding the cigarette to her lips, and the ash is certain to fall any moment. I stand there watching her. "Jesus, *move!*" she yells.

I shuffle to the side and jut out my hand. "I'm Tim. Tim Temples. I'm starting work here today." I pause for a moment, letting my words sink in. "Tim *Temples*."

She stares at my hand for a second. "Well, whoop-de-doo for you. Welcome to the mouth of hell. You're here way too early. I haven't had any fucking coffee yet." I put my hand to my side and sit down at a chair across from her desk. Her ash continues to defy gravity. She boots up her computer, which plays a tinkly *da-da-da-doooo* upon starting. "Mondays," she says.

I sit across from her and look closer at her face. She has these full lips, like Angelina Jolie without all that junk she had put in there. She has a tiny scar on her nose that splits her face perfectly. She's wearing too much makeup, particularly eye shadow; it's not Tammy Faye bad, but it's caked on there pretty good. She's wearing a cross necklace that touches the top of her cleavage; I think everything might touch the top of her cleavage, now that I look at it. It's all-encompassing. It has the gravitational pull of a thousand moons. I almost feel my chair should have a seat belt.

"Hey, eyes up, assface," she says, startling me. How

27

long was I staring? I'm usually subtle about that. "As if it isn't bad enough that I have to work in this dungeon, I have to deal with little shitheads staring at my tits all day," she mumbles.

"Well, it's not like you're wearing a baggy sweater or anything," I say, hopefully inoffensively. "You're, you know, an attractive woman." Compliments. Can't go wrong.

Her face sharpens. "Are you done? Is this over? Because I'm too old to babysit anymore." She hands me some papers and a clipboard. "Here, fill this out. Please keep your eyes on your own paper. And don't talk, or we'll send you to the principal's office." She then walks over to the coffee machine, pours herself a cup, and flicks her cigarette out the window before lighting another one.

She's a fireball. A challenge. All right. I can handle a challenge.

4.

I look down at the clipboard. Basic employment information. I take out my driver's license to copy down all my numbers. She sits back down at her desk, and I decide to have some fun.

I hide the pen from her and snap it in half. "I'm sorry, but my pen seems to have broken," I say. "Do you have another?" Without looking up from her computer, she takes a pen from her desk and throws it at me. It hits me on the chin and falls to the floor. She doesn't say a word.

I pick up the pen and start filling out the form. I come

to the question "Have you ever been convicted of a felony?" I look at her. "Hey, so this felony question . . . define *convicted?*" Normally this would get big laughs, but again she does not look up. She sighs and swats at the air like there's a bug in her face. "Having to stay after school for making fart noises in class doesn't count," she says. "So I think you're good. Now stop speaking."

The phone rings. She picks it up and her demeanor instantly changes. "Chuck Lewis's office, this is Helena, how may I help you?" she says in a schoolgirl voice. "I'm sorry, he's not in the office right now, may I take a message? . . . Okay . . . all right . . . I'll make sure to tell him you called. Thank you."

Helena. That's a nice name.

"Helena," I say. "That's a nice name."

"No speaking," she says.

I am undaunted. "So, *Helena*, how long have you been working here? Is it a fun place to work? What's the long-term health coverage like? Is it a positive work environment? Will I find this fulfilling, in a spiritual, emotional, and professional manner? Are there office retreats? Do you think there are appropriate opportunities for advancement? How about the 401(k)? Does the company match my contributions? Do we have casual Fridays?"

Her eyes don't move. "My God, you're still talking. Were you hit on the head with too many fastballs?" This is the first time she has acknowledged that she knows who I am. I am not surprised. How could she not?

"Well, I hit most of the fastballs out of the park, but I

29

guess you knew that already," I say. I have barely touched these forms. "You know, your boss has a picture of me up on his wall." Her eyes move to the picture. They go to me. She has the loveliest eyes. Topaz.

"Was that taken a few days ago?" she deadpans.

I'm about to make an innuendo-laden comment about the sexual energy of youth when Chuck comes back. He sees me filling out the papers and looks at Helena. Her demeanor changes again. She looks quiet, inward, subservient. Is she scared of *Chuck*? Other than the pit stains, he's about as intimidating as a mouse.

"Oh, Tim, my boy, don't you worry about those papers; Helena will fill those out for ya, won't ya, Helena?"

Ha. I do an internal boogie; Temples wins again.

She does her best to hide her scowl from her boss, though you can tell she'd just love to put a chair through the window right now. Chuck notices. "Oh, Helena, God forbid I ask you to do any real *work* around here!" he bellows. "Just do your damn job already, would ya? Remember who pays your damn salary." I'll admit, my victory feels a little hollow now. That seemed unnecessary. Helena glares at me to make sure I'm not smiling. I'm not. I was just *playing*.

"All right, Tim, man, let's take you out to the truck, let you meet Larry," Chuck says. He shambles out of the room. My God is he fat.

I get up from my chair. I have an urge to apologize to Helena. Before I have the chance, her eyes meet mine.

"Get out of my face," she says. There is nothing playful about this. I hand her the papers and walk out of the office. I make it about five feet and turn around. There has to be some way to salvage this. I poke my head in the door.

"Day one, baby," I say. "Day one."

5.

I catch up with Chuck—I could have walked on my hands and caught up with Chuck—and make my way out to the truck. Chuck's face is red, and he's huffing. There are few things more repulsive than a fat man who is angry.

"I dunno why I put up with her," he huffs. I'm afraid he might have a heart attack, right here, in front of me. Do I remember my freshman-year CPR training? Would I even use it? What if I performed mouth-to-mouth and he ate me?

"She's got such a bad attitude, acts like it's such a chore when I tell her to do something. She should feel lucky she *has* a job." He pauses. "Nice rack, though, eh, Timbo?"

I say nothing. I hate being called Timbo.

On the way, I run into the Horsemen, who all work on the same line. They're milling around, waiting for their shift to start. Everybody but Denny is smoking a cigarette. When they see Chuck and me coming, they put them out immediately. I meet Shad's glance. He looks nervous.

"Guys! What's up?" I ask.

Silence. Why is everyone being so quiet?

"Yeah, uh, hey, Tim, what's up, man," Jeff finally answers. "Welcome to Kraft." It's the first statement I've

31

ever heard Jeff say that

(a) Didn't contain an expletive

(b) Wasn't said with that shit-eating smirk

(c) Wasn't accompanied by a fart noise

(d) Didn't make me want to punch him.

"Hello, Mr. Lewis," Denny says. "Did you have a nice weekend?"

"I did, son, I sure did," Chuck says. "See those Redbirds this weekend? They oughta fire that La Russa, I tell you that."

"Oh, yes, sir, they sure should," Denny says. My jaw drops. Denny is the biggest Tony La Russa defender I know. We were just discussing this the other night. "He won as many World Series as Whitey Herzog did, but everyone hates him," he was saying. "It's so moronic!" He then went into this long-winded rant about how Midwestern sports fans don't like outsider Italians or some such nonsense. And here he is, pretending to be what he can't stand. What's going on?

"Well, hey, you boys keep up the good work," Chuck says. "I'm gonna show our Tim-man out to the truck."

"See ya, Tim," Shad says.

"Yeah, have fun, man. Welcome to the team," Andy says. We walk away, and I wonder which alien race just invaded our planet and replaced my friends with pod people.

6.

"This is Larry," Chuck says. "Larry, this is Tim. You'll be working together this summer. He's a good kid, Lar, so take it easy on him."

Larry is sitting in a lawn chair, smoking a cigar and cooling himself with one of those miniature handheld fans. He is wearing a Hawaiian shirt, has a Tom Selleck mustache, and is wearing a gold-colored mesh-and-foam trucker hat with a picture of a man climbing an electrical pole on it. He is built like an old fifties weight lifter: short, stocky, muscular chest like a log cabin. His thighs look like redwoods. He has a big thick gut that's round but would break a sledgehammer if you smacked it with one.

He doesn't get up. "Thank ya, Chucky," he says. His voice sounds like his esophagus is on fire, like a car whose muffler has fallen off. "Larry will take it easy on the kid, no problems. Just stay out of our way, and Larry and Tim will get all kinds of shit done this summer." Chuck frowns slightly and then slaps me on the back and says, "All right, go to it, then. You holler if you need anything," and he scuffs off, leaving a sweat trail behind him.

"So, you don't like Chucky much, eh?" Larry says. "Yeah, Larry don't much like him either. Thinks he's some kind of big shot because he's been here for twenty years. Larry's been here for twenty-five, and he don't go ordering people around. Chucky thinks what he does is important. Which is funny, because as far as Larry can tell, Chucky don't do much of anything."

Okay, so I don't like Chuck, but I'm not about to start broadcasting it on my first day. I think I really might like Larry, though. "Oh, he's all right," I say, extending my hand. "It's a pleasure to meet you, sir."

"Don't go calling Larry sir," he says. "Nothing 'sir'

about Larry at all. Larry's just a fat old fart who drinks too much. He ain't no sergeant or nothin'." I look around. Wait—*he's* Larry, right? So why is Larry talking about Larry when . . . oh, whatever.

He takes a puff off his cigar, still sitting in the lawn chair. "So, you're Bryan Temples's boy, right?" he says. "Your dad's a good man. Must get tired of everybody kissing his ass all the time, but hey, that's how she works here, right? Larry thinks everybody's just about the same in this silly world, and ain't no use treatin' anybody any differ'nt than anybody else. Seems like a waste of energy to Larry."

Seems like a waste of energy to Tim too, now that Tim thinks about it.

"Whatever, don't you pay any attention to anything Larry says," Larry says. Too late: I am definitely paying attention.

"Hey, want to see a picture of Larry's boys?" Before I have a chance to say yes, he hoists himself out of the chair and rumbles over to the front seat of the truck. He moves quicker than I would have thought; with his size and deceptive quickness, I bet he was quite the linebacker in his day. He brings out a yellowed photo of a much-younger Larry, a blond woman with big hair, and three tiny Larry clones, who are clearly identical triplets. "That's Terry, Barry, and Larry, Jr.," he says. "They live up in Kankakee. Don't see 'em much, but they're good-lookin' kids, don't ya think?" They're about four years old in the picture. "They go to school up at Bradley-Bourbonnais up there,"

Larry says. "Football players, all of 'em. Like their pops."

We played Bradley-Bourbonnais in baseball this year, and I suddenly remember three squat triplets on the team. They played first base, third base, and catcher, and they were about as mobile as ocean liners. This picture must have been taken about twelve years ago. "Yeah, sure. Good-looking kids," I say. Larry grunts, takes a puff off his cigar, goes back to his chair, and sits down.

"Larry talks too much, but hey, Larry's got a lot to say. Then again, you don't want to hear Larry babble all day, do ya? Let's get to work."

7.

This is the job: I walk into the plant, where there are boxes and boxes of Lender's Bagels, fresh off the line. These boxes weigh about thirty to thirty-five pounds apiece. I pick up a box, and I carry it about three hundred feet, past the Horsemen's line, past Chuck and Helena's office, past the break room, where some guy named Paul munches on Cheetos and drinks root beer all day. I take the box outside, walk up the ramp to the truck, and put the box down in the very back. I then go back and pick up another box and repeat this process until the truck is full. Larry does the same thing; he tells me he has been doing it for twenty-five years. It takes a full day to fill up a huge truck like that; it takes eight hours of bending, lifting, carrying, and dropping. I have a half-hour break for lunch. At 5 p.m., some guy shows up and drives the truck across town to the shipyard, where another driver takes the truck and drives it to God knows where through the night. This will be my job for the next three months. "Don't take no frigging genius, kid," Larry says. "Hell, if Larry can do it, anybody can."

Larry asks if I have any questions. I'm racking my brain, and I can't come up with one.

Wait—got it. "So what happens if we finish early?" I ask. "What if we've filled the truck, and it's an hour before the shift ends?"

Larry smiles. "Then you do what Larry does," he says. "You sit here on your ass and bullshit until the whistle blows." This is a plan I can get behind.

I head into the plant, where all the boxes are stacked. I pick one up, and it's heavy, heavier than I thought it would be. But it feels good. I feel strong. It sure beats sitting at a desk all day, waiting for Mrs. Gallagher to finish droning on about integers and parabolas.

There's a path through the plant for me and Larry, so I don't have to wait for people to get out of my way or anything. I just lift, walk, drop, stack, and do it again. Lather, rinse, repeat. I do this for about an hour. For the first half hour, I'm just concentrating on the job at hand. Mainly, I don't want to fall down and send a boxful of radioactive bagels sprawling across the floor of the plant. (I have a feeling they'd eat through the cement floor, actually.) But after repeating this movement for an hour, I find it cleansing. Any worries about the job, or Chuck, or that Helena lady, or the Horsemen's weird behavior just melt away into the monotony of the work. After a while, you don't think about what you're doing. You just do it and lose yourself in your own head. You stop thinking about having to do this for eight hours, and you start thinking how, at this pace, by the end of the summer, you're going to be freaking *ripped*.

It's nice being alone, actually. It's good being responsible for one little thing, one little job, a series of seemingly inconsequential events building up to the end of the day, when, suddenly, you've filled a whole truck. It's nice doing real work. It's not long before I'm working up a good sweat. I feel powerful. I feel active. I feel *useful*.

Which is more than I can say for Larry. I'm about two hours into the job before I realize that I'm the only one lifting these boxes. Larry seems to have vanished. He reappears about an hour later, coming around the corner, fanning himself and eating a slice of pizza. After I drop the box in the truck, he motions me over.

"So, how you doing?" he asks.

"Great," I say. "You kind of get in a rhythm, you know?"

"Oh, Larry knows. After twenty-five years, Larry *knows*."

Now, I'm not offended or anything, and Larry is starting to seem like an excellent guy to spend a summer with, but, all told, it might go by a wee bit quicker if, you know, I had a little help. "Uh, Larry . . . do you, uh . . . is it just me today?"

Larry laughs. He has such a cool laugh; it's like someone lit kindling from somewhere inside him. "Well, kid, around here we got a lot of rules, rules you'll pick up once you're here a while," he says. "Here's rule number one: on the first day, Larry don't work."

8.

I am exhausted and fulfilled as I walk in our front door. I had to hurry home to catch the opening pitch. Cards are playing the Rockies tonight, and Doug, whom I still have barely spoken to, is supposed to watch the game with me. But he's not home. Nobody's home.

A note is stuck to the oven.

> *Boys—*
> *Dad and I are at the chamber of commerce meeting. There's baked beans in the oven. All you do is heat them up. We'll be back about eleven. Enjoy the game!*
> *Mom*

I dump a spoonful of beans onto a paper plate and head down to the basement, where I flip on the plasma TV Dad splurged on. Doug is nowhere to be seen. I *did* tell him I'd be back to watch the game tonight, right?

Doug is obsessed with the Cardinals, and it's little wonder: he could have played for them. The last week of Doug's high school baseball career was a whirlwind. Every game was packed with pro scouts, all wearing doofy plaid hats and carrying radar guns. I sat behind one during a sectional game against Decatur Eisenhower and watched him. He would read the radar after every one of Doug's pitches—on days where all was perfect, he could hit ninety—and then scribble on a little notepad. After Doug fired a particularly fast one, he'd whistle. And the scout was always looking around, searching the stands for other scouts. They're apparently quite competitive.

The May amateur draft came, and we had all our extended relatives over to wait for the call. We knew Doug would be drafted, but none of us knew where. The University of Illinois had already offered Doug a full scholarship, and he had accepted it, with the caveat that he would have the option to go pro if he were drafted high enough. None of us knew how the baseball draft worked, how long it took, how many rounds there were, anything like that, so most of our eager visitors had left by the time the phone rang. It was Brian Gunn, an assistant to Cardinals general manager Walt Jocketty. Doug had been drafted by the *Cardinals*!

Gunn explained that Doug had been selected in the thirty-second round, which was a little lower than we were expecting but still high enough that they told him they felt optimistic about his chances of working his way through the minor-league system. Dad didn't trust any of the shady people who called our house all hours of the night wanting to be Doug's agent, so he did the negotiating himself. Gunn told Dad the Cardinals were willing to offer Doug a $20,000 signing bonus, and, if he accepted it, he would report to the Cardinals' Rookie League affiliate in Johnson City, Tennessee, a week after he graduated. Dad told Gunn that Doug had a scholarship offer from Illinois and asked him how much time we had to decide. "Two days," Gunn said. "That's typical for a thirty-second-round pick."

The next forty-eight hours were a never-ending series of family squabbles, most of which I was kicked out of the room for. The Templeses took sides: Dad and Doug wanted to take the money and head to Johnson City in three weeks; Mom wanted Doug to accept the scholarship and go to college. You could see both sides. Mom felt the opportunity to have your college education completely paid for was too valuable to pass up, and besides, after four years of playing in the Big Ten, he could only get better. The money would still be there, and there might even be more. He might be drafted higher after he graduated. On the other hand, my father and brother argued . . . *it's the Cardinals!*

This debate raged all day and all night. My father had his own agenda in this; he had enjoyed his own life on the road in the minors, and even though he never made the majors, he thought it would be beneficial for his son to see the country and make it on his own. But my mother pointed out that Dad had never gone to college, and in those first months after the final minor-league team cut him, he had labored for months to find a job to support him and his newly pregnant wife. "A college diploma is something he will have forever," my mom argued. "It's something he can fall back on if things don't work out, like with you." I remember my father getting angry when she said that.

40

But she was right, and Dad knew it. The night before they had to call Brian Gunn back, they sat Doug down at the dinner table and laid out their options. They made it clear that it was his decision, that they supported whatever he did, but their advice was to go to college and enter the draft later. Hiding behind the door to my room, I heard Doug protest. They worked on him all night. Eventually, they won him over.

And then it all went wrong.

Doug never got the hang of the college game; he could throw his fastball past people, but that was it. He would always cross up his catchers' signs, and he was typically too stubborn to make the right adjustments. They chalked up his freshman year struggles to the difficulty of acclimating to a new level. But he had the same problems his sophomore year, and by his junior year, they hadn't given up on him exactly, but he certainly wasn't considered a prospect anymore. He fell behind in school and took just enough classes to keep his eligibility, but not enough to graduate in the four years his scholarship paid for. That eligibility expired with a 12–1 drubbing by Michigan in the Big Ten tournament—Doug pitched three scoreless innings in mop-up work—and that was that. No one bothered to keep up with the draft this year. Everyone knew Doug wouldn't be picked this time.

Now Doug is here, home, with four years of college behind him—no diploma, no $20,000, no stories of riding buses around the country with twenty-four other hopeful minor leaguers. Doug is just here.

And Doug is not here, still not here, as I watch Jeff Suppan give up a three-run homer to third baseman Garrett Atkins. Doug would have blown that fastball by him, no doubt.

9.

I can't get over that I haven't talked to the Horsemen all week. It's like, every time Chuck comes by, they tuck their tails between their legs. Denny cornered me late Thursday, glancing around like he was pulling a drug deal. He was all shifty, nervous, and weird. "Yo, we're all gonna go out Friday night after work," he said, his eyes fixed on Chuck's back across the plant. "You coming?" I told him of course. What else am I gonna do? So here we are.

The Route is so basic and repetitive I could not only do it in my sleep . . . I probably have. You meet up at the Cross County Mall, where you kill time until everybody shows up by sneaking CDs from Mister Music under your jacket and taunting the security guards.

By the time Shad, Andy, and Denny arrive, we're ready to drive. After ten minutes of milling around the parking lot, making fun of each other's trucks—though nobody ever mocks the Blazer—we pile in my ride, crack open a six-pack, and start the Route. You turn down Broadway, past Peterson Park, past the newspaper, past the Salvation Army store, past Broadway Joe's, where all the dads and teachers and youth ministers drink. When you hit Western Avenue, you hang a left, then another left, then a right onto Lake Land Boulevard. Down you go, past the Christian bookstore, past the Hardee's, past the IGA, past Gunner Buc's Tavern, until you've actually left town. You do a couple of laps in the parking lot of Lake Land College—this is a good spot to get rid of empties and relieve yourself in one of the nature habitats they have for the agricultural department—and then head down the country roads to Lake Paradise, which is full of perfect secluded areas to take girls when you're looking to park. After a few random lefts and rights, you're back on Old State Road, which takes you back into town, back to Lake Land Boulevard, back to Broadway, back to the parking lot of the Cross County Mall. A couple of laps there, and then the Route begins again. This is what we do. We do this all night until we run into some girls. It's better than what my mom used to do when she was in high school. She's from Moweaqua, a tiny town about a half hour away. She says she and her friends used to sit at a bench next to "the stop sign" and watch the cars go by until everyone was tired and went home. We're at least *moving*.

All told, it's a mighty fine way to spend an evening, particularly when everywhere you stop, everyone wants to talk to you. I am the grand marshal of the Route.

As usual, I'm driving. Denny's in the passenger seat and the miscreants are in the back staining my interior. We're listening to Faith No More's *The Real Thing*, a CD my brother gave me a few years ago. I don't know any of the lyrics—never listen closely enough to figure out what they are. But the music is loud and angry and strange. We're

43

quiet for a while, a quiet interrupted by a loud Shad fart.

"Good one, bitchhead," Jeff brays. "You always have something interesting to say." Denny, as usual, looks embarrassed.

Andy keeps trying to light a cigarette with a malfunctioning lighter; every time he flicks it, it sends a flame six inches high, almost torching the roof of my truck.

"So, Tim, how you liking the first week?" Denny asks.

"Oh, nothing's really happening. I just pick up the boxes and carry them and drop them and do it again. Pretty brainless. I like it, though. It's real work, and everybody leaves me alone. Somebody want to hand me a beer back there?"

Andy and Shad fight over who's going to grab one out of the cooler, eventually dropping the can and spilling it. "Christ," I say, "you guys sure your parents weren't cousins?"

Everybody laughs.

Denny cleans up the mess and hands me a Bud. "It's a weird place, man," he says. "That asswipe Chuck runs the place like it's the military."

"Yeah, I don't know what your thing with that guy is," I say. "He's just a fat old man with a clipboard. You guys act like he's your dad or something."

"Easy for you to say," Jeff chimes in from the backseat. "You get to leave at the end of the summer. We gotta put up his shit for the next ten years. Asshole. I bet he beats his wife."

"I bet he beats his meat," Andy says.

"Real funny, shithead," Jeff says. "You just come up with that right now?"

Andy smiles widely in my rearview mirror. "Yeah, I did!"

"Oh, he ain't so bad," I say. "He's just a moron who thinks he's some kind of big shot because for the first time in his life, he's somebody's boss. He gets off on it."

Andy chortles. "Heh, *gets off*; I bet he—" Jeff smacks him on the back of the head.

"Well, if you ask me, someone should put him in his place," Denny says. "There's no reason to treat people like that. The other day, he was screaming at that Helena lady so loud the windows shook. I thought his head was going to pop off and burst into flames."

Jeff snorts. "That bitch probably had it coming. She's so stuck up. Those two deserve each other."

I shut off the Faith No More and turn on the radio. Some woman is singing with a sad piano. Her voice is kind of scratchy, almost snarled, and she sounds horribly unhappy. I listen for a moment, then I'm hit on the back of the head with a beer can.

"Christ, shut that girlie crap off!" Jeff says, and everyone laughs. "Anybody checked you for a uterus up there?" I snap to and change the station quickly, laughing along with them.

10.

The working relationship between Helena and me did not improve much as the week went on. Even though I pulled out all kinds of tricks. I started out by continuing that whole "day one" thing, dropping by her office at

45

5 p.m. each day and saying, "Day two, beautiful." By Wednesday she just made sure she wasn't at her desk at 5 p.m. (She even left a note: *Day three: You're a moron. Go away.*)

Thursday I decided to try something different. "Hey, that's a nice skirt. Where'd you get it?"

Her response to that one? "I stole it from your dead grandmother. Fuck off." I even put little Post-it notes all around her desk when she wasn't around, saying things like *Have a nice day!* and *It's a beautiful world! Smile!* and *Your cheerful attitude makes this world a better place!* When I went out to my truck after work, there was a pile of Post-it notes on the hood, burning in an ashtray.

I'm not entirely sure why I kept up this act. It's not a sexual thing, not at all; it just fascinates me more by the day how impervious she is to my charms. No matter how hard I try, I know I can't stop bugging her. There's something about a girl who casually calls you an asshead, I guess.

"Yeah, what do you guys know about Helena anyway?" I ask the Horsemen. "You've been there longer than me; you've probably heard some stories."

Jeff whistles. "Jesus, man, she's the coldest, most heartless bitch I've ever met, and boy, have I met a lot." I doubt he's met all that many. For all his talk, Jeff never spends much time with girls. He'll charm them for a while—partly, I'd bet, because of his friendship with me—but they usually scurry away pretty fast. Something about him inevitably creeps them out.

"I heard she was married but her husband left her and their three kids," Shad says.

"You're an idiot," I tell him. "She's, like, twenty-two or something. How in the hell would she be married and have three kids and be divorced already?"

"Well, that's what I *heard*," Shad says defensively.

"One time this dude came by the office looking for her, and the security guy had to take him away," Andy says. "He was some big Harley guy. I heard he had a gun. Or maybe it was a knife. I don't remember. I saw that happen, though. That's totally fucking true."

"Any of you guys ever talk to her?" I say. "Is she as mean to you as she is to everybody else?"

"I tried one time," Denny says. "It was late in the day, and she was talking on her cell phone, and I think she might have been crying. I asked her if she was okay. She looked right at me—right through me, really—and said, 'Can't you see I'm on the phone?' Then she flipped me off. She doesn't seem like a very happy person."

"Nothing a good shot of Dr. Jeff wouldn't cure," Jeff cackles. *"Bang bang pow!"* He and Shad high-five. I feel like I should say something, but I don't. Helena is such a strange person. Sometimes I think I'm the only one in town who has talked to her and lived to tell the tale.

I make a right turn into the Lake Land parking lot, looking for somewhere to pee.

11.

It's about midnight. Half an hour ago, Lieutenant Grierson pulled us over. He's a wiry, skinny man with a goofy mustache who goes to church with my parents and coached me in Little League. He came up to the window; we didn't even bother to hide the beers.

"Son, do you know how fast . . . oh, Tim! Hey there, kiddo! Didn't realize it was you! I hear you're working over at the Kraft plant this summer. How's it going over there?"

"Fine," I say. "It's a job." I give him a little grin and a "you know the Templeses are good kids and wouldn't get in too much trouble so let's make this quick, okay?" eyebrow waggle.

Grierson is beaming like an idiot. He looks like he wants to ask for my autograph. "So, how's your dad doing? He ready for the big event? Bagelfest is gonna be huge this year."

"Yeah, he's all right. He's got Doug helping him out."

"Doug. Good kid. Ain't nobody ever born round here with an arm like his. Certainly better than that Tavarez guy in St. Louis. Those Mexican pitchers, they can't ever keep their heads on straight."

"You know it." Jeff yawns in the backseat.

"Well, listen, you kids be careful out there tonight," Lieutenant Grierson says. "Don't stay out too late. And tell your dad I said hey, would ya?"

"No problem. Have a nice night, Lieutenant Grierson."

Maybe I should run for office here someday.

Denny's cell phone rings. "Hi, baby!"

It's Kristen, his girlfriend. Denny is so whipped. "Oh, we're just driving around, the usual. . . . You guys are at Hardee's? . . . Oh, well . . . I'd have to . . . Hey, guys, anybody hungry?"

12.

Hardee's is a fast-food joint, the only place in Mattoon open past 11 p.m., and it's always our last stop. Pretty much everyone from the high school ends up there. There they are, with their trucks, milling about, smoking cigarettes, sneaking joints, hiding from cops, trying to decide who they're going to hook up with that night. All you have to do is buy a small french fry or a shake, and they'll let you hang out in the parking lot until the police run everybody off. The employees at Hardee's are what you'd expect at that hour: teenage moms, meth addicts, the mentally retarded—all the poor souls willing to take a minimum wage job with a midnight-to–8 a.m. shift. It can take them forty-five minutes to complete an order, and your cheeseburger often has a hair in it or some sort of insect. Jeff once found a condom in his onion rings. It was fried. It doesn't matter, though, because here, you can get away with anything.

Nobody offers Denny much argument on his choice of destination, though we all make whipping sounds. He's been dating Kristen forever, and I'm sure he'll end up marrying her and having kids within a couple of years. We give him crap about this, but all told, you have to admire them. At the end of night, they always end up together, with his arm around her, her head on his shoulder. They always have each other to count on, and I suppose they always will.

We pull into the parking lot to the sound of Green Day's "Walking Contradiction"; that song sounds like someone riding a bicycle down a flight of stairs.

Shad pulls the cooler out of the truck and dumps the empty cans and ice water into the ditch. Denny immediately makes a beeline for Kristen's Ford Escort. I follow him over there, scratching and yawning. A million trips down the Route have ended like this, and there is comfort in its predictability. People are happy to see me here.

Kristen's with her usual crew—Sue Bronson, Amy Blair, and Pam Corey, her Horsewomen—but with an odd addition this time: Jessica. Surprisingly enough, she doesn't look all that out of place, though I've never seen her at Hardee's before. I don't think I've ever even seen her out past 10 p.m. She's dressed different too: she's wearing a pink T-shirt, kind of tight, and a little black skirt that stops just above the knees. She looks good, but all wrong. I thought she only owned baggy sweaters.

"Well, look who it is, Tim Temples," she says. She can't be nearly as surprised to see me as I am to see her. "What brings you around these parts?"

"Same as always," I say. "I'd be more inclined to ask you that question."

She smiles. "Well, it's not like I have to *study* or anything. Kristen asked me if I wanted to come out tonight, and hey, why not? Where else am I going to see this much chewing tobacco?"

"Your dad all right with this? I can't imagine he wants you staying out all night." I wince. Why do I suddenly sound like my mom?

"Yeah, well, no one said he had to like it," she says

with a sly grin, jumping off the hood of the car. "You want a cheeseburger? I'm going in."

"I'm all right. But you be careful in there. I think the guy behind the counter is on parole."

She heads in. I turn to Denny, but he's already making out with Kristen.

13.

"What are you doing here?" Jeff sneers to Jessica later that evening. "Don't you have a frog to dissect?"

A group has gathered around Kristen's car. Jessica is drinking a beer—a *beer*!

I sit on the front grill of my truck and hand Jeff a bottle opener. Jessica, after holding back Amy's hair while she vomits up some fried condoms, takes a seat between us. Jeff puts his arm around her.

"Hey! Keep those tentacles to yourself." She giggles, elbowing him in the ribs.

"You like to play rough, eh?" Jeff says. I shoot him a look, but he misses it.

Sue stumbles over and begins fussing with Jeff's hair, which clearly annoys him but doesn't stop him from following her down the road a bit.

"Sorry, Jeff's an idiot," I tell Jessica.

"Oh, he's funny," she says.

"Yeah," I joke, "in a Charles Manson type of way."

She clinks beers with me and takes a swig. "So this is what you guys do all the time? This is what I've been missing?"

"Pretty much," I say. "Looks like you're hanging in all right."

"Well, as much as I'd rather be in the *library*," she says with as much sarcasm as she can muster, "it's now or never, right? Just one more summer. Then we're out of here."

"Sure," I say. Then I think, *You'll be out of here, Jessica. Me . . . I'm not so sure.*

She takes another swig. "Hey, remember that time when we were kids? When we were playing wiffleball and I hit you in the crotch with the bat? You threw up all over J. P. Kirk."

"Yeah, I remember. And then he started throwing up, and neither of us could stop. I think we both lost about ten pounds." We both laugh.

She takes a deep gulp from her beer and emits a tiny burp. "Oops!"

"Four years of sitting in your room reading, and now you're out here with the common folk," I say. "What *did* inspire you to suddenly make the trip?"

"I would have come sooner," she says, brushing her hair out of her face. "You just never invited me."

I can't decide whether this is true or not. "Well, if you had spent as much time out here as I have, you wouldn't have been valedictorian, that's for sure."

"Whatever." She shrugs. "Besides, you're looking at this all wrong. Being here *is* studying—Socialization 101. I hear they have this booze thing going on at college, too."

I grin. "Cheers to that!"

We clink bottles again. I lean back on the hood of the

car and look at the clear sky above us. The stars are brighter in Mattoon than anywhere else in the world.

"You probably won't get many nights like this in Champaign," I say. "And I doubt the campus cops are as big pushovers as Lieutenant Grierson."

"That's probably true," she says, leaning back next to me. "It does seem a little easier to escape here."

What Jessica's escaping from, I have no idea.

I point out the Big Dipper. Jessica points out a constellation called Orion. I glance over at her, and for a moment I want to say the things I haven't told anyone. About how I'm feeling about college. About how I'm afraid to leave my friends. I want to tell her how I am king here, and there I would be just another faceless nobody. I want to tell her that college seems to have ruined my brother and I'm afraid it will ruin me.

But I don't. I look at the stars and say, "Yep." And then Amy pukes again, and this night fades into the rest of them.

14.

"The important thing to remember is that the problem is not your child: your problem is *you*. You have to realize the effect you're having on your children. When little Bobbie sets fire to his teacher's skirt, that's *your* fault. Bobbie is just a child. It's *learned* behavior. You're a selfish person, and there is no I in *parent*. Say that with me now: *There is no I in* parent."

I walk into the office as Helena pounds the black-and-white television on her desk. At first I think it's because she's getting bad reception, but nope: Helena's pissed off again. This time her anger is focused on Dr. Phil. "Look at yourselves. Let's face it, Veronica: you're fat. You're creating a cycle of indulgence, and Bobbie is just reacting to it. You've created this. And you're the only one who can fix it."

Helena takes a drag off her cigarette and whips it at the screen. "Who are you to tell me how to live my life? Christ! You're fucking fat too! And bald! And nice mustache, you pud!" Helena notices me. "Can you believe this guy?"

In the three weeks I have known her, this is the first time she has asked me a question that didn't involve a request either to leave the room or to do something unseemly to myself. I have no real opinion, one way or the other, but I'm not going to miss an opportunity to commiserate.

"Yeah, he's an idiot." Sure. A total moron. Um . . . Dr. who?

Helena looks at me for a moment as if she has stumbled across some strange new specimen she cannot identify. "Bah!" she blurts, tossing her hands in the air. "Whatever!"

I feel I should not let this conversation go, but I'm not sure how to keep it moving. I settle on obnoxiousness. Old reliable. I walk to the television while she's putting on some new coffee and switch it to a baseball game. She whips around and glares. "We don't watch *sports* in here." She flips it back. I playfully switch it again.

"Jesus," she says. "Listen. I'm sure this is very fun for you, but honestly, you're not cute. You're not funny. You're not charming. Stop it."

I'm not sure if she means this or if I'm just getting to her. Frankly, I don't really care. I feel like I'm constantly riding the rope with Helena; I've gotta figure this lady out somehow.

"Oh, and honestly, quit trying to grow the mustache. You look like a French porn star."

I turn the television back to the game as the phone rings. "Can you leave the room, please? It's a personal call." I step outside and listen through the crack in the door. Her voice becomes whispered, as if she's planning some sort of prison escape. She talks like someone who is walking on barely frozen ice.

"Hi, John . . . Oh, I'm fine. . . . Yeah, just the typical crap . . . The kids they bring in here are so stupid. . . . I mean, honestly . . . So, Friday . . . Yeah, I think that would be nice. . . . You don't have to do all that! I'm just happy you'll be there. . . . I'll be off work at five. . . . Oh . . . you're really working that late? . . . Uh, sure, I can just meet you there . . . and I won't see you before then? No, no, you're right. . . . I'm sorry, it'll just be good to see you Friday. . . . You only turn twenty-three once, right?"

Friday is Helena's birthday. And there appears to be some dude. My interest is piqued.

The second she hangs up, I waltz back in the room. I take the remote control and hide it behind my back. She stands up and starts to lunge for it, but I'm too quick . . .

until I trip over the chair and fall to the floor. She starts laughing and then manually turns it back to Dr. Phil, which, for a show she supposedly hates, she's awfully determined to watch. I pull myself up and flick the channel one more time. I think I see a little grin on her face—and then Chuck comes in.

"Hey, the Cubbies are on! What's the score, Timbo?" he says. "Oh, and Helena, please, I'm getting tired of waiting for those reports. Are you going to do them or not?"

The grin evaporates immediately, and her face turns to stone. She looks at me, clearly wondering what exactly is going to happen to me in hell.

15.

The mayor of Mattoon is in our kitchen, eating Club crackers lathered in melted Velveeta and stabbing blindly at a plate of Crock-Pot cocktail weenies. Mayor McKenzie is wearing a blue suit with a pink shirt and purple tie, an outfit that probably didn't fit him when he bought it in 1983. He looks like Richard Simmons on prom night. His wife seems about fifteen years older than him, with blue hair, big thick glasses, and a fluffy blouse adorned with an American flag pin. They are constant visitors to our home, and they're so silly and over the top that our whole family has a good laugh at their expense once they leave. My family really doesn't like the McKenzies much—Mom calls Mrs. McKenzie a "fundamentalist phony"—but they're always coming out here to discuss something or other. The mayor's always worried about being reelected—if he didn't win, all he'd have is the doughnut shop that he runs in town. He'd miss the glamor of being "Mr. Mattoon," and he knows he needs my father's implicit endorsement to keep his job. Kind of like President Bush making speeches with Curt Schilling in Boston.

Dad comes in from the patio, where he's grilling steaks, with a handful of beers. "Who needs a refresher?" Mayor McKenzie grabs one while my mom, wearing an apron that says, BRANSON COOKS! pours Mrs. McKenzie another margarita. Doug follows my father in and takes a beer from his hand. His beard is growing to unimagined lengths. He looks like he has been stranded on a deserted island, and, for the first time, I notice he's developing a little bit of a gut.

If this is what college does to someone, man, I really want no part of it. He's like the "before" picture in an "I cleaned up my life in two months and *here's how!*" advertisement. Except, well, this is "after." He has not spoken to anyone in days, and he's not likely to start tonight.

"So," Mayor McKenzie says in a deep Southern drawl that fades in and out depending on how many beers he's had, "did Johnson get back to you on the grandstand plans? The city council's all over me about it."

"Not a problem, Mac," Dad says. "We had the wrong parts come in from Marion in the last shipment, but we're still way ahead of schedule. Honestly, Bagelfest is going to go on without a hitch."

"Ahhh, well, the last thing we want is Jacob Kuhns

waving to the fine people of Mattoon while their bleachers collapse," he says. "Know what I mean?"

Doug chuckles in the corner. The mental picture of half the town crumbling into a heap of metal is too much for him to resist. He seems like he can already smell the carnage. My mother shoots him a deadly look.

"Mac, it's going to be fine," my dad continues. "We are on top of the whole situation. We certainly wouldn't want to disappoint the great Jacob Kuhns. After all, the kid *was* in a Gap commercial."

He was. I remember Morgan Fairchild blathering on about the cheap prices of blue jeans while Jacob, whose hair had grown considerably longer than it was when he lived here, did some sort of swing dance with a black woman with crazy Afro hair and a pair of pink overalls in the background. He looked ridiculous, with this dumbass smile on his face, but the ad ran during the World Series last year, and it was the front-page story of the next day's *Mattoon Journal Gazette*. Dad has never been a big fan of the whole Jacob Kuhns Experience. Either he did something to offend Dad when he was a young kid—or Dad resents Jacob's new place as resident Mattoon celebrity. That used to be *his* job.

"Better watch out for that Kuhns kid, Bryan." Mayor McKenzie winks. "Good-looking fella. He may end up stealing our ladies!"

Mrs. McKenzie blushes. "Well, he *is* awfully handsome!"

The mayor drinks his beer in an oddly quick fashion and reaches for another one. His hand is an inch away from the last cold one when Doug snatches it, opens it, and chugs down half of it, his eyes never wavering from the mayor's. My mother actually gasps: "Douglas!" The kitchen is silent for a few seconds until our dog, Daisy, clearly noticing something strange going on, barks and jumps up on Mrs. McKenzie's lap, causing her to spill her margarita all over the counter. "Goodness!"

I look at Doug, who is still staring at the mayor.

The mayor is startled for a moment, but he gathers himself. "Oh, well, Doug, my boy, you can go ahead and have that one if you want it." Doug stares at him a beat longer as my father, for once, is speechless. Doug then burps, turns around, and heads out the patio door and toward the garage. My mother, trying to grasp some semblance of normalcy in the situation, wipes off the counter with a paper towel, grabs Daisy by the collar to drag her outside, and then pours Mrs. McKenzie another margarita. "I'm dreadfully sorry about this, Rosemary," she says.

The mayor is calmer. "Oh, don't worry. Boy must have really needed that beer. Heck, I know how he feels sometimes." Through the window, I see Doug flip off somebody, anybody.

16.

After a few minutes of empty banter about college—

Mayor: So, Timbo, you ready for school? One last summer, then it's time to hit the books!

Me: Sure, Mr. Mayor, I can't wait.

Mayor: You just be sure to have some fun up there, you hear? You should pledge one of those fraternities. I'm a Kappa man myself.

—my curiosity about what the heck is going on with Doug overcomes me. "I'm gonna go out to the garage," I tell my mom, and she looks at me with considerable concern.

"You sure?" she asks. I realize I'm not escaping here without a joke.

"Well, you know, I gotta make sure Doug has enough beer," I say.

I laugh. No one else does.

17.

I open the door to the garage. The Cardinals game is on the television, with the sound off, and death metal is blaring.

Doug is listening to the worst song I have ever heard. I can't really make out the lyrics, but in the chorus there's something about "demon" and "semen." Doug is standing in the corner, face against the wall like the guy in *The Blair Witch Project*, holding his beer and being very still. I don't want to startle him, so I take a baseball from one of the shelves and roll it up to him until it taps the back of his foot. He jumps slightly and turns around angrily. He relaxes when he sees it's me. "Oh. Hey." He walks over to the stereo and turns the music down, mercifully.

"Jesus. What the hell is that crap?" I ask him.

"Some band called Turbonegro. Guys up at school got me into them. They're fucking insane," he says.

"Yeah, they sound like it."

We stand there uneasily for a moment until he grabs a beer out of a cooler next to him and hands it to me. He smirks. "We actually have tons of beer out here."

"Heh. Thanks, I guess."

More silence. I try again to break it, turning to the television, which I know will work, at least for a bit. I watch Cincinnati Reds first baseman Sean Casey trot around the bases after hitting a mammoth home run off Cardinals reliever Julian Tavarez. "You know, Tavarez drives me up the wall. He's such a crazy man. One game he'll be completely dominant, and the next they hit everything he throws up there. And then he'll flip out and start destroying everything he sees in the dugout. It's ridiculous."

"He's tipping his pitches."

"What?" I say.

"He's tipping his pitches. That's why he gets drilled, even though he has such nasty stuff. Watch what he does when Molina gives him the signals."

I look, intensely.

"He'll shake his head once, then nod, then shake it again, then another nod. He might as well hire a plane to skywrite what he's going to throw."

I don't understand.

"I don't understand," I say.

"Look," Doug says, watching the replay. "The first head shake is because Molina wants him to throw a

61

changeup. Tavarez always wants to go with the gas, so he shakes him off. Everybody in the league knows Tavarez likes to go with the heat when he's in trouble, and they know Molina tries to get him not to. So the first head shake tips them off that Molina called for a change and Tavarez didn't want it, and the nod shows that Molina finally gave him the fastball sign."

I listen, enraptured. "Go on."

"So the next sign Molina gives him is the one to throw low and away, because it's a one-two count. But Tavarez is a stubborn Mexican and wants to go inside. I can tell that by that second head shake, and if I can tell it, Sean Casey can sure as hell tell it. Molina gets tired of arguing with him, so he gives him the inside sign, and Tavarez agrees. That's the second nod." Doug lights up a cigarette. I haven't seen him this animated since he came home. This is the Doug I remember, and I want to keep him going.

"Well, I'll be damned," I say.

"You should really know this shit, dude," Doug says. "Maybe if you paid closer attention, you might be playing some ball up in Champaign rather than, you know, whatever the hell it is you're gonna do up there."

He's right. I love baseball, but I never thought about it as much as my coaches always wanted me to. With me, it's always been *see ball, hit ball, run.*

Tavarez strikes out Austin Kearns to end the inning, and our little session of Inside Baseball falls quiet. "Hey, so I missed you the other night," I say.

62

"Yeah, I was busy. Sorry about that. It was a shitty game anyway."

"Busy doing what?" I ask with a grin. "Tending to that garden on your face?"

Doug grins back. "You like it? I'm down with it. Freaks out Mom and Dad. I'm hoping to be able to braid it or something. I'm starting to look like a stoner. Pretty cool."

"Hell, I barely recognize you, man. You look like some Hoosier lumberjack from Cumberland County."

"Well, fuck it, you know? Got nothing much else to do here than grow a beard." He chuckles. "I think I might grow my hair long enough to wear a ponytail, just to see Dad shit a brick."

"What's it like working with him, anyway?" I've been very curious about this. Doug and I spent the first eighteen years of our lives getting yelled at by Dad for often-imagined screwups while helping him fix the car or build the shed, or do some other kind of menial junk. Maybe this is why Doug has been so cranky lately: they have to be driving each other nuts. I can't imagine having to go through that every day for a whole summer.

"Sucks, dude. I didn't even want to do it, but Dad said I had to 'pull my weight' when I was here this summer. Whole stupid town's geeked up about stupid Bagelfest. And for what? The bagels taste like petrified cat shit. And who cares about Jacob Kuhns? Ooh, he was in the background of an episode of *The West Wing*. Big freaking deal. What a fag that guy is."

Doug pauses and finishes off his beer. He pops open

63

another one and offers one to me. "Naw, still working on this one," I say. "I can't chuck 'em down the way you can."

He opens the back door of the garage and flicks his cigarette into the cornfield behind our house. "I gotta take a piss." He unzips and urinates into my mom's hedges.

18.

Albert Pujols steps to the plate and takes a strike. I hear my parents and the McKenzies out on the patio, still back-slapping and grab-assing. They're grilling steaks, talking about parade routes and the fireworks show they're planning in Peterson Park for the big day.

"So, how's your crap going over there at the plant?" Doug asks me. "You making sure enough of Mattoon's finest exports are being shipped all across the country?"

"Yep," I say, finishing off my own beer. "The money's real nice. Sixteen bucks an hour. The people suck, though, except for this guy named Larry. He keeps talking about himself like he's not there or something. I can't figure it out."

"Working world's a different place, man," he says.

"No kidding," I say. "I keep wanting to hang out with the Horsemen, but they all have these dead looks on their faces, like they're always afraid they're gonna get fired or something. They're like different people there. Even Jeff."

"Jeff." Doug snorts. "Somebody needs to knock that guy on his ass sometime. I'm surprised it hasn't happened already."

"Oh, he's all right. Just a smart mouth."

Doug is quiet for a moment. "Hey, you ever run into a lady named Helena Westfall out there?"

I laugh. "Damn straight I have. I see her every day. I work directly for her boss. She's kind of mean. Every time I try to talk to her, she throws something at me. What, you know her?"

It's Doug's turn to laugh. "Yeah, I graduated with her. I *thought* she still worked out there." He pauses for a drag. "She ain't so bad. Thinks the world owes her something. But she's gotta wade through the same muck the rest of us do. She should just shut up about it."

It hadn't even occurred to me that Helena and Doug might have gone to school together, probably because in some ways, she seems twice as old as he does. Doug laughs to himself at a private joke and takes another swig.

"So, have you talked to anybody from up at school since you been home? You hear from Lee?" Lee was a guy from the Chicago suburbs who lived in Doug's frat up in Champaign. The first time I ever got drunk was with Lee and Doug. We went to Murphy's Pub on campus, and my fake ID—along with some strategically placed lies from Lee—got me endless pitchers of beer, countless Jell-O shots, and a sleepover with a giggling sophomore named Kelly. I was fifteen. Lee's all right in my book.

"Naw, I haven't talked to anybody from up there," Doug says. "I think Lee went on some road trip for the summer with a bunch of his rich friends from home."

"You ever go to Murphy's anymore?"

"Hell, Murphy's ain't even there anymore," Doug says.

65

"They tore it apart last year and put in a Starbucks. Only freaking good bar on campus, and they got rid of it. Everything up there now is either a gay-ass dance club or some fancy-pants place where everybody drinks wine and spends Mommy and Daddy's money. It sucks now.

"Honestly, I don't know why I wasted my fucking time," Doug says, his voice rising as he chucks another empty beer can across the cement garage floor. "The whole thing was a joke. I drank a lot, I nailed some girls, I played some lousy baseball, I skipped a bunch of classes, I met a bunch of assholes . . . and I didn't even get a stupid diploma for all the trouble. Now they want me to go back there next year, paying my own way, just so I can get sixteen more stupid credit hours. Fuck that, you know?"

I sit silent.

He lights another cigarette. "Don't make no sense, man. Everyone tells you you're supposed to go to college, but why? So you can take some bullshit desk job? I don't know a single person up there who's any smarter than they were when they got there, except on the best way to cure hangovers. Chocolate milk and Aleve, by the way." He sighs and sits down on some old tires Dad has lying around. "It's just stupid, man. Stupid."

So I was right: college *has* destroyed my brother.

I remember how he used to be, cocky, indestructible. He looks like a shell of himself. I try to imagine the same thing happening to me. It's not hard to imagine. And I don't even get to play baseball.

"Well," Doug says, throwing his unfinished cigarette

into the cornfield, "I suppose the steaks are probably done by now, and Mayor McCheese has his wife calmed down. Let's go eat."

19.

I am driving to work on Friday and pull in to get gas. As I'm paying the toothless lady behind the desk, I notice one of those cheesy plastic roses wrapped in cellophane that you can buy for, like, two bucks. *Heh*, I think, *wouldn't it be funny to get Helena one of these for her birthday today? I bet she'll set it on fire right in front of me.* I give the lady a twenty, and she smiles, a huge, toothless smile, and I think I can see her tonsils, and perhaps even her soul.

I walk into the office and Helena has her head in her hands, her hair spilling all over, as her untouched coffee shoots steam that competes with the smoldering ashtray on the desk. She is motionless, so much so that for a second I think she threw out her back or something. That happened to my dad once. He was working out in the yard and he heard a crack. He sat down on the ground and didn't move for about five minutes. I tapped him on the shoulder. "Dad?" He just grunted: "Your mother. Get your mother, Tim. Now."

Helena hasn't thrown out her back. She pulls her head up, her eyes wide wide wide, brushes her hair back, and lets out a long *whewwwwwwwwww*. Her eyes meet mine. She says nothing, just clears her throat and begins shuffling imaginary papers and straightening things that don't need straightening. It's time to act.

"Hey, happy birthday!" I shout with more fake cheer than I knew I had.

She stops the pretend upkeep and looks at me. Her voice is soft. "How did you know it was my birthday?"

"Oh, a little birdie told me," I say. "Here, sunshine, I got you something." I hand her the synthetic rose, still in the wrapping, still with the green price tag that says, CITGO SPECIAL $1.99, and the three-inch-by-three-inch card that goes with it. It says:

To the happiest, most charming and bubbly person I know . . . Have an even HAPPIER birthday!
                    —Your favorite asshead

I am smiling like a buffoon. This feels like the best prank of all time. What's she gonna do now? Is she going to just throw it in the trash? Maybe she'll bite the head off it and make a big show of chewing it up.

She does none of those things. She looks at me in a weird fashion, like a pawn shop owner inspecting a cubic zirconia ring. She turns the rose over, upside down, twirling it absently for a bit. She can't seem to figure it out. I can't understand why. I'm waiting for something incredible. *Eat it!* I think. *Eat it!*

Nope. She just looks at it and sets it down among a stack of papers. Looking down, she says, "Thank you. This must have taken a lot of thought on your drive to work."

I feel like I'm supposed to say something snide, like, "Actually, no, I just took it from a grave I saw by the road," or, "Well, I thought maybe your sunny disposition could make it grow." But suddenly, I'm not really in the mood. I leave the office and walk out to the truck. I leave the door open; I hear it slam behind me, hard.

20.

Today has been particularly wearying. We got a call this morning that the plant across town was looking for an extra shipment, so Larry and I did double time today. No lunch break, no down time, no Larry sitting in a lawn chair fanning himself and talking about his kids. All we did was lift and carry and lift and carry for nine consecutive hours. I had no time to say hi to the Horsemen, no time to give Chuck bunny ears when he wasn't looking, no time to taunt Helena. It was hard work—nonstop, sweaty, exhausting, and satisfying.

Something about this always puts me in a good mood. At baseball practice, all the pitchers and catchers had to run two miles before and after every practice. I'd go out there and bust my ass for two hours and then run with the pitchers. Our tongues were hanging out, our guts were dragging behind us, our calves felt like they were being attacked by miniature railroad laborers . . . and it was incredible. You feel like you've accomplished something. That's what today was like. Even Larry felt it.

At about five thirty, panting, drenched, after stacking a forty-pound box in the truck, I walk over to Larry.

"Not a moment to breathe today, man," I say.

"You're telling Larry," he says. "Larry hasn't been able to sneak a single beer today, and Larry *needs* his beer."

Chuck comes by and nods approvingly before hopping in his truck and taking off. I don't think I've seen that guy do a lick of work since I got here, unless "supervising" counts as work. He has a slightly smug look on his face, as if he knows we're gonna be putting in plenty of overtime and knows that's something he'll never have to deal with. Larry and I share looks of hate.

The clock ticks toward 7 p.m. I'm not sure I can feel my arms anymore, and I fear I'm barely going to be able to walk tomorrow. Larry and I are the only people left from our daytime shift. The nighttime crew has arrived, with their dead eyes and sunken shoulders. There are people here who have worked the 7 p.m.–to–3 a.m. shift for thirty years. Almost all are divorced and look like life is something they gave up on a long, long time ago. One is named Otis. He sits at the end of the line and makes sure the bagels are appropriately wrapped in their packaging and deposited in the correct box. This is all he does. There might be one malfunctioning wrapper a week. He sits there and watches them, over and over, for five nights a week, smoking a cigar and staring off into space. I have never heard him say a word. This is his life.

At seven thirty, we load the final box into the truck and wave for the driver to take off. Larry sits back in his chair and lights a cigar. "That was almost too much for Larry to take, brother," he says. "Been a long time since one of these days."

I nod. "Larry, I think my *hair* hurts."

He unleashes his deep rumble of a laugh. It makes his entire body shake, and the chair looks like it will collapse under his weight. "Only one way to fix that, Tim," he says. "I think you and Larry need to get themselves shitfaced."

That sounds like a fine idea to me.

21.

Larry is talking about politics. He doesn't know anything about politics, which is what makes it that much more entertaining.

"See, here's the deal with president, Tim, and you listen up good to Larry here, got it?" I nod. "Bush says he hates gay people, right? That's why all the church folks all come out and vote for him. But did you know that his dad was gay? Bet you didn't know that. What are you looking at Larry like that for? Big Daddy was known for it during the war. Used to go out there with those young GIs and give 'em a little shot of Herbert's Walker, if you know what Larry means."

Now, I'm aware that public school textbooks tend to give major personalities of the nineties short shrift, but I'm fairly certain this bit of history was not covered in social studies class.

"So that's the deal, you see. The little Bush, little Georgie, it wasn't enough for him just to try to fix the mess his daddy made with Saddam. Nope. He had to go after the queers because his daddy was one, and like

71

any immature kid, he hates his daddy. You see what Larry's saying here? Sad thing is, these dumb folks, they bought into the whole thing. Georgie's whole life is about messing with his daddy. And he got him good this time."

I can't resist. "But Larry, what about Barbara? His wife? Didn't she know he was gay?"

"Barbara! Ha!" Larry's voice is so loud that everyone in the bar is staring straight at him. Their gazes don't last long, though. They've seen Larry like this many, many times. "Barbara's a man, man! Look at her! She's got shoulders like *Butkus*!"

I am laughing so hard that beer is coming out my pores. Larry brays and brays—so loudly I feel it in my chest—and gives me a high five.

"All right, all right, now, settle there, Larry."

The bartender of the Tumble Inn is named Gus, and he used to play ball with my dad, which is why he is freely serving me beer after beer. He has a thick white mustache and has only a few wisps of hair, which he has combed over in a tragic attempt to fool somebody. "Larry," he says, "I think maybe you're done for the night."

"Done? *Done?!!*" Larry belts. "Shit, Gus, Larry's just getting *warmed up!*" Larry suddenly turns a shade of maroon and looks at me. He leans over to my ear. "Uh, Larry just realized he has to go to the bathroom. *Bad.*"

Like a penguin, Larry shuffles off to the bathroom, holding up his beltless pants and doing his best not to topple over.

22.

Gus serves me another Natural Light and asks me about college, launching into a monologue about the great Champaign restaurants before I have a chance to respond. I continue to find it disturbing that not only does everyone know I'm going to college, everyone has an opinion about what I should do when I'm there. The single youth minister lets me know which churches up there aren't "too liberal." My dad's co-worker Buck advises me on the best place to "pick up trim." Wilma down the road says I should put a plant in my dorm room—for the "foo shwing." The lady in the hairnet at Knowles Cafeteria says I should "get to know some Asians, in case you ever have any trouble with your book work." Every time I stop anywhere, college is the number-one topic. And they all want to give me advice about it. No one ever asks me what *I* want to do.

"It's gonna be something to be able to just pop over to the Olive Garden whenever you want to, my man," Gus says. "I don't think we're ever gonna get one of those here. It's good to eat foods from other cultures, you know, Timbo. Gotta see the rest of the world."

Larry stumbles back with his shirt untucked and his gut scraping the floor. "Whew, that was a close one for Larry," he brays. "Coulda been a lot worse!" He hoists himself back onto the stool next to me and asks Gus for a shot of whiskey. Gus raises his eyebrow almost imperceptibly, then shrugs and fills the shot glass, which has an Illini Big Ten Champs 2003–04 logo on it.

Gus looks to me. "Better get yourself one of those fake IDs, Timbo," he says. "Up in Champaign, they can be real sticklers about that stuff. And ole Gus can't follow you to school." Gus laughs loudly. The sound is starting to rattle around in my head and drive me slightly nuts. I slap Larry on the back and inform him that I need to use the restroom as well.

Larry grabs my arm. "Might want to pack yourself some galoshes before ya slosh in there," Larry shouts, spittle flying in all directions. "Larry can't be held responsible for the contents of that room." Larry laughs and laughs and laughs before falling off his stool.

I pull my best Barry Sanders and deftly avoid the fat drunk falling man and make my way to the bathroom. I see some guy in an EIU athletic jacket, with three football letters, in a back booth with four cloned blond women. He's not talking much; he's just watching them talk to each other, talk over each other, talk past each other. He has a bemused, satisfied grin on his face. Whatever happens, he's going home with one of these women.

In the booth next to theirs is an old craggled man wearing a fedora, with three empty whiskey glasses in front of him. He is reading a copy of the *Sporting News*.

I walk up to the bathroom and find a woman waiting in a solo line in front of me. She is in her fifties, at least. Her skin is rawhide, and she puffs on a thin cigarette lightly, like sipping tea out of a tiny straw. She groggily bobs left and right and grabs the wall for support when she leans over too far. Her black tank top T-shirt says, ZZ TOP, LEGS

74

Tour 1984. She sees me and smiles and calls me "sugar." I nod and look at the floor and we wait for the bathroom to empty in silence.

My eyes graze the room. Old man, college punk, old woman, group of guys in cowboy hats playing poker, Larry climbing up the bar stool. They all look kind of like the same person to me.

And there, in the back corner booth, in a cloud of smoke, under an overhead hanging lamp with a miniature model of the Budweiser Clydesdales, wearing a tiny black dress with everything popping out, is the birthday girl, Helena Westfall.

23.

Traditionally, I'm excellent under pressure—and this really, logically speaking, shouldn't be classified as pressure anyway—for some reason, though, I panic. The bathroom door opens, and I push past ZZ Top and dart into the restroom, shutting the door and locking it behind me. I stand there in some sort of puddle and look at the wall.

What's she doing here? Did she see me? Is she going to throw something at me? Where's this John dude? Why did she look so sad? I know my role in this situation is to go over there and make some cutting remark, but I don't want to. I kind of just don't want her to see me.

Any measure of drunkenness disintegrates. I look at myself in the mirror and realize that I still have dirt and grime from the Kraft plant on my face. I wipe it off and take a deep breath. I decide that she didn't see me, couldn't have seen me, would never have expected to see me. I'll just wash up, sneak back to the bar, tell Larry it's time to go, and shuffle home. No one will ever be the wiser. I don't want any trouble. Whatever's going on with Helena this evening, it's none of my business, and neither one of us wants me to be a part of it.

I open up the door and am greeted by ZZ Top, who has an irritated look on her face. I give her an apologetic glance and slip past her. I'm halfway to the bar when I hear the voice from behind me.

"Tim Temples. Look at you. I didn't know they let middle schoolers into this bar."

I turn around and Helena is leaning against an empty pool table. She's smoking a cigarette and has her hand on her hip and her head cockeyed.

"Uh, hi," I say.

"I thought you had to be able to grow facial hair to drink in this bar," she says, laughing, exhaling smoke. "Citizen's arrest, citizen's arrest." Her voice is slightly slurred but steady. It's like a purr.

"Well, yeah, I, uh, me and Larry had to work late, so we figured we'd grab a beer or two before going home," I say, my voice wavering and my hands, weirdly, shaking. I feel very uneasy.

"I saw Larry stumbling around, but I never dreamed he'd bring a kid in here." Her eyes narrow, like she's close to figuring out a particularly difficult math problem. "Funny. That's funny."

I'm still fumbling for words. "So, ah, yeah . . . well, it's neat to see you here." *Neat?* "Kind of a neat co-inky-dink." *Co-inky-dink?* The brain appears to have fallen out of my head.

She smiles at me. It's the first time she's ever smiled at me. It almost knocks me over.

"I guess there *is* something *co-inky-dinkal* about the whole thing." She laughs. "Well, why don't you sit down? Might as well. Otherwise Gus will just talk your ear off."

"Ah, well, uh, we, er, could, ah, errr . . ."

"Just go get Larry and bring him back here," she says. "I'm in the corner. And grab me a beer, would you? Heineken, please."

I grunt, put my hand up in some sort of Indian "How!" motion, and turn back to the bar and Larry. What the hell just happened here?

24.

Larry is showing pictures of the triplets to Gus, speaking in a garbled syntax that most closely resembles Klingon. "Larrhh's baahhhss wit dahhh maaaaahh upstaahhhht," he warbles. "Larrrhh's gonnnnn saahhh 'emmm nerxtt wahhhk."

Gus is paying no attention; he's watching baseball highlights on the television above the bar. "Yeah, yeah, that's good, Lar, they're good kids, they look great."

I tap Larry on the shoulder. His head, like a paralyzed owl's, swivels toward me ever so slowly. "Ahhh, Timmmm . . . haaawww izzz yahhh?" I start to tell him about

Helena, about the back of the bar, about the insanity of running into her, but he interrupts me with a thunderous belch and, then, a sudden alertness. His voice sharpens to lucidity.

"Whoa," he says. "Larry seems to have drunk a wee bit much. Larry needs to lay down."

Lay down? Where? Larry cannot go home. Right now, I'm not sure Larry could find the steering wheel.

"Larry, uh, listen, I don't think you should be driving," I say. I steel myself for some sort of confrontation. Drunk people *always* think they're just fine to drive.

But Larry surprises me. "Oh, don't you worry, Tim," he says. "Larry's no dummy. He's going to nap in his truck bed. Why they hell else do you think they call it a bed! Get it? Larry's a funny bastard, yep!" He puts down his last beer, slaps a five-dollar bill on the bar, and slowly stands. For some reason, the bar stool is stuck to him. I helpfully remove it.

"Yep, Larry's pretty plastered," he says. "Stay and have a few beers on Larry's tab, Tim. When you leave, just see what you can do to wake Larry up. Punch him in the face if you have to. Larry can take it."

He then waddles to the door, opens it, and walks out. Through the front window, I see him walk up to his truck, veering left and right, almost approaching the wrong truck, and then he stops. He grabs the side of the truck, hoists himself up . . . and over. He hits the bed of the truck with a loud crash, and the entire vehicle shakes.

I see his feet hanging over the side, slowly swaying

78

before falling motionless. I sit there for a moment, in shock, really. Larry's great, but I can't *believe* he just left me alone with *her*.

Well. Here goes. I order a Heineken and a Natural Light and walk to the back of the bar.

25.

Helena is sitting down in a booth meant for four people, with two full packs of cigarettes, her purse, and an unusually large cell phone in front of her. The jukebox is playing Nelly's "Hot in Herre," which is pleasing no one but the four girls around the football player, one of whom is standing on a chair and gyrating. One of the old men glares at her, and she meets his eye and sits back down. The quintet goes quiet, and right as I walk up, they gather their belongings and leave.

Helena's smile is still clouding my brain, the same way a spot stays on your eyes when you shut them after staring straight at the sun. Right now, though, she's not smiling. She's looking at her cell phone and frowning.

A thought occurs to me: This is the Helena I work with every day. The Helena who is probably plotting to kill me. What the hell am I doing here? I'm *this* close to turning the opposite direction when her head turns toward me and she waves me over. "Bring me *beer!*" she shouts in a bemused, over-the-top way.

I sit down across from her in the booth and hand her the beer.

"What, did Larry die?" she asks.

"Oh, uh, I think he's had too much to drink," I say. "He's sleeping it off in his truck out in the parking lot. He's actually in the *back* of the truck."

Helena laughs. "That guy's a piece of work" she says. "One time I came into work at, like, eight in the morning, and I noticed that his truck was still sitting in his spot . . . and it was *running*! I looked in the window, and he was sitting in the passenger's seat, dead to the world. After his shift ended, he must have fallen asleep right there. I had to wake him up before Chuck came in, saw he wasn't on the loading dock, and fired him. He looked up at me and said, 'Whoa, it's 8 a.m. Larry musta lost track of time.'"

This story makes me laugh, though not for the reason Helena thinks (though her Larry impression *is* fantastic): I'd had to do the same thing just the week before. Except Larry was lying upside down with his feet stuck in the headrest. Shirtless.

We sit there for a moment, not sure what to say. The jukebox starts up Phil Collins's "Groovy Kind of Love," and she seems to grow even quieter. Her head turns toward me and she draws a bit of a sneer. "You're drinking Natural Light?" she says. "That's some nasty shit. That's just cat piss with the yellow taken out."

"Well, I don't drink your fancy-pants foreign beer," I say. My father once told me to never trust a man who didn't like sports or a woman who drank beers not made by Anheuser-Busch. "Just the good ole US of A for me."

"It's still beer, for chrissakes," she says, scoffing. "You act like I'm drinking sake or something."

I don't know what sake is, so I let it pass. "You want a cigarette?" she asks.

I have smoked one cigarette in my life, and it turned me thirty different variations of gray. "No thanks," I say. "I'll hack my colon up onto the table. And colons are kind of gross."

She laughs. "Hey, you actually had an intelligent thought. I'm impressed."

More silence. I'm beginning to think this was a bad idea. She finishes her entire cigarette without saying a word. Then: "Hey, how about shots?"

This is a bad idea. This is a terrible idea. This is the guy who told Noah, "Hey, no thanks, man, it's a beautiful day for a swim."

Despite this, the following words come from my mouth: "Hey, why not?"

26.

After two truly wretched shots called Prairie Fires—Tabasco sauce and tequila, a combination that really should be illegal—Helena starts to get a little loopy.

"So, anyway, I was telling my sister how I couldn't believe that Troy from *Survivor* was really a firefighter because I think he's probably gay, and I don't think they let gay people be firefighters. Do they? And he was so stupid to avoid an alliance with Gary. Gary was his only real

hope. Of *course* they were gonna vote him off after that."
Pause. "But then, reality TV is so stupid. Why do people
watch that junk? It's just a waste of time." Pause. "Did you
know that Paul Shaffer wrote 'It's Raining Men'? Can you
believe that? I mean, you couldn't even make that up!"

I've barely spoken. I have just looked at her. When
she's not chucking pens at me, I have realized, she's quite
lovely. She's very *round*, but not in a fat or porky type of
way. Something about her is almost *fluffy*; it feels like
you could just get lost in her. She's nothing but flesh,
mounds of soft, smooth flesh.

I have time to sit and think about her flesh, because she
has been talking without letting up or even noticing that
I'm there. She's talking so much that I can't believe she
was sitting by herself an hour ago. She clearly wanted to
talk tonight and would probably still be yakking away if
you set a big stuffed animal across from her.

I sip my Natural and just watch her. What a strange
woman.

Then, suddenly, she's aware of me for the first time in a
while. Her eyes narrow at me, and she lights another cigarette. She looks like she's sizing me up, like a bettor looking
at a racehorse right before the opening gun. She then sighs.

"So," she says, "you're probably wondering why I'm
sitting here at a bar by myself on my birthday."

I, of course, had been wondering that exact thing. "Oh,
is it your birthday?" I say. "That's right. I totally forgot."

"*Sure*, you did," she says, not even slowing down. "Well,
I'm not as pathetic as you think. I know you think I'm

82

pathetic. I guess I probably look pathetic. But I'm not. *You're the peach fuzz wonder, you know."* The flash of the Helena anger evaporates as quickly as it erupted. "The guy I've been seeing, he's from Charleston. We were supposed to go out tonight, but he ended up having to work at the last minute. Well, that's what he said anyway. I don't know why anyone suddenly has to work at ten o'clock on a Friday. . . ."

I don't say a word. I bet John's married, though.

"So anyway, that kind of left me hanging. Most of my friends in town have kids, and no one can get a sitter that late. And I didn't want to go to the Alamo because that's just a bunch of sleazy college brats who are just gonna try to get in my pants all night, right?"

I have never been to the Alamo. It's an EIU bar. "Right," I say.

"Oh, and on the way here, I stepped in dog shit," she says.

"Actually, that might have been Larry's," I joke.

"Ha. So, as you can see, it has been, quite literally, a shitty birthday. But I had to go somewhere. You only turn twenty-three once, right? Nobody here but drunks and other lost souls."

"And me," I say.

"Yeah," she says. "And you. For some reason."

27.

The conversation veers toward lousy birthdays in our pasts. I come up woefully short in this regard, my worst being a birthday I had at McDonald's when I was nine, when the guy dressed up as Grimace was drunk and threw up in his suit.

Helena, according to her calculations, has been broken up with on her birthday four times, been in a car wreck twice, and, the birthday after her high school graduation, had a pregnancy scare. This woman is five years older than me, but it seems more than ever like she's thirty. The drunker she gets, the sadder and older she is.

"So anyway, it turned out that it was a false alarm, but yeah, it was absolutely terrifying," she says. "I was, like, eighteen years old. Like anyone has any idea what they're doing at eight—" She pauses. "Uh, sorry. No offense."

"No worries," I say, worried.

"So, all told, this one isn't all that horrible. Sure, John's probably never going to talk to me again, all my friends have deserted me, my nice heels are covered in dog crap, and I'm sitting alone at the freaking Tumble Inn."

"Relatively speaking, I guess you've had worse," I say. "But there's still time. If you want, I could dress up like Grimace and throw up."

She laughs, then is quiet for a beat. She looks at her beer bottle and starts to absentmindedly fidget with the label, peeling it off. She peers up at me. "Oh, and I wanted to say, the rose was nice."

The rose. I had completely forgotten about it. "Really?" I say, finding myself blushing. "It was nothing."

"Well, I know that," she says. "You bought it at the Citgo. You didn't even take the price tag off. You don't have to remind me that it was nothing."

"Sorry."

"No, no. I mean, you're still the only one in that entire plant who remembered that it was my birthday. I've worked with Chuck for four years, and he didn't say a word. How'd you know, anyway?"

Do I confess to eavesdropping? Oh, shit, I'm sure she already knows. "I heard you on the phone. I think you were talking to that John guy. Hey, you should know better than to date a guy from Charleston. They're all dicks."

She holds her head in her hands. "I'm sure he's married," she says.

"Could be." I shrug.

"Oh, why do I bother?" she whines. "My cousin Jill and I will probably end up old and alone together in a nursing home somewhere."

I chuckle, already feeling sorry for that nursing home staff.

The jukebox finishes playing a Garth Brooks song. Helena perks up. "Hey, come with me!"

28.

The jukebox doesn't have any actual albums, instead just mix CDs put together by Gus. More accurately, put together by one of Gus's merciful relatives, who realized that, even in Mattoon, in the year 2005, you aren't going earn much money from your jukebox if it only plays George Jones and Conway Twitty. The CDs are labeled in a junior high girl's loopy handwriting, with little hearts dotting the *i*'s in titles like "Oops! . . . I Did It Again," "Paradise by the Dashboard Light," and, insanely, "Highway to Hell" (with a little heart over the *i* in *highway*).

Helena flips through, back and forth, trying to find something she can stomach. There isn't much.

"Janet Jackson. Her breasts sag worse than my grand-mother's.

"When did people actually start thinking Lindsay Lohan could sing?

"Do you think Jessica Simpson is actually retarded, or was she just kicked in the head by a horse as a child?

"'Hey Ya.' Jesus, white people can't get enough of this song."

I don't have many comments to add because, frankly, I have no idea what Helena is talking about. My musical taste is pretty limited. Whatever's playing is usually fine. It's not like I actually *listen*.

I chortle at the right points and play along, though, letting her rant and rave and snort.

She settles on one CD, titled *Car-Washing Classic Rock Mix*, and laughs. "Car-washing music. That's really funny. Music to wash your car in the driveway to. That's great." She cackles madly. "This okay with you? Or do you want some Avril Lavigne or something?"

I don't know who this Avril guy is, so I just shake my head and wave my hand dismissively.

Her dollar, wrinkled beyond recognition, is rejected by the machine two or three times. She smacks it and curses a bit. Finally it goes through, and the opening strummings

86

of a rock song I don't know blare through the speakers.

Helena starts dancing. Well, it's not really a dance. It's more of a leisurely sway, from left to right, her hips arriving at a point about a rhythmic half second after her torso does. It's slinky, slow, a lava lamp in a tiny black dress. Her eyes meet mine and then dart away quickly. She glances back. "I love this song," she whispers.

I'm not quite sure what to do with myself while she's dancing, and this song, whatever it is, is a little long. There aren't many people in the bar, but those who are here seem as transfixed as I am. And then, inevitably, they look at the high school kid in the Cardinals hat standing next to the chesty woman in the black dress, and then they realize it's Tim Temples, and then they wonder who the girl is, and then they figure it out, and people will talk and talk and talk, and that's going to make my nice simple brainless job infinitely more complicated. Even though it's difficult to imagine anyone believing something might be going on with Helena and me, it could still be trouble.

So, at 3 a.m. on a Friday night, almost completely alone in a crappy dive bar, I can't help thinking, *What exactly is going on here?*

Actually, better question: *With a hot woman dancing in front of me, why am I thinking in the first place?*

But still I stand here, smiling occasionally, fidgeting, doing my best to look like I belong, like I am not unbearably uncomfortable with a hot woman in a barely there black dress dancing in front of me.

Finally, *finally* the song ends, and her body slows, and

she has worked up a little bit of a sweat in her solitude, and she wipes her forehead and remembers where she is, and she sees me and she frowns and she smiles and she seems to at last notice that I was here the whole time, and she laughs and pulls the hair away from her face and takes my arm and whispers in my ear, "That was fun."

29.

"Did you love that song? I just *luvvvvvvvvv* that song."

It's two hours later. I'm laughing. We're both laughing like complete idiots.

"I don't know who that was," I say. "Was it Celine Dion?" We both explode in hysterics, though I can't imagine why this is possibly funny.

"No, you *dummy*, it's Led Zeppelin," she says. "You must have the most unhip parents on the planet. Were you raised on Pat Boone? Jim Nabors? What's wrong with your family? Hell, what's wrong with your *friends*?!"

"I just don't listen to much music, that's all," I say. "What was the name of the song?"

Helena has started to hiccup. "It's called 'Ramble On.' It was my dad's favorite song of theirs. He used to be a roadie for them."

I interrupt her. "What's a roadie?"

"Jesus Christ, Tim," she says, addressing me by my name for the first time ever. "You don't know what a roadie is? A roadie is the guy who sets up the stage for rock bands when they go on tour. Though, according to my mom, all they really do is set the band up with groupies. Wait . . . you know what groupies are, don't you?"

I nod. Believe you me, I *know* what groupies are.

"Anyway, I love that song," she says. "It's about not knowing where you're going and still knowing that you have to keep moving anyway."

"Is that why you're working at Kraft? Because you have to keep moving?" I say, and I immediately regret it.

"Hey, screw you," she says, her face steeling. "Not everybody gets to have their life freaking handed to them like you do."

I am surprised that this offends me. After all the names this woman has called me, I'm not sure why *this* bothers me so much, but it does. I look away, and she notices.

"Aw, come on, I'm just kidding," she says, though we both know she wasn't. "I'm sorry. I'm just drunk." Her eyes widen and she becomes serious, as serious as someone with the hiccups can become. "I'm not so bad, you know. I'm really not. I just hate it over there. And besides, you don't get to be all offended and shit. It's *my* birthday. You have to be nice." She puts her hand on mine, playfully, and taps my wrist.

"Niiiiiice," she repeats. *Tap. Tap. Tap.*

I look into her eyes and am startled by the way they sparkle.

It's another moment before I realize that Gus is standing right next to our table. As we snap ourselves out of the conversation, we notice that the lights in the rest of the bar are off and that we're the only people left. Gus has a white towel over his left shoulder.

89

"Thought you two were still back here," he says.

I rub my eyes. "What time is it?"

"Four thirty," he says, "Closing time."

Helena has little black smudges of eye shadow sprinkled all over her face, and she continues to spread them as she massages her cheeks with her palms. She yawns and looks temporarily horrified. A hiccup stirs her back to a reminder that she is, in fact, drunk. She takes a swig of her beer. "So, what, we gotta go or something?" she says. Gus eyes her uneasily. "Yeah, lamppost, I think you and Timbo better go."

"Thanks for everything, Gus," I say. "Have a nice night."

Helena gathers her belongings—though she only has a purse, a pack of cigarettes, and a cell phone, it takes her an awfully long time—and says she has to use the bathroom. I stand there with Gus for a moment, one of those moments that are inevitably uncomfortable, because I already said my goodbye and now we're standing here, bobbing back and forth on our heels, clicking our tongues against the roofs of our mouths, twiddling our thumbs, clearing our throats.

"So, wild night, eh, Timbo?" Gus's foot is tapping the sticky cement floor. It's clear he would have loved to close the bar hours ago. His bedroom is right upstairs.

"Oh, not a big thing, sir, no," I say. "It's her birthday, and I just kind of ran into her." Pause. "Randomly." Pause. "I was with Larry, see, and I—"

Helena comes out of the restroom and looks strangely composed and together all of a sudden. She notices my surprise, then leans over to me and whispers in my ear, "It's amazing what a little makeup will do, darlin'."

Gus shuts off the rest of the lights and heads outside with us, locking the door behind him. The stairs to his apartment are right next to the bar's door. He looks us over slowly. "You kids gonna be all right?" he asks.

I stopped drinking a while back. I feel all right, I guess. "We're fine," I call out to Gus.

Helena whispers in my ear, "I'm fine. But *you* are an assface."

Aha! I silently rejoice. That's the Helena I know.

The night is crisp for June, and the sky is clear and full of stars. They stretch on forever. Helena lights a cigarette and puts her elbow on my shoulder. "All right, how we gonna do this?" she says.

What does she mean? How we gonna do *what*?

"I wouldn't admit it to that prick, but I really don't feel all that comfortable driving home. I'm pretty sure I can make it, but I'd feel better if you followed me back. Just drive behind me, make sure I don't go flying off the road or anything." She pauses. "You're okay to drive, right?"

I tell her I am just fine. Which I am. I guess. Pretty much. Mostly. Sure.

"Good," she says. "So let's go. It's just a mile up Broadway. Real close. Just don't tailgate me or anything. Last thing I need is some cop pulling us both over. Your parents would probably kill me."

We walk over to our cars, parked a couple of spots away from each other. She's driving a 1993 Toyota

Camry; I recognize the year and model because my older cousin Mike has the exact same one.

I unlock the door to my truck, and I'm struck with the thought that I'm forgetting something. It has been a whirlwind evening, and much is escaping my mind at the moment. Keys? Got 'em. Wallet? Yep. Sunglasses? Still in the truck. I look around the backseat to see if anything looks out of place or missing. Everything is tip-top back there. I have tons of room in the Blazer, and I always keep it real clean. You could sleep back there if you wanted.

Sleep . . . wait . . . Larry!

Right as Helena starts her car, I leap out of the Blazer. She looks at me with alarm. "Larry!" I yell. "I completely forgot about Larry!" Her eyes grow very wide, but she's doing her best to hide a grin, I can just tell.

"We should go check on him," I say.

"Yeah." She whistles. "I dunno, though . . . I'm almost afraid to look."

We walk over to Larry's truck together, parked on the other side of the rock-paved lot. With serious trepidation, I look into the truck bed. There is Larry, lying there, dead asleep, peaceful. His huge chest is heaving up and down, and he's snoring like a dump truck, not a care in the world.

"Awww," she says. "He looks so cute." She turns, walks back to her car, and opens the trunk. She brings out an oversized blue comforter and a big fluffy pillow. I look at her with amazement. "Hey, you never know when you might have to lie down somewhere," she says.

She gently lays the blanket over Larry and carefully

props the pillow under his enormous head. "Sleep tight, sweet prince," she whispers. "Be safe through the night."

30.

Helena is driving *slowwwwwly*. If I had my windows rolled down, I bet the bugs would come flying in. I'm barely touching the gas pedal. This mile down Broadway is going to take a long time.

This is such an odd assignment I've been given. I'm not sure what Helena expects me to do if she *does* go careening off the road. I'm in a *truck*. If anything does happen, she has merely assured me an excellent front-row seat to the carnage. I take out my cell phone just in case. I dial the 9 and the 1 so I'll be ready.

Then I wonder, what will Monday be like? Will Helena be as rude to me as usual? Will she loosen up? Or will she feel like she has a rep to uphold, that she has to be the Office Bitch? And won't it look weird if we're suddenly friendly? My head spins as I flip through all the different permutations. Of course, if she *is* still mean to me, I think I have a trump card. It's hard to be aloof and dismissive of someone who has seen you hiccup for two hours.

She makes a right turn past a house with a sign out front: SHEAR ESSENCES. I've been there; it's where my mom gets her hair cut. Some lady named Dorothy runs it out of her living room. Every time I drop by to pick up my mom, a mean dog barks at me like crazy. I hear him barking now, at four thirty. It makes me nervous.

Helena makes a slow left turn, turns her lights off, and pulls into her driveway. I am not sure what to do here. Do I wave? Give a little "All right, you made it, have a nice night" salute as I scoot by and head home? Should I get out? What's the protocol here? She shuts her car off and steps outside, stopping, then walking toward me. I pull my car to the curb and leave it running as I step out myself.

She is smiling. "Well, thanks for following me home, Skippy."

Skippy? "Hey, no problem," I say. "Um, it was a nice night."

"Yes, it was actually," she says. "You be careful going home."

I nod. "No problem." What happens now? Do I shake her hand? Give her a playful pop on the shoulder? Just turn around and start running? "So, uh, happy birthday. I'm sorry it didn't quite work out the way you had planned."

She looks down and brushes her hair out of her face. She tucks it behind her right ear. She looks up at me. "Hey, it's just a birthday, right?" She stands there for an infinite second, then moves toward me and gives me a hug. I hug her back, awkwardly, and she holds the hug for longer than I expected. She whispers into my chest, "Thanks for not making me spend my birthday alone. Oh . . . and thanks for the rose. Really."

I hold on to her and catch a whiff of her hair. It's nice. Some kind of flowery scent. "No problem," I say. "Anytime."

She pulls her head up and slowly, *so slowly*, kisses me on the cheek. She holds her lips there a beat. Instinctively,

I caress the back of her hair. Her face moves to the left, a bit, a bit, a bit . . . and then she kisses me on the lips.

It's soft. I do not resist. I am hesitant at first, but then muscle memory kicks in, and there we are, in her front yard, with my truck running, with the dog barking in the distance, with the sound of the birds starting to replace the crickets, in the wet grass, together, just us. I am no longer kissing her. I am summoning up something from my toes, and it is working its way through my legs, through my waist, through my chest, and it is pouring into her.

We are there on her lawn forever, and then forever ends, and she looks up at me, and her face is sharp, focused, intent.

"My mom's asleep. Come inside."

I can think of nothing on earth I have wanted to do more. I have no idea why. And I do not care. But is it supposed to be like this? She's *plastered*. Will she even remember this? In the past, I might not have cared. But it seems wrong now. Cheap, somehow.

"I don't know," I say. "Maybe it's not a good idea."

She kisses me again, harder this time. "Probably not," she purrs into my ear. "But we'll never know if you don't come in."

Without a word, I separate myself from her, which makes her frown slightly. I walk over to my truck, turn off the ignition, and leave the keys on the driver's seat. I turn around and look at her. Her head is cocked slightly; she looks like she's waiting to see if a stray dog is going to keep following her home.

I move toward her. She turns around and tiptoes toward the house. She silently opens the screen door and turns the door handle just enough so that it clicks. She looks back at me.

"Come in."

I walk through the door, following her to who knows where.

JULY

1.

Chuck is reading the newspaper with his muddy boots propped up on Helena's desk. She is trying to file some papers. She is looking at Chuck with a considerable dollop of hate. Chuck hasn't noticed.

"Heh, heh, heh, that Kerry Wood got hammered last night," Chuck says, scanning the sports page. "Big dumb Texan. Couldn't happen to a better guy." He is chewing tobacco loudly. Every few minutes he'll spit in his empty coffee cup. Helena just sits there, waiting for this fat man with the boots on her desk and the brown spittle to go away.

I am on my lunch "break," which basically consists of grabbing a package of Cheese Nips from the vending machine and gulping down my fifth Coke, roaming around the office, making a nuisance of myself. The Horsemen are never around during my lunch hour. I never see them take lunch, actually; they always seem to be on the line, working slowly, zombies, never looking up.

I'm pacing around, doing nothing. I look at a picture on the wall I hadn't noticed before; it's of a *somewhat* thinner Chuck and Kurt Kittner, former quarterback for the University of Illinois football team, the one that won the Big Ten and was slaughtered by LSU in the Sugar Bowl. It is not signed, and Kittner appears to be talking to someone just off camera.

"He just got cut again, Timbo," Chuck says, noticing my attention to the photo. "Bears had him for a week, then the Niners, and now he might go play Arena League, if you can believe that. I told him when I met him that he needed to work up his arm strength. Guess he didn't listen."

I acknowledge his name-dropping with a noncommittal grunt and look at Helena. She shoots me a stare: "What are you doing in here?" she says. "Don't you have anything better to do than pick your nose and get in everybody's way? I mean, should we give you a coloring book or something?"

Chuck laughs loudly. Pieces of chaw are flying in all directions, and I think his gut is slapping the top of the desk. "Now, you leave Timbo alone, he's got as much right to be here as you do," he starts, cheerily. Then he switches, anger turning his fat face bright red. "Besides, if anyone is sitting around picking their nose, it's you. Instead of complaining, why don't you try getting some goddamned work done?"

Helena looks down at her desk and I feign interest in Chuck's son's perfect attendance awards. Finally he stands, twists on his overworked, tragic feet, and heads out the office door, slamming it hard.

Helena looks at him and flips off his back as he walks away. She then takes a Kleenex and wipes the mud from Chuck's boots off her desk. I walk over to her and grab a napkin to help.

I look at her. "I bet that guy has never been laid in his entire life," I say.

Helena smiles, puts down her Kleenex, and taps me on the forehead playfully. "Good thing you don't have that problem," she says. She glances over my shoulder to make sure no one is looking. No one is. She presses herself against me and leans close to my ear. "You don't, do you? No. You. Don't."

She pulls away with a grin. This has pretty much been the routine for the last two weeks. Sly, whispered looks at work, leaving an hour apart so no one suspects anything, meeting up at her place, taking one car wherever we can slip away unnoticed and undisturbed. Not a day has gone by when we have not spent the evening together. It helps to have parents who are busy and trust me.

"So, where are we going tonight?" I ask.

"My cousin Jill works at the French Embassy in Arcola," she says. "I think you'll like that place. It's right up your alley."

"That sounds great to me," I say. "Make sure you bring plenty of Skoal." I turn to go back to the truck, back to work, and she smacks me on the ass as I walk out. I utter a girlish "ooh!" and she laughs as she goes back to her papers and her filing.

I'm not sure how to explain these past two weeks, except to say it's the first time I've ever really wanted to hang out with a girl—not for the hookup, but because I actually like her more each day than I did the day before; each day is a different adventure. Everything about her is different from anyone I've ever been with before—*everything*.

But what does it mean? I have no idea, and, frankly, I'm in no hurry to ask.

2.

Arcola is a tiny town about thirty miles outside of Mattoon, with a population of about two thousand. One stoplight, a Red Roof Inn, a Shell gas station, a high school, and a McDonald's. The drive out there, on Route 45, is littered with trailer parks, poorly lit sharp turns, and the occasional pig farm. The stink at times can become unbearable.

Already, Helena and I are to the point that we can take a thirty-minute drive where we just listen to music and don't talk. She knows all kinds of music I've never heard, and she loves to introduce it to me. Currently, we're listening to a band called the Smoking Popes, a name that sounds vaguely sexual to me. But the music is nothing like that. It's upbeat, and it's sad; it's a guy trying to put the best face on a broken heart. The songs have titles like "No More Smiles." It makes me drive faster, yet with unusual care.

"This is really good," I say.

"You like them?" she says. "They're great. An old boyfriend of mine turned me on to them. They broke up a few years ago." She giggles uncomfortably. "Of course, so did we!"

I turn off the interstate and take a left at a White Hen Pantry that advertises LIVE BAIT INSIDE. "It's kind of funny," I say. "I never listen to music when I'm driving."

"What do you do? Just sit here in silence?" she asks.

"Naw, I'm usually listening to the ballgame or sports radio," I say, feeling embarrassed, feeling kind of stupid. "I don't know why. I'm just used to it, I guess."

Helena blows some smoke out the window. "Most of those talk radio guys are lame," she says. "I mean, all they do is yammer about how the Cards should fire La Russa all the time. They don't like him because he's Italian, but, you know, how many World Series have *they* been to?"

I look at Helena, astonished. "Wait—you follow baseball?"

She turns to me and smirks. "Please," she says. "You think you can be a girl in this town and not follow baseball? Even if I didn't like it, I'd have to study the box scores just to have something to talk about." She leans over and pinches my side. "Besides, guys look great in baseball pants."

I jump, laughing. I'm pretty ticklish.

We listen to a couple more songs before I wonder where the hell we're going. "Where is this place?" I say as we arrive in Arcola proper. She tells me to take a left at

103

the stoplight, and we drive for another couple of miles and turn right on a dirt road. I see lights in the distance. "Is that it?" I ask. "It looks like a roller rink."

I'm not far off. The parking lot, paved with loose rocks, makes no sense: it's half pickup trucks, half BMWs and Mercedes. (Not surprisingly, they are parked on opposite sides.) But the building itself is what stuns me to silence. There is a door right in the middle. On its left is what seems like the most fancy-pants restaurant you can imagine. The windows are tinted, and I see flickers of candles and outlines of people dining in a prim fashion, cloth napkins in their laps, wearing suits and evening gowns. On the door's right: a bowling alley. A huge one, with blank but glowing fluorescent lighting, Budweiser neon signs, a guy in a paper hat making hot dogs, some kids milling outside smoking cigarettes and sneaking sips from a brown bag.

"What the hell is this place?" I ask Helena.

"Oh, just wait," she says, giggling.

Next to the door, there is a plaque with a laminated newspaper article encased. It is from the *New York Times*, February 21, 1996. I scan it quickly. Some famous French chef moved to Arcola with his wife. He wanted to start a restaurant in town but couldn't find any open real estate—except for the old skating rink, now closed, next to the bowling alley. So he started his five-star restaurant, with which he shares a lobby with a bunch of guys in funny shoes.

I look at Helena. "You have to be kidding me."

She takes my arm. "Come on, it's funny," she says. "Be

a sport." She leads me in. To my relief, we turn right, not left.

3.

We sit down at a molded plastic booth with molded plastic chairs, and Helena tells me she'll be right back. I look around. It's late Friday, and the lanes are nearly empty. A young couple takes turns aiming at pins; one fires the ball down the lane, the other one tries to calm their wailing baby. An old man is in the far lane, alone, scribbling down his scores furiously. Starship is playing on the jukebox. *We built this city. We built this city on rock. And. Roll.*

Helena returns with a rundown-looking woman wearing a white shirt with black pants. Her face is wrinkled and leathery prematurely; she's either thirty years old or fifty, I can't tell, and I wonder if it matters, even to her. She is carrying a bottle of wine, and Helena has two large plastic foam cups.

"Jill, this is Tim. Tim, Jill. She's my cousin. She's totally hooking us up tonight."

Jill shakes my hand, limply. I try to make a joke. "Horse walks into a bar. Bartender says, 'Why the long face?'"

Jill stares at me blankly.

"Uh, never mind," I say.

She speaks: "So anything you guys need, just come and get me. We're hardly busy, and Jean-Georges is drunk again anyway." She walks away, sullen.

Helena sits down and pours the wine into the cups. "You sure you don't want a straw?" She smiles. We cheer each other—"Tink!" she says as our cups meet—and she lights up a cigarette.

"So, what's with your cousin?" I ask.

"How do you mean?" she says, frowning slightly.

"Well, she looks kind of sad," I say, sipping the wine. It tastes like motor oil with a drop of jalapeño in it. I could really go for a beer. "She doesn't seem to like her job very much."

Helena drinks the wine in great, round gulps, clearly enjoying it. "Oh, she's fine. Just had a hard time of it. She got divorced recently. Now she's just kind of filling time, not sure what to do with herself. She lives just down the road."

"In the trailer park?" I blink, surprised.

Helena's eyes narrow. "Yeah, in the trailer park." She has an urgent look on her face. "Nothing wrong with that."

"No, of course. I didn't mean . . ." I trail off. If I'm living alone in a trailer park when I'm thirty-slash-fifty, I will kill myself. But the whole topic seems to frustrate Helena, so I try to recover.

"This wine is, uh, really good," I say, hoping my face isn't scrunched.

"Do you like it?" she says. "It's a 1998 Bonaccorsi Syrah."

"1998?" I say. "Like, that's when it was made? Jesus, it must be spoiled by now."

"No, silly," she says, laughing. "Wine gets *better* with age. Surely you know that. It's kind of an interesting story, this wine. The guy who made it actually is from the Chicago suburbs. He went to the U of I, like you. He was in business school, but he met this girl there and they fell in love. She loved wine, and she turned him on to it, and next thing you knew, he dropped out of college and they moved for a while to Burgundy."

I look at her quizzically.

"That's in France," she says.

"Oh."

"Anyway, he learned all he could about wines, and then he started his own vineyard. What was strange was that he did it in Santa Barbara, California, where nobody grows wines because it's too far south; the temperature doesn't vary enough. But somehow he did it, and he's considered one of the greatest winemakers in U.S. history. He just died a few months ago. He never had kids or anything, just him and his wife, living on a vineyard, stomping grapes."

"That's an amazing story," I say, and I mean it. I always thought they made wine pretty much the same way they made bagels. "Have you been to that vineyard? What's it like?"

Helena smiles. "Oh, no, I've never been there," she says. "I've never been *anywhere*. But I watch the Discovery Channel a lot. You can learn just about everything you need to know about the world from the Discovery Channel."

"I guess I should watch that channel more," I say.

Helena raises her right eyebrow. "I guess you should," she says.

There's something about the way she looks at me—all sexy and playful—that makes me want to take her in my arms and spin her until we both fall over.

Helena's cell phone rings. She gives me the "Sorry, gotta take this" look and answers. It's her mom.

"Yes . . . Oh, no . . . All right. Just stay calm, Mom . . . Listen, which pill did you take? . . . The gray bottle or the brown one? . . . That's good . . . that's the right one. . . . All right . . . No, you *should* be tired, it's a narcotic. . . . No, Mom, not that kind of narcotic . . . Just relax and go to sleep. . . . I'll be home late, all right? . . . Yeah, love you too. 'Bye."

I look at Helena with concern. "Everything okay?"

"Oh, she's fine, she just gets confused about the labels on the bottles," she says, frowning. "It's so much simpler than she makes it. If I didn't keep it straight for her, she'd probably OD every night."

"I'm sorry," I say, not sure what I'm apologizing for.

"No, it's good," she says. "She needs me there. And besides, nothing says mother-daughter bonding like a reliance on pharmaceuticals." She laughs to herself.

I shift gears. "You look lovely tonight, Ms. Helena," I say. Women like it when you refer to them as "Ms." before their first name. It sounds formal yet charming— quirky. "Your eyes, uh, your eyes, are . . ."

"My eyes what?" she says, breaking into a smirk so charged with irony that it nearly melts the plastic table.

"This glorious bowling alley lighting really brings out the beauty of my eyes?" She laughs and pops me on the shoulder. "Come on, Temples, you can do better than that. That line might play in the sticks, but did you forget who you were talking to here? I'm a *real* woman."

I blush for a moment before breaking into a grin. "Oh, all right, I'm busted," I say. I lean back, lounging. "They're not all gold, baby!" I decide to do my Dean Martin. "You're dazzling, baby, dazzling! You're like a great big shining star, a great big star! You're all pizzazz. Pizz and azz, that's you, baby! You a model? You gotta be a model, baby!"

"Who, me? Little old me?" she says, playing along.

"I tell ya, kiddo, ya stick with me, you'll see your name in lights, baby, lights!"

"Whee! I'm the luckiest girl in the world!" She laughs and pours more wine.

4.

"So, how did you lose your virginity?" Helena asks, and I spit up my wine. We have been here for several hours now. They've closed down the bowling alley and the restaurant; Jill gave Helena the keys and asked her to lock up "when you're finished doing whatever the hell you do." All the lights in the alley are off except for the ones above us. It has the effect of making the alley look like, well, like a fancy French restaurant.

"How did I *what*?" The wine is now going down

smoothly. I guess it's like beer that way; you just have to get used to it.

"First time you ever had sex," she says, blowing out smoke. "What was it like? Who was it with?" In this light, with the smoke in the air, she looks like a fifties movie star.

I think for a moment about how much of this story I want to tell Helena, and I decide I'll tell her all of it.

"Her name was Amanda," I say. "She was a senior and I was a freshman."

Helena raises her eyebrows. "So you've always had a thing for older women?"

"Oh, we didn't date or anything," I say. "She came over to see my brother when he was home from college one weekend. He wasn't around, and neither were my parents. She told me I looked like him, kind of, only younger. And then, well, then she just kind of pounced on me. I really didn't know what was happening. It was very romantic."

"How long did you last?" she asks with a mischievous grin.

"About thirty seconds," I say. "It would have been even shorter, but I think I think I blacked out for the first twenty."

Helena laughs. "Well, I'm pleased to see that you've improved."

"How about you? What was your first time?"

"It was one of my dad's old roadie friends," she says. "I was fifteen. He was working for some metal band, and they were playing in Champaign. He came by and hung out with my parents. They let me stay up, and after they went to bed, he kissed me. And then one thing led to another. I didn't really want to at first, but I figured I'd have to learn how to have sex sometime, and he was a friend of my parents, so I figured he was okay."

This story disturbs me, and I tell her so.

"I know!" she says. "I saw the guy again at my dad's funeral, and he was totally afraid to talk to me. Who knows what he thought? But it was no big deal."

I try to picture the fifteen-year-old Helena at that moment. The image hurts. She seems so sad. I want to help her. "What was the first thing that made you so happy that you cried?" I ask.

"Easy," she says. "I won a gymnastics competition when I was eight. I did everything perfect. They gave me the best scores, and I got to stand on the podium and everything. My dad was so proud, and my mom was crying, and it just made me so happy. I cried so much that my instructor thought I'd hurt myself. I still have the picture from the day next to my bed."

"That's a wonderful story," I say. I like this game. I want to keep it going. "Favorite stuffed animal?"

"I have an Alf doll my mom got me when I was a kid," she says. "He's wearing a chef's hat."

"First time you felt like a grown-up?"

"I am not a grown-up."

"Favorite day of the year?"

"New Year's Eve. It's the one day of the year where the only requirement is that you have fun."

"Ever wish you had a brother or sister?"

"No. I'm too much of an attention whore."

"Favorite movie?"

"*Singing in the Rain*. It makes me really happy."

"Favorite ice cream flavor?"

"Rocky Road. Though I think vanilla tastes really good. Is that weird?"

"First time you ever slapped a guy?"

She smiles. "When he asked me too many questions." She leans over and nibbles my earlobe, then puts her cigarette out and yawns.

"You know, I've always wondered what it looks like behind the pins in a bowling alley." She stands up and takes off her shoes. She slides like an ice skater across the dimly lit lanes, and as she's gliding, I see her, from the back, unbutton her blouse and drop it behind her.

"You're not going anywhere without me," I shout at her as she prances off.

She turns and looks at me with those topaz eyes. "Come on. Catch me."

I stand up from my chair and hustle toward her, chasing her down the slippery lanes. With each step, my feet threaten to slide out from under me. But finally, I reach her. I grab ahold of her, and I do not let go.

5.

I have always dreaded Saturday afternoons. My mother and father always, and without fail, pack Saturday full of chores until the whole day is one big long Temples family to-do list.

But as I grow closer to potentially having to leave this place, I'll confess, Saturdays are building up a bit of nostalgia in my brain.

Take today, for example. After last night's festivities, I'm in a very pleasant mood. It surprises me—a night out with a girl that's not only fun in and of itself, but actually fills you with enough warmth to last through the next day or two. It's a new thing, and I like it. I'm washing the car while bobbing along to my own internal rhythm. Scrub, scrub, scrub, rinse, rinse, rinse, dry, dry, dry, la, la, la. I'm too happy, frankly, to feel even the slightest bit self-conscious about it.

My family is out on the lawn, on a gorgeous Saturday afternoon, doing chores, like we have our entire lives. The riding mower broke down again this morning, so Dad's out in the garage messing with it, cursing, calling it terrible names. Mom's cleaning out our spare room, taking old family mementos and knickknacks she can't bear to throw away, putting them in boxes and taking them in the attic above the garage. I'm on car duty: during the summer, the only time we take the Camaro out, we clean it and wax it every two weeks. When you have a car like that, you don't mess around.

I look at my parents, functioning so well together, so smooth that they don't even have to talk to each other. Mom will hand Dad lemonade, and Dad will hold the ladder for her, and each instinctively knows what the other is doing and what the other is needing. It's like a silent ballet. I envy them this and I wonder if I will ever have something like that. Then I think of Helena, and I think I should stop thinking like this before I scare her away, because that happens sometimes, I hear.

And Doug? Doug's sitting on the porch, smoking cigarettes, listening to his Discman. Because he has his headphones on, he's pretending like he can't hear everyone talking, but I know this game. It's one of Doug's old tricks. He only listens to one headphone so he can tell what's going on. Doug doesn't like to miss anything, but he also doesn't like being addressed directly. Especially not these days.

Mom clearly notices I'm in a good mood. "What's gotten into you?" she says, smiling as she puts some old Christmas lights in a box labeled USELESS PAPERS AND JUNK. Dad always labels our boxes like this, in case we're ever robbed. He thinks the criminals will be less likely to steal, say, a microwave if they think what's inside the box is worthless. This in spite of the fact that we don't have anything all that valuable and, of course, the day someone drives all the way out to the country just to steal our stuff will be the first time. Hell, we still don't lock our doors. Dad's quiet paranoia about crime has always confused me.

I'm spraying the tires with the water hose, grinning like an idiot, and I look up at Mom. "Oh, nothing, nothing," I say. "I just love washing cars! Woo!" I then playfully aim the hose at her, and she scampers off, giggling. She isn't watching where she's going, though, and she bumps into my dad, knocking his toolbox on its side and sending wrenches and hammers spilling in all directions. He growls at her for a moment—"Jesus, Sally, watch it!"—but she's still laughing, and she musses up his hair as he halfheartedly bats her away. To make sure he's playing along, I spray him with the hose too, and he does his best to look mean and angry and annoyed, but he's really trying not to laugh. We're on to him.

My mom loves this stuff. Like all moms, she becomes a little misty-eyed when she has everyone in her family together, and now that I'm supposedly going off to college, she sees this as one of the last times everyone's going to be under the same roof, save Christmas. You can see her looks of appreciation and worry fighting each other for face time. Nobody handles the growing up of kids worse than mothers, and my mom is no different.

As she picks up Dad's wrenches and gets ready to go back to her boxes, she stops and walks toward me. I pretend like I'm going to spray her with the hose again, but she has a sad look that I know a goofy sprinkle won't evaporate.

"Oh, Tim, I can't believe you're leaving us," she says, starting to tear up. "I remember when you were just this tall." She holds her hand about three feet off the ground. It's the type of thing out-of-town aunts who haven't seen you in ten years do, and, frankly, I thought my mother above it.

"We used to take you for drives, and you just *loved* going on drives. You would look out the window and read the street signs. You could always read before anyone else could. Remember how he used to do that, Bryan?" My father lets loose something that's halfway between a grunt and a fart noise and doesn't look up from the tractor.

"And now look at you, going off to college, a real college boy." Her voice quivers. I can't help but groan. Birds are falling dead out of the sky, and the dog's ears just started bleeding.

"You're going to have so much fun! I can't wait to see you grad—" She stops herself, looking ever so slightly in Doug's direction. Convinced he didn't hear her, she still lowers her voice almost imperceptibly. "You're going to be such a good student, and you'll graduate, and you'll be able to do anything you want. It'll be *wonderful*."

I silently question just how sad my mom would be if I *stayed* because, hey, I'm not at college yet. I haven't signed any papers. Nothing is set in stone.

Dad notices my discomfort and shoos her off gently, like wiping a dry-erase board. "Sally, he's not moving to China," he soothes. "He's just going to college, like Doug."

Mom looks at him as if she wants to say something, but she doesn't. Deciding she has gone far enough with this, she gives me a hug, and, just to lighten the mood, I spray her feet with the hose, and she scurries off, tittering like a junior high girl.

6.

The wax is now all off the car, and to make sure I did an adequate job—adequate in Dad's stringent terms, that is—I spray it with the hose one last time. You want to make sure the water doesn't stick to the car; it should roll off the hood and the roof, gliding, so smooth that it makes an outline of the car in the driveway. It is a long process, which must be done to perfection, a perfection that, unlike just about everything else my father insisted upon, I have down to a science. Nailed.

It looks immaculate. My father would never acknowledge this, but he knows, I know he knows, and he knows I know he knows. That's enough.

After mowing the lawn earlier, there are stray blades of grass and clippings strewn across the driveway. Since the driveway is paved with asphalt, using a broom won't do much good, so I begin to aim the hose at the grass, pushing the blades back onto the lawn, where they vanish, as far as I'm concerned. Mom asks Dad what he wants for dinner, he mumbles something about pork chops, and she readies herself to go inside. A long day in the yard is wrapping up.

I spray the driveway, imagining I am an omniscient god, releasing plagues on the placid and unwitting citizens of Blade Grass Nation. Look out! It's a flood! Women and children first! Circle the wagons! Aaaaaaah!

I'm unleashing hell on their populace when Doug, still sitting on the porch and listening to his music, flicks a cigarette right in front of me. He doesn't appear to be looking at me.

I've pretty much left Doug alone all afternoon. Whatever shit he's getting from my parents, I'd just as soon stay out of it. But I can't resist a little joke. "Oh, hey, Doug, don't worry about it, I'll get that," I say. I aim the spray so that it pushes the cigarette without dousing it. Blade Grass Nation has a new seed of destruction: smoldering ash! *Whoosh!* I am God! Feel my wrath! *Whoosh!*

Out of the corner of my eye, I see Doug stand up quickly and tear off his headphones.

"What'd you fucking say to me?" he yells.

Whoa. He's joking, right? With my lighthearted, nothing-to-see-here tone, I say, "Just saying I'd take care of that dude, no worries."

Doug stomps toward me. "No, seriously, what'd you say, you little shit?" I'm stunned. I look at him, grin in a "Hey, bro, it's me" type of way, and say, "I was just joking. Don't strain yourself; I'll take care of your mess." Our noses are now about a foot apart.

"Mess?" he seethes. "My mess? What, you mean *this* mess?" He takes his latest cigarette and throws it right where he threw the first one. He then takes another one, crumples it, and throws it down too. "Or this?"

"What the fuck, dude?" I yell, my voice squeaking and quivering a little more than I'd like it to. "What's your damage? I'm just cleaning the driveway. Jesus!"

Doug still has the fury in his face, but it seems directed inwardly now. That, and he appears to be out of cigarettes. He takes the empty pack and flips it toward me. He seems shorter all of a sudden.

With all he's got left, he spits, "You're so smart, Mr. *College Boy*, you fucking figure out what my problem is."

118

With that, he turns around and stomps inside, slamming the screen door behind him. My mom stands there, speechless, before whimpering, "Tim . . ." I look at my dad, still working on the tractor like nothing happened.

"Did you see that shit, Dad?" I say.

He stays where he is, loosening something or tightening something, I can't tell which. Without even looking up, he says, with no emotion whatsoever, "Watch your mouth around your mother."

7.

Right now, I'm driving. The whole Doug incident is still on my brain. What *was* that about?

As Helena and I hang out more and more, we're discovering that it's difficult coming up with places to meet up without the prying eyes of co-workers, friends, and/or family. We've had to be resourceful. That's why I'm headed to the Sunny Lane Residential Community, which is in Humboldt, just outside of Mattoon on Route 45.

Today's illicit hiding place is the home of her cousin Jill. She's working at the restaurant all night and staying with some guy she met at the Tumble Inn last week, so she let us have the whole place to ourselves. Helena is renting some DVDs, and I'm in charge of grabbing some Villa Pizza. I'm so absentminded, though, that I stop by Domino's and Monical's first before remembering that I'm an idiot.

As I pull into the place, I notice that it's about 35 percent wind chimes and stained-glass frogs. Like all trailer parks, more dogs seem to live in the area than people, and they're all off their chains, starving and grumpy. I shut the truck off, and, like, five of them immediately run toward me, snarling. I roll down the truck's window. "Helena! Hey, Helena!" She opens up the screen door, wearing a T-shirt, a beaten-up cowboy hat, and jean overalls. Somehow, I notice, she even manages to make this look hot. "Can you get these damn dogs out of here? They're gonna scratch up my truck." She whistles and claps loudly. Not only does the clap send the dogs scurrying in all directions, but it also shuts off all the lights in the trailer. Jill has a Clapper. Of *course* she does.

Helena laughs, shrugs, and claps again. "Howdy, stranger, welcome to La Casa de Luxury."

I open the door and step in a deep puddle, even though it hasn't rained in days. Nobody needs lawn mowers in a trailer park; almost everything is gravel, except the areas surrounding the park, which probably haven't been mowed in years. They look like a rain forest. And why wouldn't they? Nobody who lives here wants to, and nobody imagines living here very long. The pride one takes in a well-put-together lawn is nonexistent here; it would be like putting premium gasoline in a rental car. The whole scene makes me uneasy and a bit surly myself.

I grab the pizzas off the dashboard and head inside. Helena greets me with a nibble of my ear. She always does this when we first see each other, and usually I can't help but giggle a bit. But I'm not really in the mood right now; I'm still brooding over the Doug confrontation.

120

"Well, *fine*," Helena purrs. "Be that way."

I bring the pizzas into the kitchen, which barely seems to have room. It is stacked with dirty dishes, cheese-stained paper plates, and empty beer cans. "Christ, it's like a tornado came through here," I say, disgusted, and not just because I sound like my mom again.

"Well, we *are* in a trailer park." Helena chuckles. "A tornado probably did come through here." She clears out some space on the counter, takes the pizza boxes from me, and grabs a couple of beers from the fridge. As I look around, I realize that Helena has attempted to create a little romantic oasis among the filth. The makeshift coffee table—a beaten-up air hockey table sitting on two cinder blocks in front of the television—has some freshly picked flowers in the middle, along with two candles. She's playing jazz music in the background, and she has closed the window shades for more ambiance. She's trying to make the trailer into something nice, and she did it for me. I'm touched, and it almost melts my grouchy mood. Almost.

She hands me a beer, but I decline. "No thanks." Helena might have been more surprised if I'd shown up with a third eyeball, but I doubt it. "What?" she gasps. "Tim Temples, turning down a beer? It's icy in hell today!" She opens her own can and grabs a slice, bouncy, unfazed, ain't nobody here but us chickens. She spreads herself out on the saggy couch, takes a bite out of her slice, and lights a cigarette. The idea of eating and smoking at the same time turns my stomach.

"Ugh, I don't know how you can do that," I say. "Why

121

don't you just use the ashes in the ashtray as salt while you're at it?" I grit my teeth. Those dogs outside are *still* barking.

Helena frowns. "Jesus, what crawled up your ass and died today?" I don't answer, just snatch a slice of pizza and shoo off one of the fifty cats in this place so I can sit in the chair across from the couch. We sit there quiet for a bit, eating our pizza, looking around the trailer rather than at each other. A stack of CDs, out of their cases, have been tossed hitherto in the corner and appear to be caked in some sort of syrup. An empty birdcage hangs where a ceiling fan should be. A loaf of bread molds. A picture of Jill and Helena sits sideways on a dresser, cracked. Helena would have needed a leaf blower and loads of duct tape to even *start* to make this place presentable, no matter how hard she tried.

"Are you sure you don't want a beer?" Helena says, trying to fill the air with *something*. I decide to fill it with some more poison.

"No, I don't want a beer. Is that a problem? You know, why do we have to drink all the time? Is that all you want to do? Just drink?"

Helena recoils as if slapped. *That,* I think a beat too late, *was a bit too much poison.*

But to my surprise and relief, Helena quickly composes herself. She moves from the couch and positions herself directly in front of me—crouching so that we're eye to eye. "Jesus, Tim, what is *wrong* with you? Seriously. I want to know."

I put down my pizza, humbled a bit. This is the first time Helena and I have had anything resembling a bicker since, well, since we hated each other. "I'm sorry," I say. "It's just my brother."

Helena says, "Oh," really fast, for some reason.

"Wait, you know him, right? He says he graduated with you," I say.

"Yeah, yeah, I knew him a little in high school," she says. "He was Mr. Big Shot Athlete, though, so we didn't really hang in the same circles. Anyway. What's the deal?"

I take a breath. I suddenly feel like I want to talk for days, like a hose with a kink in it that's finally been straightened out.

"Well, he's really weird since he's been home," I start. "Every time I'm around him, he's scowling around, in a pissy mood, bitching at my parents, really angry and shit. And I don't know what his problem is. He's even yelling at *me* now, and he didn't even do that when we were kids. I know he didn't like college much, and I guess it's hard to blame him, but I mean, he looks *terrible*. He's got this nasty facial hair that probably has bugs in it, and he's even getting kind of fat, which I *never* thought I'd see. I dunno. I look at him now, and I think about the big brother I remember, and they're two different people." I pause. "And I feel like college did it to him or something. I know, that sounds stupid."

Helena has been looking at me very closely this whole time. "I don't think it's stupid," she says. "Some people just aren't into college very much."

"Really?" I say. The thought hadn't occurred to me. *Some people just aren't into college.*

123

"Oh, I wasn't, not at all," Helena says.

Jesus, another bolt from the blue: *Helena went to college once.* I am the biggest moron on earth. How did I not guess that?

She continues, "I mean, I guess I never really gave it much of a chance. Dad died right when I was starting up, and Mom couldn't really take care of herself, so I was only there for a few weeks, and it was Lake Land anyway, so it hardly counts."

I've never understood why anyone from Mattoon would go to Lake Land, the community college just a mile from my house. Either you leave town and go to a real college, or you stay in town and you work. Lake Land is like some half-assed compromise, a commitment to nothing, an empty promise to go somewhere and make something of yourself that is backed by nothing. It's like saying you're going to be a carpenter but not buying a hammer.

I don't share this, of course. "Well, that was a tough situation," I say.

"Yeah, but I was never really into it," she says. "Some people, college just isn't for them. Not everyone's like you, you know."

I'm not sure what this means, but I let it slide. "How is your mom, anyway?" I ask. Helena is always alluding to her mother ailing somehow, but I've never quite pinpointed what exactly is wrong with her.

"Oh, she's fine," she says. "It's just—something's always acting up with her. Either she forgot her insulin, or her back hurts, or she doesn't take her pills, or whatever. You just have to keep an eye on her. It's pretty stressful sometimes." She lets out a big sigh. "But that's just the same old bullshit you've heard over and over," she says, even though I haven't. "Boo-fucking-hoo, poor me. It's nothing that should get in the way of our fun, right?"

She's right, though I sense she's holding back in a way I didn't. She must have noticed me thinking this because she lays her hand on mine and says, "Listen, we all got our problems. If we didn't have someone to bitch about them to, we'd go insane, right? And we're not insane. Are we?"

"I'm not, but you . . ." I trail off, smiling.

"That's the spirit!" she yells, standing. "I'm a nut job, and you're my cute little boy toy."

"That's sounds fine to me," I say.

"Well, it *better*!" she says, cracking up. "Because that's what you are, college boy." She walks to the fridge, slipping slightly on an indecipherable pool of goo on the floor. "All right. So *now* do you want a beer? Now that we've all had a good cry?"

I feel like a weight has been lifted. Just talking to Helena has made the whole Doug situation seem bearable.

As for that beer? Don't mind if I do, actually.

8.

Helena does the funniest thing. When she's sleeping, she snores like a lumberjack. It surprises me how cute I find it. She breathes in all she can and gives out all she takes in, even in slumber. It is a strangely soothing rhythm that helps me drift off to sleep.

9.

Helena is still snoring when my cell phone rings at 11 a.m. It's Denny.

"Dude, where the hell you at?" he says, too loud for this early. My pants are hanging from a novelty lamp in the shape of a naked woman.

"Uh, nowhere," I cover, "just, uh, running around, that's all." Helena stirs a bit and looks at me quizzically. I give her an "It's nothing" shrug, and she nods and falls right back into her snoring.

"Well, your mom just called me, wondering what time you were coming home for dinner tonight," he says. "She says your grandma's coming over or something. Dude, when you tell your moms that you're staying with me, you gotta warn me, all right? I covered for you, but just barely. I told her you ran out to get everybody doughnuts."

Denny has been lying to my parents for me since we were kids. My personal favorite: I once spent a weekend in Champaign with some chick named Michelle I'd met at a party on a Friday night. I'd forgotten to tell my parents I was even leaving the house. Denny was on vacation with his parents in Cincinnati and only found out my parents had called to check on me when his dad checked their messages at home. Denny somehow, some way, convinced not only my parents that I was with him, but also *his* parents that there was no reason to call the Temples, even though they had irrefutable evidence of my lie. When my parents ran into his a week later, *they* even lied for me. Honestly, the kid's amazing.

"Okay, okay, man, sorry about that, I owe you," I say.

"So who's today's lucky girl?" he says, with a hint of suspicion.

"I'm sorry?"

"Well, just curious which of Coles County's finest the great Tim Temples decided to grace with his presence this time," he says. Denny is the only person I would let jerk me around like this, because I know he's half mocking me and half envious. Kristen is the only girl he's ever slept with—he had to wait about three years for that—and she's assuredly the only one with whom he ever will. I find this admirable (mostly) and idiotic (little bit, gotta admit). I'm pretty up front with him about everything, which allows him to gently scold me and still live vicariously through my exploits. It works out well.

That said, I'm still none too eager to have the entire Kraft plant gossiping. I'm taking no chances, particularly with a nude snoring Helena lying right next to me.

"Oh, just drank too much last night and crashed over at a buddy's place," I say.

"Really?" he says, his voice arching slightly. "Which buddy?"

"You don't know him. Some dude from Charleston I ran into at a party."

"Uh-huh," he says, not convinced. "Well, he must be a pretty good pal because we ain't been seeing much of you lately. Andy and Shad are running out of replacement asses to kiss."

In all the bustle of unexpected Helena developments,

I've barely seen the Horsemen at all. This was supposed to be our last summer to rip it up, and they've mainly been the silent, sullen guys I walk past and nod to at work. Denny has a point.

"Yeah, well, I've had a lot going on," I say, yawning. What time is it, anyway? "We should hang soon, definitely."

Denny is quick on the trigger. "What you doing tonight?" he asks. "The other Horsemen and me, we're gonna meet over at Jeff's garage, play some asshole, pound some beers. You should come by. Unless your *Charleston buddy* has something better for you to do."

I look over at Helena, who shifts slightly and lets out a little *mmmmmmm*, followed by some indecipherable mumblings that sound like a bathtub draining. She has a tattoo of the masks of comedy and tragedy on her back. I wonder what she'll think about that when she's eighty.

I wonder what I'll think of it when she's eighty.

Jesus. Where did that come from? I swat the thought away.

"Well, we'll see," I say. "I could maybe make it over there. We'll see if I have time."

"Six thirty, right at Cards pregame. Pedro Martinez is pitching tonight. Just come by. Oh, and call your moms so she doesn't call my parents or anything."

"Yep," I say. "See ya."

I hang up and Helena turns over. "Who was that?" she says, drowsiness leaking out of every breath.

"Oh, just my friend Denny," I say. "The guys are playing cards tonight. Don't know if I'm up for it, though."

128

She raises an eyebrow. "Really?" she says. "You'd be the first guy I've met who turns down cards with his buddies. Though I can't imagine those guys play for much money. Wait. It's not strip poker, is it? Is it one of *those* parties? I've always had my suspicions about that Jeff guy."

I laugh. I love it when people make fun of Jeff, particularly people who don't buy his act for a second. "Naw, it's just asshole. We play it as a drinking game. Other than that, the whole thing gets a little old. You know, the same arguments about baseball, debates about which girls they would get with—if they ever got off the couch."

Now that I think about it, it *is* starting to get a little old.

"Well, you gonna meet them?" she asks.

"I dunno," I say.

Frankly, I'd planned on spending the evening with Helena. And to be honest, I don't see any real reason to get out of this bed for quite a while. "I mean . . . well, what are *you* doing tonight?"

She grins in a weird way, like she's bitten into something sour. "Well, I was just kind of hanging out at home tonight," she says. "My mom loves to watch that *Monk* show on Saturday nights, and I thought I might just spend the evening with her."

"So wait—you don't want to hang out with me?" I say. I sense a weird tone of desperation in my voice, and I really, really don't like it.

"Aw, that's cute," she says, exhaling. "Don't worry, Timmy. Go out with your little friends. I'll see you tomorrow."

"Really?"

"You should go."

"You sure?"

"Tim. You should go."

"Yes. I should go." She then kisses me, hard. Hey, we've got a couple of hours before I have to be anywhere.

10.

Asshole is the game we've been playing since we learned that if you drank enough beer, it started to taste somewhat tolerable. Asshole is not a real card game, though it uses cards. Its only service is the rapid distribution of alcohol; it performs this service extremely well.

Here's how it works. We usually have six players. In our case, that's the Horsemen and whatever girl is with me. (Kristen always finds it "juvenile," which, of course, is the whole *point*.) You distribute all fifty-two cards to each player. Whoever sits left of the dealer plays first; ace is high card, three is low. The point of the game is to get rid of your cards as soon as possible. If the first player lays down a three, the next player can play anything higher than that. You can play a five, an eight, a king, whatever. You can also, if you have a pair, play both of them; the next player then has to have two of something higher than your pair, or they skip their turn and, of course, must drink. You go until either no one can play any higher cards or until someone throws a two, which "clears" the whole hand and starts everything over again. If you have to skip a turn because you have no cards that will trump what's in the middle—you drink. Also, if someone plays a four at any time, it's called a "social," and *everybody* has to drink.

The first one to get rid of all his cards wins and is declared "president." Whoever finishes second is "vice president," third is "secretary," fourth is "treasurer," and fifth, last place, is "the asshole." This is where the drinking really kicks in. During the next round the president, being president and all, can command anyone below him on the totem pole to drink—for any reason, at any point. The vice president can do this for anyone below him, and on down the line. The asshole cannot tell anyone to drink; he just sits there and gets loaded, on demand. The roles switch every round—which leads to a ludicrous game of drunken musical chairs as everyone sits themselves down in order—affording everyone the opportunity to order everyone else around, at least for a bit. The best part about being president is that you *don't* have to give any reason to anyone at all. Don't like that look on Jeff's face? Drink. Tired of Shad's dopey grin? Drink. Want to make sure your date is plenty bombed? Drink. Drink. Drink.

I arrive at Jeff's right at six thirty, and the Horsemen are all already there, milling around. I walk into the garage, which is filled with calendars of women in bikinis modeling power tools, and I am greeted with the usual "Tim Dog, yo!" Andy and Shad push each other for room in front of me, Denny slaps me on the back, and Jeff lurks in the corner, smoking a cigarette, hankering for trouble as always.

"Glad to see you could make it," Denny says, offering me a beer.

"Hey, anything for my niggas," I say. I never like saying this, but it inevitably makes everybody laugh and try stupid gimmick handshakes.

Andy now has Shad in a headlock, for some reason, so I drift over to Jeff. He clinks my beer with his, wearing that smirk of his that both makes me grin and makes me want to slap him.

"Ain't seen you around here for a while, man," he says. "Thought you might have made some college buddies already."

"Oh, I wouldn't do that to you, Jeff," I say. "Who would be the main character in all your wet dreams if I weren't around?"

Jeff shows those wolf teeth. "I'd surprise you, punk," he says. "I got plenty to work from, I guarantee that."

Denny turns the sound up on the game, and Joe Buck chronicles the last week in Cardinal baseball. Denny rattles off statistics of various Cardinals hitters against Pedro Martinez, Shad smacks Andy in the nuts, and Jeff lets loose a juicy fart. All is normal in the world, and okay, fine, I *have* kind of missed these guys.

11.

We sit around the main folding table, and Denny heads out to his truck to get the playing cards.

"So, you got a little over a month left, right?" Jeff says.

"You ready for that shit? Bunch of classes with lesbian professors telling you about how *women* should be spelled with a *y* because they're not subservient to men?"

I ignore his question. "So how come you guys didn't invite Chuck to play with us tonight?" I say. "It's a shame. I would have loved to see you guys soil yourselves when he looks at you wrong."

"He's a dick!" Shad blurts.

"Yeah, a dick. That guy sucks," Andy says.

"I don't know why you're all so scared of him," I say. "One of you should just tell him off sometime."

Andy and Shad recoil, as if I just said we should set fire to a church. Andy instinctively looks over his shoulder. "Relax," I say, "he's not behind you, you wuss."

"You don't get it, man," Shad says. "You don't have to deal with the guy all the time. I mean, I *need* that job, you know? I don't want that guy pissed at me."

"Whatever," I say. "You guys are like zombies over there. I don't even recognize you."

Jeff clears his throat. "Well, not everybody gets to take off at the end of the summer to study philosophy—or whatever useless crap you *special people* do up there."

I shoot him a look but decide to drop it. Denny comes in from outside with the cards, looking at his watch. He is nervous and distracted.

"Well, all right, we ready to play?" I say. "You ready to be my assholes, bitches?"

Denny opens up a beer. "Well, actually, we're still waiting on our sixth," he says. "Should be here any minute."

"A sixth, huh?" I smirk. "Is one of you turds humping around? Look at you! I leave you guys alone for two weeks, and you start picking up my chicks. Good job!" I smack Shad on the back of his head, knocking off his South Carolina hat. "It's you, right, boy? You pick up one of those Neoga ladies I'm always hearing about?"

Headlights appear through the windows in the garage door. Denny starts to stand, then sits back down abruptly, looking around at nothing in particular. Jeff snorts.

The door to the garage opens.

"Hey, guys! I hope Heineken's okay. Oh . . . hey, Tim. Wow. You made it!"

It's Jessica. Carrying a twelve-pack of beer. Wearing a summer dress that accentuates all the stuff I never realized Jessica had. She's wearing makeup. And she's in Jeff's garage. To play asshole.

"So, who's dealing?" she says, sitting down, looking around at everyone but me.

12.

Denny is dealing the cards as everyone starts chattering. The table is a whirlwind of activity that I'm no part of.

"So Denny, I was talking to Kristen this morning," Jessica says. "She's *very* curious as to what's on tap for her birthday next week." Denny blushes somewhat, and Andy and Shad start chuckling. Somehow I ended up sitting in between the two of them, which is the worst place: it's like being stuck in between two boulders who keep trying to talk to each other.

134

Jessica is sitting between Denny and Jeff, on the other side of the table.

"Oh, I got a few ideas," Denny says.

"I mean, she's gonna be eighteen this year!" Jessica says, her eyes full of excitement. "She's finally *legal*!" She laughs and takes a tiny sip of beer, and her face scrunches, though she tries to hide it.

Some people just never get into beer. I guarantee you Jessica ends up a fancy-pants wine drinker. Maybe she'll drink that Bonaccorsi stuff Helena told me about.

Denny passes all the cards around. I have a perfect ass-hole hand. I have a two, a ten, a K, two nines, two Js, and three sixes. It's pretty much unfair; this hand is going to be unbeatable.

Shad plays a single three, a terrible lead. Andy plays a double five, an even worse follow-up. We should really start playing these games for money. I clean up. My cards are gone in two minutes.

"You suck," Jeff says. "And Denny, you're a crappy dealer."

Jessica laughs, way too loud and way too emphatically for something that wasn't all that funny. Jeff looks at her and smiles.

Wait a minute . . .

Andy's the next one out of cards, then Denny, then Shad. Only Jeff and Jessica are left. Walking behind them, I see that Jeff has a two, a seven, and two jacks left. Jessica has a four, a nine, and two threes. She's toast: all Jeff's gotta do is throw the jacks, then the two, then the nine,

135

and she's the asshole. I feel bad for her; she probably doesn't know how to play very well.

And then I feel *really* sorry for her, because Jeff, in his twisted, socially retarded way, is flirting with her.

"Let's see, let's see," Jeff says in an exaggerated, Dr. Evil type of way. "What cards does the lovely Jessica have left? Hmm."

She smiles at him, like she knows what he's up to, likes it, even. "Funny," she says. "You're a real comedian. Just show your cards, goofball. Sheesh."

My God, she's flirting back.

Jessica plays her four. All Jeff has to do is throw his two jacks, then his two, then his seven, and he wins. Jeff is an excellent asshole player; he knows this. But that's not what he does. He throws his two, clearing the hand. Then he throws his seven. Jessica trumps it with her two threes, and then she plays her nine, and she wins.

There's no question—Jeff threw the game. I look at him, and he smirks back at me.

"I won! Woo!" Jessica exclaims. Jeff pretends like he's really disappointed, and Jessica rubs his back playfully and consoles him. "Aw, it's okay, Jeff," she says. "You played real well. I just had a good hand!"

I know what Jeff is doing. I know what he's doing because I have done it countless times before, with countless different girls. He's playing the game I taught him. But he's playing it with *Jessica*. I'd tell him to knock if off, but I have absolutely no room to talk. And he knows it.

Jeff gives that "cat that ate the canary and then ate anything else alive it could find" smile. "I guess that makes me the asshole," he says, mock dejectedly.

"It definitely does," I say. "Now drink, asshole. Your president commands you."

13.

Here's how you get there:

Old State Road, the road that takes you to my house, has a quiet, out-of-the-way cemetery across from where my old friend Kyle Gill used to live. Right before you turn into the cemetery, there's a little side road, unnamed, that's made entirely of dirt and tiny pebbles. You sneak that turn and drive for another empty two or three minutes, where there are no cars and no lights and no houses and no nothing. When you look around you, you will not see a thing. This is exactly you want: after all, you're parking. This spot is my favored terrain; as far as I know, nobody else knows about it. It took me years to find the exact right one, and this is it.

A couple of years ago, my parents, for one week, hosted a family whose daughter was here for a cheerleading competition. They were from the Chicago suburbs; it was some sort of exchange program, where they would stay with a local family and get a feel for the small-town atmosphere or some such bull. The daughter was named Mandie, and she was blond and gorgeous. We took an instant "liking" to each other. So I told her I knew of a place, an area I simply called "the Spot."

To appropriately impress her, I sneaked out the Camaro in the middle of the night. Honestly, had he caught me, Dad would have shot me right there. Knowing how much the legal titans of Coles County appreciate a quality automobile, he likely would have been acquitted.

We drove to the Spot, and she was astounded. Here was a place in the middle of nowhere, just a mile from my house, where we would not be bothered. "There's no place like this in the suburbs," she said, giggling, and I told her, once again, this is why Chicago sucks.

Helena and I have been appropriately unencumbered here at the Spot. We lie here in my truck. Helena is wrapped in my arms, smacking mosquitoes, content. She usually likes to have a cigarette afterward, but we've just finished now, and we're both trying to catch our breath in that level of realization that you were just doing something that caused you to forget everything that was going on in your life and now it's over and you're satisfied and thrilled yet vaguely aware that you have to, slowly, gradually, go back to being who you were beforehand. She is silent, her breath warming my chest, her hair everywhere.

We lie there for a few minutes, with an occasional contented hum from Helena. She whispers, "I'm a little cold," and I grab a ratty old sleeping bag I have in the truck for this very purpose.

She thanks me and then feels the sleeping bag. "This thing is kind of gross," she says. "When's the last time you had it cleaned?"

The truth is that I have no idea (sophomore year?

Freshman?), and since I think this answer won't be acceptable, I try a different tack. "Well, I think Dad took the truck hunting last week and used the blanket to wrap up the deer he shot," I say. "But, um, he probably washed it afterward. Does it smell like venison?"

Helena smacks me playfully and tells me to shut up. "Yep, I'm twenty-three years old," she says. "This is me, still parking."

"Hey, nothing wrong with parking," I say. "You like this spot? Years of research went into this spot. You have no idea how many times Lieutenant Grierson would flash his light in the window until I found this place."

Helena smiles broadly, pulls herself up, and rests her elbows on my chest. "Yeah, this is a pretty good spot," she says. "I think I was here six years ago."

"What?" I swivel my head to look at her. "Really? You're kidding me."

"Tim, come on," she says. "It's a small town. I guarantee you you're the hundredth person in Mattoon history to think they 'discovered' this spot." She leans down, puts her mouth on my ear, and tugs. "It *is* nice, though."

As if on cue, a car appears in the distance. Helena scampers up to the front seat and taps the brakes. This is the universally accepted sign for, *We're parking here. Please, don't hit us.*

The car flashes its brights in return code: *We saw you. We know what you're up to. Good for you.*

The car passes and Helena returns to the backseat. She lights a cigarette, cuddles into my arms, and smokes out the window. She's shivering slightly but at ease. I am calm—at peace. *Still* in a way I've never been before.

"You know, you look fantastic," I say. "Like some movie star from the fifties."

"That's silly." She waves the comment away. "All my makeup is gone."

I hold her more tightly. "Doesn't matter. You look better this way."

She turns her head slightly, and she's beaming. "Well, I never heard that one before."

"Maybe no one was paying close enough attention," I say, and she nestles her head into my chest. Neither of us wants to move. We lie there for hours, days.

Eventually she gets up, stretches her arms in the air, and unleashes a yawny *ahhhhhhhhh*.

"So who's this woman you're house-sitting for?" I ask.

"A friend of my mom's," she says. "Over in Charleston. She and her husband are, like, crazy rich, and they just want me to stay there and water the plants and feed the cats. It's like having my own huge house, all to myself, for two weeks!"

I pause. *All to myself?* What does that mean? Does she want me to leave her alone for these two weeks? Am I reading too much into this? And why am I asking all these questions all of a sudden?

I usually pride myself on being able to hide whatever I'm thinking, but Helena, once again, seems to have opened up my skull and peeked inside.

"It'll be great," she says. "They have this enormous

kitchen; it's like the size of Jill's whole trailer. We could have a big feast together. We should *totally* do that. I'll make Italian, and we'll watch DVDs on their big screen. Let's do that on Saturday. Friday I'm thinking we should just lie around and watch TV. The workday wears me out."

My smile is the size of the moon. "Sure. That would be cool," I say, trying to contain myself.

Helena gasps. "Oh my God, you haven't had my fettuccine yet! It's so good, it's been known to make people *kill themselves!* I'll make it and we can spend the whole weekend lying in bed and eating. Hell, we can spend *both* weekends doing that!"

It is one thing to go parking, which I have done repeatedly. But to spend a whole weekend with Helena—*two whole weekends!*—sounds amazing. It will be like living together. I wonder if we will walk around the kitchen, communicating silently like my parents do, handing each other salt and pepper and spices, dancing around, our own ballet to our own orchestra. Things may not be entirely smooth the first weekend, but the second weekend . . . that second weekend—oh, *wait.*

"You mean, the *next* two weekends?" I ask.

Helena nods.

"Shit. I have my, uh, I have my college orientation the second weekend. A friend and I have to go up to Champaign and listen to them tell us What College Life Is Like. I'm supposed to stay in the dorms and everything."

Helena frowns. "Really?" she says, running permutations in her head. "Oh, well, one weekend will be fine, I guess."

I've been dreading this orientation weekend. It just seems like one of those situations where Jessica and I are going to have to *talk*. About college, about Jeff, about all of it. And for what? So I can see how shitty my dorm is going to be? So I can stand in line waiting to get a fake ID so I can get into bars? So I can see a bunch of people who are smarter than me and know it?

Doug says nothing happens at orientation *at all*. You just sit around listening to boring speeches by the types of nerdy students you would never hang out with in the first place. And the worst part: you're just another kid on the assembly line. No one knows you there, and no one cares. Not like here.

The whole thing kind of sucks, and I really wish I didn't have to go.

"So, you know," I say, choosing my words carefully. "I could just skip it." Helena acts like she didn't hear me.

"Really," I say. "I didn't want to go in the first place." A thought buzzes through my brain: *Why should I go when all I need is right here, in this truck?*

Helena suddenly looks very tired. "Don't be ridiculous; you *have* to go to your orientation," she says. "I mean, you're going to college. Of course you're going to go to orientation. That's part of the drill, right?"

Our conversation is all serious—immediate, for some reason. I feel urgent, like I need to tell her everything I've been thinking.

"I dunno," I say. "It's just that I'm not even sure I want to deal with the whole mess. It seems like it's coming up

142

on me real fast. Everything has been, um, I dunno . . . so *nice* this summer. It seems kind of strange to just, uh, dump it all and take off in a month."

Helena looks at me like I'm a kindergarten kid trying to figure out how to make Legos fit together. "Oh, that's perfectly natural," she says. "It's a scary thing to leave something that you know and go to something that you don't. It would be weird if you *weren't* concerned about it." There is a lackadaisical tone to Helena's words, like she'd rather not be talking about this. Like she wishes I would drop it. But I can't, not yet.

"I mean, what's college going to do for me, anyway? Doug looks like college stole his soul. I mean, here, I've got this great job that pays a ton of money, I've got a home I don't have to pay a cent for, everybody knows me, I can get into any bar I want to, all that. When I get there, I'm going to have to make all new friends and a whole new life. But I kind of *like* my life here, you know?" Another thought: *I like my life here with you.*

"Please," she says. "You're too smart to hang around here. What are you going to do, carry boxes the rest of your life? This is what you want?"

I grab a beer. What am I failing to get across?

Helena speaks before I have a chance. "Tim, seriously. You're great. And this is real nice. But you *have* to go to college." She pops me on the shoulder lightly. "If you don't, I'll just have to dump you. And we don't want that, do we?"

She's joking. But not really. But is she? Why does this

143

conversation make no sense all of a sudden? I'm about to say something, Lord knows what, but more headlights appear behind us.

"*Car!*" Helena screams, laughing. "Hit the brakes, Tim."

So, that being that, I hit the brakes, and hard.

14.

It's after work, and I'm waiting at Denny's car. He walks toward me, yammering on his cell phone—Kristen, surely. He looks up and seems legitimately surprised to see me milling about. He tells whomever he's talking to that he'll call them back and acknowledges me.

"Well, Mr. Temples, what a rare surprise," he says. "I don't owe you money, do I?"

"You probably do," I say, shaking Denny's hand, an action we both realize is incredibly formal and unnatural. It's been a while, but for God's sake, we're not strangers. We drop each other's hands as if we've touched something hot.

I recover quickly. "I just stopped to say hey."

Denny looks dubious. "Yeah, that would be a first. You must want something." Before I have a second to protest—and I *am* a little offended—Denny's face lights up: "Dude. Oh, man. You like a girl. I mean, you, like, really like a girl. That's totally it, isn't it?"

I blush immediately. I hate blushing. It's like your face is a stool pigeon, eager to give you up to the cops at a second's notice. "Well, I, uh . . ."

"Man, I gotta play some more poker with you," he says. "I could clean you out in an hour. Ha. Tim Temples. Really likes a girl. And is asking *me* about it. That's totally what you were going to do, weren't you?"

I can't help it; I nod sheepishly.

"Ha," he says. "I'm a fucking genius. Man, I dunno who this girl is, but I gotta meet her! She's tamed the great beast!" I try to punch him on the arm, tell him to knock it off, but he's twittering madly, *extremely* pleased with himself. He's moving at about ten speeds faster than I am. He has already run to the other side of the car, unlocked the door for me, and zipped back to the driver's side.

"Let's get a cheeseburger," he says. "I want to hear everything! Tim Temples. All in *luvvvvv*. Oh, man, have I been waiting a long time for *this* conversation!"

He starts the car and sits idle for a moment.

"Before we take off, I want you to apologize," he says.

"What?"

"You heard me. I want you, Tim Temples, to apologize to me, Dennis Strong, for calling me whipped all those times. Do it, or I won't tell you what you want to know."

I shake my head. "No way."

"All right, then," he says. "Have a nice walk to your truck. Lemme know how it all works out for you."

I seethe. *Fine.* I raise my right hand. "I, Tim Temples, do solemnly apologize to Dennis Strong for calling him whipped because he was really into his girlfriend."

"Why?" he says, grinning.

"Because I really like this girl." I'm beet red.

Denny starts the car. "Damn," he says. "That was even better than I imagined."

15.

We have a Burger King in Mattoon, but it's not like any other Burger King on earth. In the fifties, the Mattoon Burger King was the hot downtown spot, where all the bachelors and bobby-soxers would take their main squeezes for milk shakes and pronto pups after a night at the movies. (This is the way it seems, at least, from all the black-and-white pictures outside.)

But in the sixties, the other Burger King, the big national chain, started popping up all over the country. The Mattoon BK owners saw this as copyright infringement, and the little Davids took Goliath to court. And wouldn't you know, they won. The verdict: an undisclosed amount of cash and a ban on national Burger King chains within forty miles of Mattoon city proper. I'm told they have a Burger King up in Champaign; if anything good comes out of college, I'll at least be able to try those guys out.

Mattoon's Burger King is run by the same family who has always run it. The hamburgers are flat and greasy, the waitstaff all wear white paper hats and ugly white shirts, and some guy who sounds like his nostrils are being attacked by weasels announces everybody's order with a nasal, *"Forrrrrrrttyyyyyy-threeeeeeeeeee."* The patrons are either ninety-year-old ladies who have chosen the Burger

King as the one place they're going to visit "in town" this week or young punks like me and Denny. The owners always look askance at us when we come in, like we're going to set the place on fire or something. And I'll say, we have been prone to pranks here; my favorite is to put five bucks in the jukebox, play the same song twenty times, and then leave.

I'm digging into my fries, but Denny has yet to touch any of his food. I don't think I've ever seen him look happier.

"So, who's this special lady?" he starts. "Oh, wait, let me guess. She's from Charleston. She has to be. I think you've sampled all the merchandise Mattoon has to offer. Where'd you meet her? How do you know her? You clearly like this girl, 'cause we ain't barely seen you—on your supposed last summer—for a month, man."

Denny is usually so quiet and reserved, but it's difficult to fault him for his glee. We've been making fun of him for so long, he's probably been waiting since freshman year for one of us to fall for some girl. (Is that what I've done? Fallen?)

"Listen, there might not be any 'special lady,'" I say, trying to throw him off the scent. "Maybe I'm just curious about girls I'll meet up at college. They'll be more sophisticated, and they might fall for more of your nice-guy bullshit than the chicks here, you know? Like, I might have to know their names or something."

Denny isn't buying this for a second. "Please," he says. "Don't insult my intelligence. Some girl's got your panties all in a bunch. I can't believe I didn't notice this before." He is actually cackling now.

My facade is crumbling. I try one last trick: Denny or no, I still feel like I should keep Helena and me quiet, if just for her sake. (Why? *I don't know*, I realize. I promise myself that I'll figure it out later.) "Well, fine. Yes. There is a girl," I say. Denny raises his hands in the air as if he just hit a half-court jumper. "But you don't know her. She's from somewhere else. Like, really far."

He begins to say something, but I stop him. "Look, we're off the point anyway. I just need you to accept that I'm seeing someone. You don't know who it is, and I'd kind of like to keep it quiet for a while. Can you do that for me? Because, I dunno . . . this girl's *real* cool, you know? And Kristen seems pretty happy, and I guess I was just wondering, you know, uh, um, how you do that."

Denny's face turns smug in a way I haven't seen before, and I shoot him an angry look that he knows I don't really mean. I lean in closer. "You mention any of this to the Horsemen, I'll kill you."

Denny laughs. "I'm not going to tell those chuckleheads. They don't *deserve* this information."

I keep eye contact. "I'll kill your family. And your dog. And I'll burn your house down."

"No worries, dude," he says. "Honestly."

"Okay. Tell me how to keep a girl happy, you know, so she'll *stay* with you for, like, a really long time."

He takes a sip of his milk shake and sets it aside. "All right," he says. "Here's what you need to know."

16.

Over the next twenty minutes, Denny gives me four major tips on making a woman happy and keeping her happy. He describes them in such detail that it's clear he's been wanting to give this speech to somebody, anybody, since he *met* Kristen. He starts off by explaining that everything I know is wrong. My interactions with women have been in the short term, not the long term; actually making a woman stick around that you *want* to stick around is a skill I have never used, so it needs to be developed.

The pretend-like-you-don't-like-them rule? The one that has *always* worked for me? Apparently it's the complete opposite if you *want* a woman to stick around. (I know. That part threw me for a loop too.)

Here are Denny's four rules to keeping a woman happy ("Jesus, Tim, get out a piece of paper and take some notes already," he said. "This is gold I'm giving you here, man. Gold."):

1. *You are always wrong.* He said this with a certainty that terrified me. "If you disagree with her, you are wrong," he said. "Always. If she tells you that you are an aging black woman, you are. If she says your chicken cutlet is trying to kill you, it is. There are no exceptions to this rule. None."

2. *Her friends are your primary enemies. This is why you must kiss their asses and treat them like they're your own best friends.* "When women get together, all they do is bitch about the guys that they're

with," he said. "Thing is, though, every girl is secretly jealous of the other ones. If you're good and they like you, they'll think, 'Well, if he were *my* man, I'd appreciate him more.' Which, of course, is total crap, but whatever. This works the other way too. If they hate you, it doesn't matter what you do: you're screwed. They'll fill her head full of so much poison that she'll never wade her way out. You could be Mother freaking Teresa, and she'd still think you're not nice enough to her. Make good with the friends. Absolutely vital."

3. *Be there when she needs you.* "Realize that your only real job is to be around when they want you to be. Anything you do in addition to that will come as a pleasant surprise. Make sense?"

4. *When in doubt, get flowers.* "Not those cheap Citgo ones either," he says as I cough. "Real flowers. Girls just melt at the sight of 'em. Never fails. You could run over their foot with the car, and if you had flowers with you when you did it, they'd forgive you. Craziest thing. I mean, it's a *plant.*"

Denny sucks down the rest of his milk shake. "So, you got all that?" he says.

"I guess," I say. "It seems kind of cynical. I mean . . . I thought you were *happy* with Kristen. That all seems like the kind of stuff you could do for any girl."

Denny smiles. "Dude, I am totally happy," he says. "I'd be completely lost without her. She's the first person I talk

150

to in the morning and the last person I talk to at night. I wouldn't want it any other way, and neither would she. But that doesn't mean there isn't strategy involved. It's just a matter of giving yourself a little outline and then sticking to it. It just makes it easier."

I shrug. This really can't be all there is, is it? I mean, does it really all come down to *flowers*? "But dude, I don't want strategy, and I don't want rules," I say. "I just want her to like me as much as I like her. I want her to stay with me."

Denny gives me a funny look. "*That's* what you wanted?"

"*Yes*," I say, exasperated. "I don't want to lose this girl."

"Well, that's different," he says. "To ensure that she likes you, you have to tell her how you *feel*. And don't pussyfoot around, either. You only get one chance at this stuff. When that moment hits, the one where everything's perfect, you just have to lay it all out there."

"Lay it all out there?" I repeat.

"Yep. Just don't *screw it up*," he says. "And don't be an idiot. That's all. Lesson over."

And I smile, pleased that it really could be so simple. "Wow," I say.

"So now that that's cleared up," he says, "you around this weekend?"

"No," I say. "She's staying at a friend of her mom's this weekend, and we're cooking dinner."

"Wait," he says. "Are you cooking dinner, or is she?"

"We're working on it together," I say.

151

"Oh." He shrugs. "Well, in that case, you're completely screwed. Have fun!"

17.

We're walking out to the truck when Denny mentions that they're planning another game of asshole this weekend, if I can fit it in.

Which reminds me . . .

"Uh, Denny," I ask hesitantly. "So, does Jessica hang out with you guys all the time now? I mean, like every night?"

Denny's eyes start shifting around, like he's afraid someone's wearing a wire. "Off the record or on the record?"

I don't know what this means. "On the record?"

Denny stiffens and begins to talk like a robot. "Kristen believes Jessica should have more fun before she goes to college. Repeat. Kristen believes Jessica should have more—"

I interrupt him; that doesn't make any sense at all. "What are you talking about?"

Denny is still talking like a robot, and now he's even moving around like a robot, in place, joints rigid. He clearly finds this amusing. "That is the official story, and Robot must stick to the official story."

I smack him upside the head. "Knock it off, man." He straightens up, and life returns to his eyes.

"So, you want the real deal?" he asks.

152

"Of course," I say.

He gets a conspiratorial look. "I'll tell you, if you tell me who this new lady of yours is."

"Christ," I say, exasperated. "You're like a gossip columnist all of a sudden."

"Hey, you want to know or not?"

I think it over. Is this something I *really* want to know? Denny's clearly hinting at something. And you know what? I'm kind of tired of Helena being some big secret, no matter how much she insists she has to be.

Besides, if I can't tell Denny about this, who can I tell? "Deal," I say.

Denny doesn't hesitate. "Jessica and Jeff have a little thing going," he says. "Kristen says she finds him 'charming.' I don't know how far it has gone, but it's going, whatever it is."

I'm slack-jawed. Astonished. The woman is valedictorian of her class and she starts something with *Jeff* a month before she leaves for college. *Why?* And deep down, I fear I might know.

"All right, spill," he says. "Who's the lady?"

"Well . . . you know that girl at work?" I say, choosing my words carefully. "Helena?"

Denny's face does something strange. It somehow rises and falls at the same moment. It looks like his face is fighting a war with itself and both sides are losing. "Westfall?" he says, choking on his words. "That lady who works for Chuck? The mean one?"

"Hey, she's not really—"

"Wow," he says. "Um . . . well . . . that's nice, I guess. Kind of a summer thing, maybe?"

"Well, actually, I was kind of thinking it might be more than—"

"Uh, listen, I gotta get going, man," he says. "Hop in. I'm supposed to meet Kristen in an hour."

The drive back to the Kraft plant goes by without a word.

18.

On Friday night, Helena is lying on the couch. She's wearing a pink T-shirt with a picture of a cute bunny smiling and waving on it. Beneath the bunny are the words *Sometimes You Make Me Want to Throw Up a Little.* The shirt cracks me up. Her head is in my lap, and I'm stroking her hair while she flips through the channels. There are a million of them.

This house looks just like every other house that's owned by grown-ups in Mattoon, except a little bigger and with some *Mission: Impossible* security system. The kitchen is huge and immaculate, the family room has pictures of Jesus and little signs that say, BLESS THIS MESS, and the television is placed in the strategic center. The whole place is designed to funnel you into the television room. If you brought a caveman who had no knowledge of modern technology into this house, he'd walk through the door and inevitably gravitate toward the couch, where he would sit and see if any NASCAR was on. The only two rooms that really matter here are the kitchen and the television room. Everything else is apparently where you rest up between those two.

I won't lie: we would love a home like this.

Helena flips past two old white men yelling at each other on the news channel, a group of midgets playing tug-of-war with an elephant, and an inexplicable rock-paper-scissors tournament. She lands on some sort of reality television show where people tear apart a house. Girls always end up on the wrong stations when they have the remote.

"Yes!" she shrieks. "I *thought* this was on tonight!"

A young, blandly handsome man is telling us about the Bluth family. They live in Omaha, Nebraska, and their family home has fallen into decay. Mike Bluth, the dad, looks into the camera and says he'd love to fix the place up but just doesn't have the money. The blandly handsome guy comes back, puts on goggles, and smiles. "It's time to change the Bluths' life . . . *EXTREME MAKEOVER STYLE!*" He then takes a sledgehammer and smashes it into some worn plywood posing as a wall, and the camera starts zagging all over the place and some cheesy music starts playing at a frenetic pace.

"I *love* this show," Helena says, smiling. "Do you like it? Do you want to watch it?"

I never understand why people love these shows so much. I mean, when is Helena going to renovate a house? She can't even keep her room clean. I decide that these shows are like porn. People can't stop watching them, even though they're full of stuff they'll never actually do.

"That part where he started hitting stuff with the sledgehammer was pretty cool," I say.

"Oh, come on, you'll like it," she says. "Half an hour in, you'll be begging for more."

So we watch the rest of the show. For the first half, the handsome guy—who never wears his goggles after that first shot—destroys everything in sight, and they show him firing up a chain saw ominously, though, to my eye, he never actually uses it (which is a shame). The family is sequestered somewhere, where they talk about how miserable their lives are and how that house is all they have in the world. The second half, after the place is a mess of drywall and two-by-fours, a perky, well-chested woman who absolutely cannot stop smiling comes in with some kind of crew and changes their entire house around, bringing in new furniture and painting it and turning it into something that doesn't even remotely resemble what it was before. The place looks nice, I suppose, and the family starts crying when they see what Blandly Handsome Man and Smiling Breast Lady have made for them.

The whole thing seems empty and brainless to me. So some people got a new house. Big deal. The way that house looked initially, they're destined to make a disaster area of the new place within a couple of months anyway. I'm about to make this observation to Helena when she looks at me, lit up and nearly teary-eyed.

"Wasn't that *incredible*?" she says. "That place is beautiful! God, I love that show."

"Really?" I say. "I mean, I guess the house looks nice, but so what?"

"So what?" she says, her voice rising. "Don't you get it? Their lives have totally changed—like *that*. They were stuck in that place, stuck in their lives, and then, before they even realized it, they had a brand-new start. They can do whatever they want now. Wouldn't that be great?"

A single happy tear rolls down her cheek.

"I guess," I say. "It's just a house." But in that moment, I see it. I see it all through Helena's eyes.

I see the disappointment she's had to live through and the shitty hand that life has dealt her. I see what her dreams were—and how those dreams never came to be. I see where her anger comes from—and her hope—and exactly how a show like this can move her the way it does.

I know. I look at her, and I know.

I want to change Helena's life. And mine. There is no question. I want them to change together.

19.

Saturday morning, my dad made me go see my grandmother in Toledo, just twenty minutes outside of town, in notoriously redneck Cumberland County. Some hooligans snuck in to her backyard earlier this week and spray painted anarchy symbols on her shed, and Dad and I were painting over it for her. She's seventy-four years old and has been a widow for thirteen years. She was married at twenty and had eight children. All she really does anymore is play bingo on Wednesdays, watch *Wheel of Fortune*, and wait for any of her thirty-four grandchildren to come visit.

We paint the shed blinding white, and Dad pauses only to fire menacing looks at anyone under the age of thirty he sees in the general vicinity. He protects Grandma, like a good son. But he never stays over there any longer than he has to. As soon as we're done with the job, he hugs his mother, and so do I, and we head back home.

It's about 3 p.m., and as usual, the only thing Dad and I are talking about are the Cardinals. I will know something is seriously wrong with my father if he ever mentions anything that, you know, *matters*. We're not that kind of family, and I prefer it that way; everybody just *knows* everybody loves each other. There's no need to *say* it, for crying out loud.

It's starting to rain a little, with the promise of more to come; it'll be a perfect evening to spend inside, drinking wine with Helena, cooking, staying away from the scary, dreary outside world. Dad's complaining about the big contract the Cardinals gave to Jason Isringhausen when we see a beat-up Ford Escort pulled over to the side of the road, its hazard lights flashing. It has a bumper sticker: MY DAUGHTER IS AN HONOR STUDENT AT MATTOON HIGH SCHOOL. Its license plate border says, EASTERN ILLINOIS UNIVERSITY FACULTY.

"Dad," I say, "isn't that Professor Danner's car?"

My dad breaks into a wide grin. "Heh, I'll be damned. Herb, Herb, Herb. What mess did you get yourself into this time?"

We pull up behind Jessica's dad's car, which is littered with dents and has various empty packages of Cheetos and

158

Funyons clogging up the back window. It looks like a college student's car. Little could offend my father's sensibilities more than an ill-kempt car, but he always takes a playful, "There he goes again" attitude with Professor Danner.

Dad hops out of the truck and taps on Professor Danner's window. Standing behind Dad, I see the professor leap up in his seat and start frittering about madly, looking around for some sort of identification or paperwork or some such nonsense. Dad knocks again and waves. "Herb, it's Bryan, relax," he says in a soothing voice I rarely hear.

Professor Danner rolls down the window. "Oh, oh, hello, hello, Bryan, hello there."

"What seems to be the problem, Herb?" Dad says. The professor scampers out of the car and looks down at his feet, afraid to look at my father. The rain picks up.

"Oh, well. It appears, you see, it's been a very busy day, and I was just so caught up in everything, it seems that I, well, I might have run a bit low on gas," he sputters.

"You ran out of gas," my dad says, mystified, more to himself than the professor. "Jesus. They don't teach you what the *E* means up in college, Herb?"

Unsolicited, Dad heads to the back of his truck and grabs a container full of gas. My dad always is always prepared for situations like this. Professor Danner tries to protest. "Oh, no, no, Bryan, that's nice of you, but I've called Jessica, you see. She's already on her way."

Dad isn't waiting around. He opens the gas cap and pours the gas into the car. It's an Escort; Dad'll probably be able to fill the damned thing with that tiny container.

The professor turns to me and talks to me like we're old friends. "I just don't see how this could have happened. I kept such a close eye on it, but it's difficult sometimes. I get caught up in matters, and it's hard to keep focused on all the little details, you know?"

His glasses are soaked. I hand him a paper towel. He wipes his glasses, but a speck of paint on the towel smears his lenses, making him look even more ridiculous. This tiny man, standing in the rain, next to a car with no gas, wearing glasses streaked with white paint. And *he's* an academic giant.

I hear a car horn behind me. It's Jessica, in a matching but much cleaner Escort. She parks behind the truck and runs out of the car, holding a towel, which she drapes around her father. "Oh, Dad, I told you the car was near empty. How many times do I have to remind you to check the gauge?" She looks tired and embarrassed, and she barely notices me as she puts her dad back in the car.

Dad empties the gas container into the car and walks over to Jessica. "Everything okay here?" he says, putting a fatherly hand on her shoulder. "Your dad all right?"

Jessica is looking at some space in the distance where there is nothing. She looks up at my dad. "Thank you for helping out, Mr. Temples," she says. "He gets absentminded sometimes." My dad nods; he *knows*. She pulls out her purse. It's beginning to rain even harder. "How much do I owe you for the gas?"

Dad waves off her offer. "Hey, just happy to help, kiddo," he says. "Keep an eye on your old man, would ya? He worries me sometimes."

Jessica tries very hard to smile. "Will do," she says. She walks up to her father's window, which he rolls down. "Okay, Dad, now, just follow me to the gas station up ahead, all right? Make sure you don't turn your brights on, because those make it harder to see in the rain. I'll drive slow, all right?"

Jessica thanks Dad again. I wonder if she has even noticed that I'm there. She starts to drive off into the rain, and we hear a screeching crunch as the professor accidentally shifts into reverse. My dad flinches, and we hop back in the truck.

My dad chuckles, but it is a sad chuckle, the one of a man who realizes a situation might just be hopeless. "It's a wonder that guy can write his name in the ground with a stick, let alone shape young minds," he says. "Old Herb is going to be lost without Jessica around."

This last comment strikes me particularly hard. I hadn't really thought about what Jessica's leaving for college might mean for anyone else.

"I don't know, Tim," Dad goes on. "They said Einstein couldn't tie his shoes. Well, I believe them."

20.

I never know quite what to do in supermarkets. I haven't spent enough time in them to know where everything is, which puts me at a considerable disadvantage. It's strange how people act in supermarkets. They're either dead serious and determined about it, running over anyone who

161

stands in their way, or they're contemplative and philosophical . . . *Do I want this cheese or this one, or maybe one of those grapefruits, no, these.* . . . Supermarkets are like complicated freeways I've never driven on before: the regular commuters all seem to know the rules much better than I do.

That said, I'm feeling rather free in the Jewel-Osco with Helena. Especially as I revert to the supermarket experience I had as a kid—when I could just ride in the cart and point out all the stuff I like.

Example:

Helena: So, what kind of pasta should we get?
Tim: Ooh, ooh, Super Golden Crisp! Look, look, Sugar Pops! Sugar Pops!
Helena: (eyes rolling) Yeah, so . . . the fettuccine.

We're flying through the store at a breakneck pace, but we're still having a grand time. On our list for tonight: pasta, pasta sauce, garlic bread, some sort of salad thing for her, and, of course, a whole bunch of wine. (I do not understand why Helena barked at me when I suggested we buy the box of wine. You get more and it's cheaper. So what's the problem?)

I love this whole idea. We are out shopping *for food*, which we will bring back to *our* (temporary) *home*, where we will make the food *together* before zoning out in a food coma in front of a movie with a bunch of explosions. I could do this every night. I *want* to do this every night.

Helena is giggling as I pretend to put a frozen turkey on my head, and we turn the corner toward the checkout. There, pushing a cart and looking surly, is Doug. I actually let out an audible gasp, and so does Helena. Doug turns his head slightly and breaks into a wicked smile.

"Well, hey there, shitface," he says. "Fancy running into you here." He looks at me, then at Helena. He twists his expression into something resembling constipation. Then his face releases and he looks very, very pleased with himself.

"Helena Westfall!" he says, grinning like a cat playing around with a mouse. "How long has it been? And here you are, with my little brother. I'll be damned."

Helena has eaten something sour, apparently. "Hello, Doug," she says, gritting her teeth.

"Hey! What are you doing here?" I say, trying to sound jovial and plucky.

"I had to pick up some steaks for the park grill tonight, *Squirt*."

He hasn't called me Squirt since I was in the third grade. I hated it then, too. My stomach clenches. Doug goes on. "I got stuck with the shit detail. But man, this trip is surely worth it now." He eyes Helena. "So, you still out at the plant? Wait, I guess you must be if you know Squirt here. You out buying stuff for the boss tonight?" He pauses. "But wait . . . it's *Saturday* night! That seems odd, no?" If he weren't my older brother, I'd definitely be punching him in the face right now.

"So, Helena, you ever talk to Rob anymore? Or Frank?

Or Mike? Or Ted? Ever seen any of them around?" I
know that Doug is trying to get under my skin, or
Helena's skin, or *somebody's* skin, but I have no idea what
the hell he's trying to imply. Helena shakes her head
meekly and mutters something about being real busy and
not being able to stay in touch with everyone anymore. I
sit there and stare at the grinning Doug, trying to figure it
all out. He catches me.

"Oh, don't worry, Squirt, I won't tell Mom and Dad
that you're not with Denny. Your secret's safe with me."
Then he winks at me, the smug prick.

"Well," he says, turning his cart in the opposite direction, "it's nice to see you two kids out, having a nice
romantic time. Enjoy your dinner. Oh, and Tim, she's
allergic to shellfish. Just keep that in mind." He saunters
off, the winner again.

I look at Helena. She turns away, then looks back. "I
think we need more wine," she says.

21.

On the drive to the house-sitting job, she breaks a lengthy
silence by turning to me.

"I knew your brother in high school," she says. "He
dated a couple of my friends. I don't mean any offense,
but he was kind of a jerk to them. I don't think about it
much. And I'd really rather not talk about it anymore, if
that's okay with you."

That is just fine with me.

22.

Helena is already onto the second bottle of wine by the time we've even figured out how to turn the oven on. She isn't talking much, just watching TV.

I know Helena's upset. If I can just keep her mind on the matters at hand, I think everything will be okay. We have a dinner to make. *Together.*

"Hey, so, should I start stirring the pasta sauce?" I ask as she fidgets and curses at the remote. She nods at me. I turn the stove top on—this button, right?—and dump in some random spices I see lying around—whatever the hell *cumin* is. I sip a glass of wine halfheartedly; Helena has lapped me twice over.

"So, listen, I'll put the garlic bread in the oven, all right?" I tell her from the kitchen. How did I end up the one in here?

She stumbles into the room, knocking over a cat figurine on her way in. "Oops!" she says. "Well, she's got a million of these stupid things; she's hardly going to miss this one."

I steer us back to common ground. "So, yeah, um, I had a dream that Chuck was being smothered by members of the Wu-Tang Clan," I say, lying. I never remember my dreams, but I've found making up dreams about someone two people mutually know never fails to spark conversation. "Except the Wu-Tang Clan were all made up of stuffed animals, and they had these big furry feet and talked like sheep, only with these really long tongues."

Helena, pouring herself yet more wine, interrupts me.

"I don't know what you're talking about, but I really don't feel like thinking about Chuck and work, okay?"

I must look a little hurt, because she puts her arm around me and kisses me on the ear. "Oh, lighten up, Tim. It's a little joke. You like jokes." I laugh, though I don't see what was funny about her comment. I don't have much time to figure it out: I think I smell something burning.

"Do you smell that?" I ask.

She sniffs the air. "Maybe the sauce? Have you stirred it?" I haven't. I rush over to the pot, turn down the heat, and start stirring feverishly. Helena says she has to use the bathroom and walks off.

I stir, and I sniff, and things aren't getting better. Then, suddenly, an alarm blares. Helena comes stumbling out of the bathroom holding her pants at her waist, yelling, *"What's going on?"* and I'm waving my hands in the air trying to shut off the smoke detector and now the phone is ringing and the alarm is still blaring and I'm thinking only one thing: *Jesus, we just got here.*

23.

I eventually get the alarm shut off, the phone answered (it was the security people, making sure the place wasn't in flames), and the smoke cleared. The whole sequence of events happened so fast that as I stir the sauce on a lower heat, I have to remind myself it happened at all.

Helena is watching television again, calmed down by wine, obviously. The sauce is simmering, should be ready anytime now, really, and the replacement garlic bread should be perfect in about fifteen minutes. All Helena has to do is boil the pasta and strain it.

I'm still trying to figure out when this "special evening" went off the rails. The easy answer? When we ran into Doug. God, he was such an ass. What *was* that about? But was Helena acting odd at the supermarket before that? Was it me? Was I acting too much like a little kid? Is she wondering right now what the hell she's doing here?

Get a grip, Temples, I order myself. *You sound like a girl. The evening is under control. Everything's fine.*

The sauce is finally ready. I call for Helena. "Hey, it's time to boil that pasta now." No answer. "Hey, Helena, the sauce is done." She remains on the couch, motionless.

I turn the stove top off and walk over to her. "Helena?" I hear a faint whisper, almost a growl, coming from her direction. I sit down next to her and discover the source of the rumble.

Of course. She's snoring. And she has spilled her half-full glass of wine on the nice leather couch.

I've seen her asleep like this before. It would take a jackhammer to her skull to wake her from this. She has passed out.

It seems there's only one thing to do. I pick up the wineglass, set it on the coffee table, and wipe up what I can of the wine off the couch. I grab a pillow from the end of the couch, prop it under her head, and lift Helena's legs up so she's lying more comfortably.

I take the pot of sauce back into the television room, sit

167

down on the La-Z-Boy, and prop up the footrest. I quietly slip the remote control out of Helena's hand and flip to the Cardinals game. They're down 5–1 in the sixth. As Mike Shannon tells us the play-by-play, I look over at Helena, sleeping peacefully.

This might not have been what I had planned for the evening, but all told, it's not so bad. I dunk my garlic bread in the pasta sauce. You know what? It tastes pretty good.

24.

I wake up to the smell of coffee. I look down at myself. The pot of pasta sauce is gone, but I'm still wearing my clothes and I'm covered in bread crumbs. The television is blaring highlights from the baseball games the night before. Hey, Pedro Martinez threw a no-hitter. Good for him.

Music is playing in the kitchen, some sort of poppy crap that they'd play in a dentist's office. I hear the spray of cleaning products and the squeak of diligent scrubbing.

Helena comes out of the kitchen with two cups of coffee. "Good morning, sleepyhead!" she says. "I made you coffee! Thought you might need some."

I feel unusually groggy, almost drugged. My words feel like they're slurring. "I don't drink coffee," I say. She jumps back a step and says, "Oh, of course, I totally knew that."

I'm looking at her, and I'm wondering if she has any

recollection of last night at all. She certainly isn't acting like it. *I might need some coffee?*

She heads back in the kitchen, and I hear her dump the coffee down the drain. She struggles in there, trying to light a cigarette, cursing to herself. When she comes back in, I'm watching highlights of some soccer game in some country I have never heard of and will probably never visit—except maybe via the Discovery Channel.

"Tim, listen," she starts. "I'm real sorry about last night. That wine just went straight to my head. I know it was supposed to be our fun night. And I just punked out."

Trying not to sound pathetic, I say, "You know, the sauce *did* turn out really well."

Helena smiles sweetly. "I'm sure it did," she says. "Honestly. I'm really sorry. You were very sweet last night, and I just drank too much, too fast. I'll make it up to you tonight, all right?"

I am not convinced it was simply a matter of her drinking "too much, too fast," but it's way too early in the morning to argue, and besides, she's only wearing a T-shirt.

"You could make it up to me now . . ." I say.

She laughs. "I'd love to, but I have to shower and go check on my mom." She frowns in a fake pout. "But tonight, okay?" I try to grasp at her and pull her close, but she's already on the way to the bathroom, out of my reach. I stand up, brush the crumbs off, and pour myself a glass of water.

I see a cork on the counter from one of Helena's wine bottles, and, for reasons I can't put a finger on, I sweep it into my pocket. Something about it seems worth keeping around, worth remembering.

25.

Sunday night. A call to my cell phone.

Tim: Hello?

Helena: Hi, it's me. Listen, my mom's not feeling well. I think I have to cancel tonight.

Tim: All right.

Helena: So I'll see you at work tomorrow?

Tim: Yep. I'll be there.

Helena: Tim?

Tim: Yes?

Helena: I am really sorry about yesterday. Really.

Tim: Sure. Listen, I gotta go.

Helena: (playfully) Got a hot date?

Tim: Yeah, that's me. I'm the ladies' man.

Helena: Are you mad at me?

Tim: I don't know. I'm just confused.

Helena: I'm sorry. It's my mom. I can't exactly leave her alone right now. She's running a fever, and I wouldn't feel right taking off on her.

Tim: I understand. It's totally fine.

Helena: Really? Because you sound weird.

Tim: I'm fine.

Helena: Well, all right. Good night, sweetie.

Tim: Yeah, you too.

26.

Monday morning. 1 a.m. Another call to my cell phone

Tim: Hello?

Helena: Are you awake?

Tim: Yes. You're talking to me.

Helena: Were you really awake?

Tim: No.

Helena: I was lying here, thinking about you.

Tim: What are you wearing?

Helena: (giggling) Nothing.

Tim: Really?

Helena: Well, actually, I'm wearing a baggy T-shirt and a pair of huge old lady underwear.

Tim: I liked your first answer better.

Helena: (sighing) My mom's real sick. She's been throwing up all night.

Tim: Jesus. Is she going to be all right?

Helena: She'll make it. She's just really flushed.

Tim: Lemme know if you need anything. I'm really sorry.

Helena: Tim?

Tim: Yeah?

Helena: Do you mind talking awhile? It's been a hard night.

Tim: Of course.

Helena: I'm just lying here listening to Liz Phair. Have you ever heard of her?

Tim: No. Who is she?

171

Helena: She made this album called *Exile in Guyville*, like, twelve years ago. It's so sad. It's all about the terrible things she had been through. I feel like sometimes she broke into my brain and stole everything I ever thought.

Tim: Twelve years ago . . . is she still sad?

Helena: No, actually. She ended up getting married and is all happy now. Her music isn't as good as it was when she was depressed. It's like her heart isn't in it anymore. But that's okay, you know? She still made this album. It's about being afraid she's going to spend her whole life alone, and it turns out that she didn't. It turns out that she found someone and could be happy. I think that makes up for her songs not being so good anymore.

Tim: I'd guess so. I don't know, really. I don't know who she is.

Helena: (*pause*) I get really sad sometimes.

Tim: That's okay. Me too.

Helena: Really? What the hell do you get sad about?

Tim: (*silence*) I don't know, honestly. (*pause*) I've been a lot happier lately.

Helena: Yeah, me too. Hey, Tim?

Tim: Yeah?

Helena: I wish you were here. I wish I were with you right now.

Tim: So do I.

Helena: I feel safer with you. I feel like it will all be all right.

Tim: It will be. I promise.

Helena: Really?
Tim: Really.

27.

Chuck is in his usual egomaniacal state on Monday morning.

This would be repulsive anytime. Today, when everyone's still recovering from the weekend—particularly one as bewildering as this one—it's just too much.

But he's Chuck, and in Chuck's miniature world as king of this plant, this is the type of crap he can get away with.

"So what'd you do this weekend, hot stuff?" Chuck asks Helena. "You meet up with some big stud? I bet the guys just crawl all over you, wherever you go." He gives her a salacious look. His eyes crawl all over her.

I don't know why this sets me off the way it does. I've seen Chuck do some repugnant shit, everything from passing gas in the break room to what he calls "land mining" one of the Horsemen. He has tossed every horrible name in the book at Helena, belittling her, calling her a moron. . . .

Helena has always just taken it because, as she said, "I need this job." But I don't need this job. And she shouldn't have to deal with this. No one's ever stood up for her before, but that's all about to change. Because I have seen enough.

"Chuck, honestly, what is your problem?" I shout.

In a movie, the needle would have scraped off the record. Helena stares at me with her mouth wide open. Chuck has his usual stupid, blank stare on his face, but his eyes are quivering, like he can't decide whether or not he's angry. I *am* angry, though, so I decide to give him more reason.

"Seriously, where do you get off?" I say. "You prance around here like you run the place, and you never do a second of work. You just sit there, annoy everyone, and make you like you're somebody when you're *nobody*, man. Helena's got more class in her snot than you do in your whole body, so why don't you leave her alone?" I find myself walking toward Chuck, fast. Before I realize it, I'm standing right in his face, and I'm on a roll.

"How's it feel, Chuck?" I yell. "How's it fucking feel, someone lording over you, treating you like ass? How's it feel to having somebody call you on your shit? Huh? How's it feel?" I pull back my right arm like I'm going to punch him, and I take considerable glee in watching him flinch. I hope I've made him soil himself. At this, Helena jumps up from her chair and grabs my arm. We have a quick conversation with our eyes.

Her: Oh my God. What are you doing?
Me: What's wrong? I wasn't really going to hit him.

I glare again at this waste of life. "You're not worth the scrape on my knuckles," I say. (Doug taught me that line many years ago. One thing that maybe I should thank him for.) I then turn around, slam the door behind me, and begin to assess the ramifications of what just happened.

28.

I go about my work all morning, picking up the boxes, setting them down, not even talking to Larry. My adrenaline is carrying me; I could juggle these boxes today. All things considered, though, I suspect that might not be appropriate.

Right before lunch, Larry pulls me aside. "Uh, Chuckie-poo wants to have a word with you in his office," he says. "Larry wonders what's got Chuck's panties in a bunch. He was all red-faced, heart-attack lookin'. Good luck, kid."

I work fifteen minutes into my lunch hour, wondering what will happen. Will he fire me? I figure he probably will. I guess I knew that when I did it. It's certainly no big deal. I only had a couple more weeks here anyway, and you'd have to say I got my money's worth out of my time. Will he hit me? I'd like to see him try. He'd be on the ground before he even knew what happened. Heck, it might even be a nice touch to pick my nose and flick it on him as he lies there bleeding.

Yet, I dunno. I kind of feel bad about the whole thing. It's like beating an infant in arm wrestling. He's pathetic. Everybody knows that—even *he* has to know it. So why do I feel like I just set an ant on fire with a magnifying glass?

I knock on the door to Chuck's office and he says, "Come in." Helena, thankfully, is not here. "Have a seat, Tim," he says. He looks small, shrunken behind his desk.

"Tim, there's a lot of things I'd like to say to you," he starts. "But first off, I want to say I'm sorry."

This, this I did not expect. "Uh, what?"

"Yeah," he says. "You know, I'm not that bad of a guy. It's just not easy being the boss. I know I didn't come up through the plant like a lot of people here, and people look at me like I don't deserve this job. And you know what? I probably don't."

I sit there, speechless.

"So I try to show people that I should be respected, that I'm someone to be reckoned with, you know?" He is jittery, playing with a paper clip on his desk, bending it, straightening it, twisting it back to its natural shape. "Sure, yeah, sometimes I overdo it. I know I do."

I snap out of my shock long enough to speak up. "You were being really rude," I say. "Helena doesn't deserve that."

"I know," he says. "And I have apologized to her. And she has accepted it. She asked to go home for the day, and I let her. I know she's had a hard life. I'm just, I dunno, trying to toughen her up a little bit. Does that make sense?"

"I think she's plenty tough without you," I say, calling him on this latest load of crap.

Chuck smiles. "I know, kid," he says. It bothers me that Chuck is starting to seem like a human being. "And I respect you for saying so. So thank you." He extends his hand to me, and I eye it warily. I then accept it.

"So are you going to stop being such an ass?" I ask.

"I'll be honest with you, Timbo," he says. "Probably not. But thanks to you, I'll feel real guilty about it. You're a good kid. We'll sure miss you around here come August." He opens the door for me and pats me on the back, and I leave, and I wonder just how our small little town ended up with such a ludicrously high percentage of complete weirdos.

29.

Message on my voice mail:

Tim, it's Helena. Listen, I really don't appreciate the little stunt you pulled today with your dumb redneck bullshit. You made me look like a complete idiot in front of my boss. I'm a big girl. I can take care of myself. I know you were just trying to help, but I don't need your help, okay? I'll be at my mom's friend's place later, if you want to come by and talk about this, though I'm not sure what more there is to say. See ya.

As I listen to her message, I notice myself breaking into a sweat, and for the first time I can remember, I'm dreading going to see her.

Denny's advice echoes in my head. *Don't screw it up. Don't be an idiot.*

Jesus. What have I done?

30.

I'm lucky not to be caught speeding between the Kraft plant and the house-sitting job; I was going so fast, the Blazer's dashboard started vibrating. I knock on the door, and Helena is standing there drinking straight out of a bottle of wine. I open the screen door, she offers me a swig, and I decline.

We sit down on the couch. There are still crumbs everywhere. Helena lights another cigarette.

"You know, I don't know what you were thinking today," she says. "I mean, who does that? So what if Chuck's a moron? He's my boss. You don't do stuff like that to people's bosses."

Before I have a chance to protest, Helena says what's really on her mind. "Seriously, Tim, you could have blown the whole thing. Thank God Chuck's such a knucklehead that he didn't catch on."

"Wait—you're upset about *that*?" I say, hearing the words come out of my mouth. "You're afraid that Chuck might catch on to our little *secret*? You know what? I don't *care* if Chuck knows. I don't care if anybody knows!"

Helena is quiet. She's counting the tiles on the wall, I think. "You know, Tim," she says in barely a whisper, "maybe you should care."

I don't understand this. "What's that's supposed to mean?"

"You know, I'm not some great person," she says. "I've got all kinds of history and baggage. If you knew some of the things I've done, you might not like me anymore."

I'd like to tell you my first instinct here is to say, "I don't care about anything in your past," but that would be a total lie. My first thoughts are rather intense speculation on what these "things" could be. But I remember Denny's advice: tell her how you feel. "It doesn't matter," I say. "I just want you to be happy."

She pulls her hair out of her face. "You don't get it, do you?" she says. "What happens if everybody knows? What happens when you go off to college and I'm still here? Then everyone says, 'Oh, poor Helena, her boyfriend left her.' I'm pretty tired of that role. Pretty fucking tired."

To this, I have no response. I lean over to her and kiss her on the cheek, and she burrows her head into my shoulder. I fear that she's going to cry, but she doesn't.

I think maybe she'd be better off if she did.

31.

It's two in the morning of the following Friday, and she has woken me up by *not* snoring. I've been spending so much time with her, the absence of the noise is enough to jolt me out of sleep.

"Everything all right?" I say.

"Are you ready for orientation tomorrow?" she says, lying there awake.

"I guess so," I say. "I don't really have to do much. Just be in front of my house at 8 a.m. so Jessica can pick me up."

"You're going to have such a good time," she says, smoking another cigarette. It mixes with my just-woken-up breath and almost makes me gag.

"I always wanted to go to the U of I," she continues. "All kinds of interesting people there."

"I guess," I say. "I just want the whole thing over with as soon as possible so I can get back here."

"Will you call me tomorrow night?" she says. "I'd like to hear how it's going."

"Of course," I say. "I wish you were coming with me."

"Don't say that." She puts out her cigarette and lies back down, silent, hearing only the stillness of the Mattoon night.

32.

When I was about thirteen, my neighbors Eldean and Lori gave me the key to their house to make sure their dog was fed. It was the summer, so I didn't have much to do other than finish whatever menial, moron lawn task Dad had assigned to be completed by the time he returned from work. I had a lot of free time. And Eldean and Lori had cable.

This was one of those old cable systems, before everything went digital. I always ended up on channel 158. It was called American XXXtasy. For a considerable fee, you could watch all the porn you could handle, all day and all night. I, of course, didn't have either the fee or the access, so the signal was scrambled, an indecipherable mix of random colors and twisting vertical reception. But it had the sound. And that was enough.

I would go to the backyard and dump a bag of industrial-sized Sam's Club for their three snarling Dobermans. Then I headed inside, where I'd fix a glass of milk, eat a couple of cookies Lori had set out for me, and turn on the television. I'd go directly to channel 158, darting glances out the window to make sure none of the retired neighbors were keeping an eye on what I was doing. I would stare at the hodgepodge of rolling images on the screen. I'm lucky my eyeballs stayed inside my head. The scrambled American XXXtasy was a visual obstacle course. Was that a nipple there? A woman's face?

I could only take the sounds I was hearing at face value and use my imagination to try to figure out what else was going on. It would always give me a headache, and sometimes I'd even get nauseous, but it was always worth it, it always captivated me, it always riveted me, even though, when you really broke it down, I hadn't the foggiest idea what was happening, what I was actually looking at.

Talking to Helena reminds me of those afternoons at Eldean and Lori's. Our conversations are a puzzle I can't quite solve, a maze I can't find my way through. They're a struggle to see something, anything, that might give me what I need. And yet, no matter what, I'm there, every day, hoping that today the picture becomes clear—that nothing is scrambled—that it's all in focus. And even if I don't get that, even if I'm confused and dizzy afterward, I'm still enthralled.

33.

Jessica is so cheesy sometimes. She's wearing an orange University of Illinois T-shirt and blue jeans with

Chief logo sewn on them. We hop in her car, and I ask, "Are you wearing that in case you get lost?"

"Very funny," she says. "I'm just trying to show a little school spirit."

"You look like a Japanese tourist," I say, and she slugs me on the arm. "Hey, you and your dad make it home all right the other night? You looked a little flustered."

She sloughs it off. "Oh, yeah, it was fine. He just ran a little low on gas."

The radio plays a rock song where the lead singer is screaming. His voice makes him sound like he's about fifteen years old.

"What is this?" I say.

"I don't know, actually, but I like it," she says. "It's 107.1, the college radio station. Did you know it's run entirely by students? The students get to pick the songs and be the DJs and everything. Can you imagine? You could have a *class* with one of the DJs!"

"Every time I hear those DJs, they sound like idiots," I say. "All they do is make a bunch of stupid noises and lame jokes."

Helena told me a while back that she used to date a radio DJ, which is probably the real reason I hate them.

Jessica drives the car—*slllooooowly*. She sets the cruise control right at the speed limit and putters along. Ordinarily, I'd be annoyed by this pace, but I am in no hurry.

"You know, I don't understand why this whole thing is necessary," I say. "We're just gonna have some dork show

182

us around. I mean, I'll find my own way. I don't need this guy telling me where to go."

Jessica makes a perturbed face. "Honestly, why can't you just get excited about this? If you're going to sit there and whine the whole time, I don't want to be next to you."

Jessica is scolding me. This amuses me somehow . . . but I still have a point to make. "Well, it's real easy for you," I say. "You were valedictorian. College is something you've always wanted. It's easy."

Jessica's voice rises, to the point that I—finally—realize she's angry. "Jesus, Tim, do you think this is *easy* for me?" she says. "Have you ever *met* my dad? Do you know that was the fourth time in the last few months he's run out of gas? He can't cook, he can't clean, he can't even keep his shoes tied. My mom used to do all that stuff for him. Without me, he's going to be alone and completely helpless. You think I feel *good* about that? God."

The car goes quiet. I look out the window and try to think about something else. *Helena.*

"So listen," Jessica says, eager to change the topic. "We're supposed to meet at the Illini Union, where some student rep is going to take us, and some other people, I'd assume, around campus. It's pretty regimented, so don't go trying to roam around like you do."

I tell her no problem. "I wouldn't even know where to go."

We're passing the Tuscola outlet mall when I work up the nerve. "So, um, hey, uh . . . is there something going on with you and Jeff?"

She looks at me like I've slapped her. "That's none of your business," she says in a harsh tone that kind of reminds me of Helena. "I don't go asking you about your million little affairs, do I?"

"Oh, so it's an *affair* now?" I say, trying to keep the tone light. "Come on, I'm just asking. You guys have been hanging out a lot lately. And anyway, all I'm saying is, be careful. Jeff can be kind of a jerk sometimes."

Jessica looks at me like I am four feet tall. "My dad's the one who needs taking care of," she says witheringly. "Not me."

34.

We drive around the Champaign campus for at least twenty minutes trying to find a parking space before finally accepting that no matter where we stop, we're going to get a ticket. We are supposed to meet our guide at the front desk, so we walk there and run into two other fresh-faced losers who seem marooned. I peg them immediately as incoming freshmen, because they look just like Jessica and me. Except that, well, they're twins.

"Hey, you here for the campus tour?" I ask one. They're a pair of reed-thin guys with bushy hair and coke-bottle glasses. "Hi," I say, extending my hand. "I'm Tim. This is Jessica. We're from Mattoon, just about an hour south of here."

"Oh, well, hello there, Tim, it's a pleasure to make your acquaintance," the one on the left says. "I'm Eric; this is my brother Gabe. We're from Skokie. Perhaps you've heard of it. It's where the Ku Klux Klan is always petitioning to march every year, on account of all us swarthy Jews."

Eric has this overly proper way of speaking that sounds completely different from everyone I know. I can't decide if I like it or if it's just plain weird.

Gabe snickers. "Where did you two say you were from?"

"Mattoon," Jessica says, shaking their hands. "Go, Green Wave!"

"Wild," Gabe says. "I always thought it was pronounced 'Ma-TOON.'"

"Wait. You know our town?" I ask. "I thought nobody knew Mattoon."

"Oh, Gabe's quite familiar with it," Eric says. He wipes his brow with a handkerchief that seems to have his initials on it. "He wrote his senior term paper about it."

"What?" I yelp. "That must have been the most boring paper of all time."

"No way. Check it," Gabe says, all excited. "I did my paper on traditional Jewish conventions being taken over by Gentile culture. I read a newspaper article on this tiny town downstate—your town—that claimed it was the 'Bagel Capital of the World.' I did some research and was like, how can you claim to be the public center of what is traditionally known as Jewish food, when not a single Jewish family lives in your town?"

"Tim works at the plant that makes the bagels," Jessica says, smiling broadly. I'm looking at Jessica, and I know

185

she's imagining having arbitrary encounters like this every day for the next four years.

"The Kraft plant?" Gabe asks. "Eric and I did a tour of that place."

"We certainly did," Eric says. "And it was *fas*cinating! Though I wish I could have seen your 'Bagelfest.' Perhaps I would have enjoyed it. Though I doubt Mattoon has much lox. Oh, and I liked your Burger King. Gabe, did you know they make a chocolate Coke there? It's in*cre*dible."

Eric has an almost fey way about him; I'd get the feeling he was making fun of me if he weren't so darned *enthusiastic* about everything.

Gabe snorts. "It's probably just regular Coca-Cola with a few shots of chocolate syrup in there."

Eric's face falls. "Well," he says, grimacing, "I suppose that's what it is, yes."

Gabe motions to me. "So, the point is, your town is not boring at all. Which is more than we can say for Skokie. Have you been there?"

Jessica chuckles. "I've only been to Chicago three times, and those were just for band trips. I've never been anywhere else."

"Yeah, me neither," I say. "I've just been to Wrigley a couple of times." I pause, realizing something else. "Actually, I think you might be the first two Jews I've ever met."

Jessica does her best to hide a gasp and fails.

Eric reveals a small, clipped smile and places his hand on my shoulder in an odd *"dahling"* type of way. "Oh, well, you'll find that we're quite friendly people," he says. "Except for the ones who control the media. But they're such an *unseemly* sort."

35.

We stand with the brothers, talking about broadband connections and other things I don't understand. I don't have much to say since none of them are big baseball fans. But it turns out that Eric is gay, a proclamation that startles me in its matter-of-factness.

After this revelation, Eric turns to me: "Did you know that the high five was invented by a gay baseball player?" I tell him I didn't know there were gay baseball players, and he laughs long and hard at that one.

I'm starting to think I kind of like him, even though I'm probably supposed to pop him on the nose.

After about five minutes, a tall, skinny, Indian guy, with a tightly groomed goatee, brown corduroys, and a baggy flannel shirt shambles in the front door of the union. He's carrying a backpack with stickers on it that say things like, TAKE BACK THE NIGHT '03 and BUCK FUSH. His hair is shaggy, unkempt, and he carries himself with the grace of a man who is always in a hurry yet never particularly stressed out about it. "Hey, are you guys the new students?" he says. We all nod, and Jessica shoots out her hand. "Hi, I'm Jessica!" she says. "I'm a music major!"

He smiles slyly. "Hey, nice to meet you, Jessica. I'm Munesh, and, um, I go to class occasionally." He speaks perfect English. The brothers and I laugh at his joke and introduce ourselves. He shakes our hands loosely, casually, trying some kind of special handshake that involves, as far as I can tell, a slap, a tickle, a pound, and a wiggle.

"So," he says. "I could just take you guys around the campus, show you historic buildings, let you know where your classes are gonna be, but that's all totally boring, to be honest, and you're gonna have to figure that out on your own anyway. This is the first time I've done one of these, and I figure you should just ask me questions about what it's like here, and I'll answer them. That okay with you?"

Jessica, who was inexplicably looking forward to hearing about the Altgeld building, starts to protest, but I glare at her and she shushes.

Munesh rubs his hands together as if he's about to start making something out of clay. "So I was figuring we'd just hit the White Horse, have a few beers, and we'd chat," he says. "That sound cool to you guys?"

That sounds cool to the brothers and me, though Eric asks if it's okay if he has a vodka and tonic. (Answer: "Whatever, man.")

Jessica takes on the role of the true wet blanket. "Well, honestly, um, Munesh, are you sure that's the best thing? I mean, don't you have to be nineteen to get into the bars here? None of us are nineteen."

Munesh licks his lips. "Oh, don't you worry about that, Jennifer."

"Jessica."

"Whatever. I know the bartender at the Horse. He'll

hook us up." Munesh looks around, hopping slightly on his feet. "You guys ready? Let's do it."

36.

"You know, I have to say, this is a fine vodka they have here," Eric says. "Do you know who the distiller is?"

Munesh, smoking a strange cigarette called a clove that gives off a scent that's overwhelmingly pleasant, smirks. "Yeah, I think it's called Popov. It's, like, four bucks a bottle. Goes well with Jell-O."

The White Horse is surprisingly bereft of patrons, though I guess it *is* summer. We're out in the beer garden, and as the night approaches, the air is cooler, crisp, agreeable. Munesh calls over the waitress and orders two pitchers for the table, even though he and I are the only people drinking beer.

"So, Munesh . . . wait, is that the right pronunciation of your name?" I say.

"Yep, that's it," he says, chewing some leftover french fries the bartender gave us.

"So, um, where are you from?" I say. "Like, what's your homeland?"

"My homeland?" he says, smirking again. "Uh, let's see . . . *Chicago*. Well, Naperville, actually, but I think you get my point. You're obviously from downstate." Jessica laughs, and Eric gleefully conveys my first-ever-Jew anecdote, cackling. I blush, but I laugh too. "Sorry."

"Oh, hey, not a big thing, man," he says. "Whole different

universe out here. Wait until you start meeting"—his voice lowers to a sarcastic whisper—"*the black people. They're just like us, except taller.*"

"Yes," Eric puts in. "Shame they can't dance, though."

The table explodes in laughter, and Eric claps me on the shoulder. In that moment, I decide I do like him. And all told, I like being the butt of the joke. It's a refreshing change of pace.

"So, Munesh, what are the professors like here?" Jessica asks.

Deadpan, Munesh says, "Oh, they're just like me, except they have more time on their hands. Most of your teachers the first couple of years will be graduate students, which is good, because they really don't want to teach and are all full of liberal guilt about failing anybody. Just turn in everything on time and show up enough so that they vaguely remember your face, and you'll be fine."

Munesh goes on for a few hours like this, dispensing pearls of wisdom. The Tao of Munesh is less about thriving in the classroom than it is about doing enough to get by and making your social life as rewarding as possible. I think I could be a disciple.

"You won't learn anything you really need to know from class until your advanced-level classes, and those aren't until your junior and senior years. Your first two years are all about making sure college is actually your type of thing. I mean, when I got here, I didn't know anybody. I knew I was smart, I knew I kind of liked science, but that was about it. Now I'm an engineering major, I'm the president of the campus chapter of Amnesty International, all that stuff. I've got more friends than I can count. I know all the best bars, the best places to pick up girls. . . . That will be your job. Seeing if you *like* it here, you know? Finding your place. You do all your real learning outside the classroom. The rest of that stuff, the classes, all that, if you're not a drooling moron, you'll be able to figure that out."

"Kind of like high school," I interject, immediately wishing I hadn't. I brace myself for another joke at my expense.

But Munesh just smiles. "Actually, yeah," he says. "It's pretty much like that. Except the girls here are a lot hotter, man . . . and they're *legal*."

37.

Any hesitation Jessica had about this unexpected excursion from her much-anticipated "tour" has evaporated. I can see her absorbing everything that surrounds her, from the waitresses wearing bows in their hair to the jukebox that has two Roy Orbison discs right next to two Marilyn Manson ones. I see how she watches a girl in the corner of the beer garden, drinking a beer while reading a book. I see the longing on her face. I can see that not only does she realize that she desperately *wants* to go to college, she is realizing that she *belongs* here.

And I cannot escape the nagging feeling that I'm settling in real comfortably too.

38.

Next thing we know, it's 11 p.m., and, as the brochure for orientation clearly stated, *your residential living arrangements lock up for the night at 11:30, so all orientees must return to their location before then.* Munesh leans over to me. "Hey, man, you learn everything you need to know?"

"I think I learned enough," I say. "This was certainly fun."

"Cool," he says. "I gotta scram. I have three dates tonight."

"Wait . . . *three* dates? Tonight?"

He cocks an eyebrow and gives a "Whaddya gonna do" shrug. "Hey, college is where it's at, man. And brown's the new black, baby." He takes a puff off his clove cigarette. "Oh, by the way, number-one most important lesson I can give you: college students never have any money. You think you guys can cover this?"

I laugh. "No problem, dude," I say. "This might be the last time I have any money, after all."

"Yeah, no kidding," he says, and he gives me a fist pound, and slaps the brothers on the back, and kisses Jessica on the cheek. "You all give me a call when you get to campus, and I'll set you guys up, definitely." And he leaves, knowing full well that none of us have his phone number and that that's fine too.

39.

I take the surprisingly long walk back to the Florida Avenue residence halls with Jessica, who is practically floating.

"Oh my God! Wasn't that *great?*" she's singing. "I could have stayed there all night!"

I feel the urge, even though I don't really want to, to play devil's advocate. "Well, Jess, to be fair, that's not all that different from what we do back in Mattoon."

Jessica kicks me lightly. *"Please,"* she says, laughing. "You *know* it's different. For one thing, nobody here tries to set stuff on fire at the end of the night."

"True," I concede. "I guess the conversation is a *wee* bit better." I pause. "And no one farted."

"See?" Jessica says. "You had a great time. Don't lie."

I did. Of course I did. I talked and laughed and listened to people who come from someplace completely different from me. Not just from a different town, but from a different perspective—a different mind-set. The more Eric and Gabe and Munesh talked, the more I could feel myself opening up.

It was a feeling I liked, a feeling I want more of.

We make our way through the quad, past the undergraduate library, past the Krannert Center, where all the music majors like Jessica will spend four years convincing themselves they'll be opera singers or whatever. I look up at the stars. The night is perfect. I want to walk forever. But we have to hustle. I look at my watch. 11:24. We're gonna cut it close. Jessica is thinking the same thing, and we start to jog, right beside each other, and it feels perfect, it feels like we could run forever.

We arrive at the front door with two minutes to spare.

"This was really great, Tim," she says.

"It was," I confess. "It really was."

"Did you ever think, when we were kids, that we'd end up going to college together?" she asks, with a dreamy look in her eyes. "I think it was destined to happen."

"Honestly, when we were kids, I was just worried about you peeing in your eye." This is a famous Jessica incident. When she was four, we were playing in the backyard, doing somersaults and playing with little plastic soldiers. Jessica did a little handstand and then, out of nowhere, peed all over herself. My mother ran out from the house, mortified, thinking that Jessica's parents would wonder what the hell kind of operation the Temples were running over there.

That would have been, let's see, three or four years before Jessica's mom died. She was a really nice woman. She always made Kool-Aid and Rice Krispie Treats for us, and she always rubbed my scrapes with rubbing alcohol and made me feel better. Funny how I forgot about that until just now.

Jessica turns pink. "Great. Thanks for bringing that up," she says.

We stand there, quiet for a moment, looking at each other, outside the front door. "Well . . . thanks for coming up here with me," she says.

"Yeah, you too," I say. And she gives me a hug, and it feels good, it feels warm.

The janitor walks to the door, jangling keys, ready to lock up. We see him and start toward the door. I open the door quickly. "We're good, right?" I say. He gives us a dirty look and waves us inside. The girls' dorm is to the left, the boys' to the right.

I head up to my dorm—a tiny, compact room with sliding glass windows. I crawl into my bed. It's next to another bed, which is supposed to have another incoming freshman in it. He didn't hit the eleven thirty curfew. A soldier who didn't make it back. A man left behind.

I salute you, Private, I think, smiling. *You made us proud.*

As I'm drifting off to sleep, I have a feeling I'm forgetting something—something vital has slipped my mind. I can't imagine, as nice as tonight has been, as fulfilled and exhausted as this has left me, that it could have been all that important anyway.

40.

I meet Jessica at her car at 9 a.m., way too early, but the time we promised we'd leave so we could tell our families just how much fun we had, how much we love college, how much we're excited about our new opportunities, so on, whatnot.

I had been concerned I wouldn't have that much to tell them. I am now afraid I will not be able to stop talking.

We drive down 57 toward Mattoon, listening to the radio. Jessica has more interesting taste in music than I would have thought. That is to say, I don't know a single song or band or album she's playing, but I kind of like it. It sounds chaotic but lovely.

195

"Who is this?"

"This is the Butthole Surfers."

"What? That's disgusting."

Jessica laughs. "So I don't suppose you'd like the Flaming Lips either?"

"Sheesh," I say. "Lips and Buttholes. Sounds like a hot dog factory."

We hit the Mattoon city line, and, like clockwork, my thoughts return to Helena. I'm running low on time; I told her I would come by her house-sitting place at noon, and it's already ten thirty. Jessica keeps the car running outside my house. "Well, that was certainly something," she says.

"It really was," I say. "So . . . I guess I'll see you around, eh? Next game of asshole?"

"Only if you want me to kick your butt again," she says, with a grin that lights up the car. I get out, and she speeds off. I head inside to see Doug sitting on the couch, flipping through infomercials. I try to sneak past him but fail.

"Good time at camp, Squirt?" he says.

With one sentence, Doug has once again brought my mood crashing down. Half of me wants to know what his damage is. The other half just doesn't care. "Went all right," I say, through gritted teeth.

"Well, good," he says, ending all conversation. I hop in the shower and get cleaned up to head to Helena's, wondering what she's been doing. Did she make dinner last night? What will she be wearing when I get there? Was there anything good on the Discovery Channel last night?

196

Oh, and: is there any way I could spend Monday through Friday in Champaign and Saturday and Sunday with her? *Hypothetically speaking.*

41.

I find myself, as I drive to Helena's house-sitting gig, mentally editing the story of the day to make it more palatable, easier for her to digest. We're gonna have to leave Jessica out of the story, I realize; don't want Helena to feel jealous.

But nothing happened with Jessica, and I have nothing to be ashamed of. Do I? No. Of course I don't. I know! I'll just alter her a bit; she was off talking to some guy! That'll work. Or how about: she was off looking at boring buildings and hearing about classes while I was hanging out with Munesh. That's totally believable. Oh, and the day itself wasn't really that much fun. Sure, the campus was impressive, but socially, everyone was lame and I'd much rather be back here spending time with her.

Or wait—maybe she would like it up there. Maybe I should make it like this wonderful place she won't be able to stop herself from visiting? Maybe I should tell her about the White Horse, and the cool music, and the drink specials, and the vibe that makes you realize there's a whole other planet out there? Come on, Helena, let's go!

I pull into the driveway and . . . something's wrong. Her car is parked half in the garage, half out. The passenger side door of the car is hanging open. There is also a beer huggy lying in the grass and a half-full pack of cigarettes sitting on the hood of the car. The front door is flung wide, swinging like a loose tooth. All the lights in the front room are on, and, as I move closer to the house, I realize that the television is blaring. An elderly woman coming down the street looks at me, concerned. I peek my head in the door and swivel around. "Helena? Hello? It's me . . . hello?"

I turn to the television. It's playing some kind of strange Asian film where everyone is naked and running around, screaming. I hear music from the room Helena is staying in. A CD is on at full volume, but it's skipping, the same loop over and over, some kind of techno garbage, *ta-da-DUM, ta-da-DUM.*

I tiptoe to her room. "Helena?"

She is lying facedown on her bed. She is topless, wearing a skirt that's half hiked up. The ashtray next to the bed is stuffed full. Empty beer bottles are everywhere. A bottle of wine lies on the white carpet, spilling a trail from the door to the bedside table. A jean jacket, not hers—a man's jean jacket, with an AC/DC patch sewed on the shoulder—is draped over the door handle to the closet. She is snoring.

I survey the scene, then back slowly out of the room.

I turn around, leaving everything where it sits, and leave the house, shutting the door gently behind me.

AUGUST

1.

"You know who it was who framed O.J., don't ya?" Larry is telling me. At least I think he's telling me this. His lips are moving, and there seems to be some vibration that could pass for sound, but right now, I'm not sure.

I try looking at him closer. Perhaps if I squint and move toward him a bit, I'll be able to understand him, the same way that if you lean your head to the dashboard when you're driving during a rainstorm, you can hypothetically see your way through the downpour. I try taking in the words phonetically. *"Mar. Kuss. Al. Lin. Wuz. Gel. Us."* None of this makes any sense. The sounds he's mouthing surround my head, dance around for a while, never finding their target.

I don't know how long I do this, but eventually Larry realizes that I'm not paying any attention. He takes the water bottle he keeps next to him for hot days and squeezes its contents into my face. Even with this, it takes me a few seconds to snap to.

"Jee-zus, Tim, Larry lost ya there for a sec." Finally I comprehend him. Where am I again? It's hot out. I'm outside. I'm with the Larry human. I must be at work! Yes! Work! All right. That's a start. I work here. I carry boxes of bagels. Larry works with me. He talks to me a lot. This happens all the time. This is a regular day. I'm Tim. I work at the Kraft plant. I'm going to college, I think, in two more weeks. I remember that! Cool. We're making headway.

"You all right, Tim?" Larry says. "You got yourself a funny look on your face, like you're trying really hard to crap or somethin'."

I cock my head down a peg so I'm no longer staring at the middle of his forehead. I blink a few times, *fwap fwap fwap*. I crick my neck and then shake my head back and forth rapidly. I might be coming to.

"Sorry, Larry," I say. "I think I spaced out for a second there."

"Spaced out? You were spending some time in La-La Land," he says. "Larry don't know where you went on your little vacation there, but he'd sure like to go sometime." His laughter rumbles the cement and comes close to crumbling his lawn chair. He coughs up something horrendous and spits it into the grass. He pulls himself up from his seat and brushes imaginary dirt off his Hawaiian shirt. "Well, Tim, break time's over," he says. "You and Larry got a buttload more boxes to carry. Whaddya say we get to it?"

2.

As I cart four ten-pound boxes out to the truck and pass Chuck's office, everything my brain had shut down to avoid returns—against the brain's best efforts. For the second consecutive workday, Helena is not here. I've been trying to piece together what in God's name happened the other night, the night I was gone, the night I wasn't there, the night I forgot to call. I haven't had much more luck making any sense of it than I did when I walked in that house.

Let's retrace. I saw the mess in the yard. I saw that weird tape on the television. I heard the music blaring . . . the CD was skipping. I saw her in her room, or the room she was staying in, anyway, though it already has morphed into her room, her room at home, with the Lake Land Lady Lakers stuffed bear on the wicker chair and the pictures of her at her high school graduation, with her bearded, leather-jacketed dad, with her then-made-up mom. I saw her lying on the bed. I saw her not wearing a shirt. I saw a jean jacket. I saw a patch.

I don't remember much after that. I don't remember much after that until now, actually.

The boxes are feeling oddly heavy. I set them down for a moment to catch my breath, to collect my strength. I see Chuck pass by me on my right. He is holding a clipboard. I wonder if he needs it. I wonder if he really writes anything of importance on it or if he just carries it around, stops occasionally, looks at someone working, someone who has noticed him and is now nervous, and he jots down, *Eggs. Milk. Toilet paper. Porn magazines,* followed by a disapproving glance and a clicking of his tongue. Chuck's eyes meet mine. I nod, subconsciously—or maybe I really did it; I just don't know. I pick the boxes back up and take them out to the truck.

I repeat this for a while, as the job requires. My shoulders hunch. A secretary at the plant's front desk walks by me, pats me on the back, asks me if I'm okay. I nod—for real this time, I'm fairly certain.

She's still not here. How can she still not be here? It has been *two days* now. The first day, all right. Maybe she was just feeling sick from whatever the hell went on Saturday. Maybe she was embarrassed. But today? Two straight days? Even Helena doesn't get that hungover.

I know one thing for certain: this is my fault. How could I have forgotten to call her? I was so wrapped up in myself, in Munesh, in the twins, in Jessica—no . . . not Jessica . . . I wasn't wrapped up in Jessica, I *wasn't*—that it just slipped my mind.

I told her I would call. I said those exact words. *Of course I will call you,* I said. *I wish you were coming with me.* But I didn't call, now did I? I can't even excuse myself by saying that I got home too late. I have called Helena at all hours of the night. She has called me. That's a horse-shit excuse.

Why wouldn't she be mad? Her boyfriend—that's what I am, after all, her *boyfriend*—told her he would call her, and he didn't call her, and she punished him. But *how*? What *was* that? Whose jacket was that? What was on that tape? Where did she even get that? Where was her shirt? How could she forget to *park the damned car*? The front door was hanging open. Why was the front door hanging open?

And I still haven't talked to her. I haven't even called her. What would I say? How could I get more than a sentence out before she hung up on me? What in the world is going on? And goddammit, goddammit, goddammit . . . *why is she not here?*

Seconds pass, minutes pass, hours pass, maybe, I don't know, it could have been forever, it could have been nothing, I have no idea. Right now I'm just the guy carrying boxes, lifting them, transporting them, dropping them, lather, rinse, repeat, it's all I know how to do, it's the only thing that makes sense, I think it's a Tuesday, I think my name is Tim, I think I live in Mattoon, I think I'm going to college soon, I think maybe I might be losing my freaking mind.

3.

It's late in the day. I'm drenched in sweat; though it doesn't feel like I've been working that hard, I guess I have. I guess we all have. Larry offers me a swig out of his water bottle, but I wave him off; don't take me out, Coach, I want to stay in.

I lift, I carry, I drop.

I have no idea what time it is when Larry stops me, talking to me like I'm wearing headphones. "Kiddo, it's

205

time to go home," he says. "You put yourself through a helluva day today. You wore ole Larry out." I take the last box to the truck and walk back into the plant. There's the office, the one without Helena. Chuck is sitting at his desk, reading the *Sporting News*. I open the door and walk in. I am not sure why.

Chuck sees me and puts down his magazine. "Christ, Timbo, looks like you went through a car wash," he says. "You're gonna have to peel that shirt off of you." I turn around to leave.

"Wait, Timbo, wait, got a question for you," Chuck says. I'm in no mood to chat, something Chuck wants to do with increasing regularity since our little talk, but I turn my head and then the rest of my body anyway.

He puts his boots up on his desk and motions for me to sit down. I oblige him and start fidgeting with one of those little black paper binders, the one with the two metal clips. Whatever he has to say, I know that I don't want to hear it, so I spread the shiny clips out like they're wings and pretend they're a Star Wars TIE fighter, battling the empire, *vroom*.

"So Timbo," he says, and I have a sudden, panicked dread that he knows something is going on with Helena, that he's going to lay it out on the table for me, that he's going to ask me a bunch of questions that I absolutely cannot answer right now, of all times. "I was wondering if you might know of anybody who might be looking for a job, maybe somebody from your class or something."

"I'm sorry?" I say, sputtering.

206

"Well, don't know if you've heard or not, but Helena quit today," he says.

He says something after this, but he sounds like the adults in a Charlie Brown cartoon. My world goes hazy. The walls are melting to the floor all around me. The back of my head starts producing a sound like my parents' alarm clock, *bam-BAM!, bam-BAM!* The noise is relentless. The room is red, bright, bright red.

I do the lean-toward-the-windshield thing again. I am able to focus a bit. I can make out Chuck, who has taken his boots off the desk. "What?" I say.

"Yep, she called me this afternoon. Says she just doesn't want to work here anymore. She's just gonna come back today or tomorrow and pick up her stuff. Didn't even give me two weeks notice. Well, I guess I shouldn't give her too much crap. She probably had all kinds of shit she wanted to say to me. But she held back, and I gotta give her that."

I stand up and hold on to my chair for support. I feel like I am growing old right here, going bald, going gray, shrinking. The room isn't spinning, necessarily; it's just rocking up and down, like in a horrible earthquake, one of those that happen in Spain or Egypt or wherever. One of those where they spend weeks searching for survivors and find none.

I stagger toward the door and reach my hand out for the knob, but it's far away, it's running. *Get back here. I'll catch you, you sonuvagun.*

I hear Chuck's voice over my shoulder. "Well, anyway,

if you know anyone, I need a new assistant, and I bet you know some hot pieces of tail. Let me know, Timbo. I'd like to maybe find another one with a huge rack, you know?"

His words fade away into nothing and, somehow, I make it to my truck.

4.

Three hours later, I am still at my truck. For a while, I sat inside, trying to listen to the radio. That didn't last long at all. This sent me into a weird cycle of standing outside the truck, then taking a lap around the truck, then walking to the front door of the plant, then walking around the plant for a while, then back to the truck, then inside the truck again, fiddling with the radio.

I was waiting for Helena. I am still waiting for Helena.

I walk into the plant, which now has only the sad souls on overnight shift. I'm looking for someone I recognize, someone who knew Helena, someone who might have an idea if she's coming by tonight. This is not a rational thought, but I don't care. I'm clueless as to what else to do with myself.

I see old man Otis at his lonely job of ensuring the bags of bagels make it into the boxes, the one he has done all night, every night, for decades and decades and centuries. He has eyed me a few times pacing around. And then, he makes a motion that is not part of his fossilized rotation of staring at the bags, staring at the boxes, and chewing slowly. He raises a bony arm and waves to me.

He's calling *me*. As if sleepwalking, I glide to him. I have never heard him speak before.

"She's not coming, kid," he wheezes, as if talking through a garden hose. "You should go home."

5.

Four voice mail messages:

Number one: *Helena. It's Tim. Um, call me, if you get a chance. Thanks. 'Bye.*

Number two: *Hey, Helena. It's me. Uh, hi. Listen . . . ah . . . I haven't talked to you, and I want to, I need to, I need to talk to you. Did you really quit work? What's going on? Will you call me? Please?*

Number three: *Helena, it's Tim again. I don't know why you're not picking up your phone. Well, I guess I know why you're not picking up your phone. You're mad at me, and I understand, I do, but I think if you'd just pick up the phone or if you'd just call me back, we could work this out. I know it's not fair to ask you to call me when I didn't call you, but, uh, well, I guess that's what I'm asking you to do. So just call me back, okay? I'm here. My phone will be on all night. I need to talk to you. If you get my voice mail, it's only because I'm getting bad reception, but I'll call you back the second I get your message. Because I'm here, all—*You have exceeded the message time limit. Please press one to send your message, two to listen to your message, three to re-record, or four to hang up.

Number four: *I'm sorry, Helena. I'm sorry. I screwed up, and I'm so, so sorry. Please call me back. Okay? I'm sorry. Seriously. I'm so sorry.*

6.

Twenty-two hours after Otis the Crypt Keeper talked to me, I am sitting in my truck again, waiting for Helena to come and get her stuff. It was tempting yesterday to go back out to my truck and just sleep there, but that seemed ridiculous. So I drove home, where my parents were actually surprised to see me. They even asked me if Denny, who has been my fake companion for the last two months, was finally spending a night with that nice girlfriend of his. Dad said this in an odd way. He said it like he knew I was full of it, that *something* has been going on. Like with everything else, he didn't push any further, a reliability I love him for.

My cell phone rings. I grasp at it hungrily. It's Denny. I hate him for not being her.

"Dude, where are you?"

Before I realize I should probably lie, I say, "I'm sitting in the parking lot at work."

"What?"

My mind unfogs. "Um, uh, I was just heading home," I say. "Stayed a little late tonight."

"Why the hell would you stay late? They don't have anything for you to do," Denny says. I silently beg him to stop pushing me on this. He must have telepathically heard me. "Whatever. Listen, why don't you come out with us tonight? Kristen and Jessica are insisting on driving around tonight, and I really don't want to get stuck with just them and the Horsemen."

This doesn't seem fun to me at all. You know what does sound fun? Sitting in this truck. "I dunno, man, I'm pretty tired," I say, trying to freestyle enough to come up with something convincing. "We worked real hard today. I have some packing to do. Dad wants me to help out with some Bagelfest crap. Mom's making lasagna. I think I ate something bad. My feet hurt. I'm feeling kind of—" Denny interrupts me, for which I am thankful; I was two or three free associations away from saying I had a sticky film on me that just wouldn't rinse away.

"Oh, come on," he says. "You only got, what, like a week and a half left? For Christ's sake, dude. Just come by." Denny has a whiny insistent tone in his voice that reminds me of, oh, just about every girl I've ever been with. And me: it reminds me of my voice mail messages. Then, without warning, his voice hardens.

"Look, bro, I don't care what the hell's going on with that lady of yours," he says. "But whatever it is, *she's* not there, and *we're* around, and you should get over here, because you won't find a single prick in Champaign who can shotgun a beer like Shad can. Don't you want to see that one last time? Come on. You know you do."

I sigh. I know Denny will stay on this phone for days until he gets the answer he wants. It's no wonder he gets along so well with girls. "Fine," I say. "Lemme run home and shower and eat dinner, and I'll meet you guys at . . . well, where should I meet you?"

Denny's voice rises with incredulity. "Hardee's, man," he says. "Where the hell else we gonna go?"

7.

I pull into the Hardee's parking lot, which is surprisingly crowded for a Wednesday night. I farted around at home just long enough. I'd thought that my crew would give up on me coming, and there wouldn't be many people left. No such luck.

Shad has the tailgate of his truck down, and a gaggle of our classmates are standing around it. He installed his speakers himself, which is why they're constantly short-ing out, and they're blaring the country music station. It's a song about loving America and not knowing the differ-ence between Iraq and Iran. It's just ending when I pull in, and I hear an advertisement for Rush Limbaugh's radio show. My parents hate him, but I always think he's kind of funny.

As always, everyone gravitates toward my truck when I get out. I realize then that I haven't been here for a while. Since last time, I was harboring illusions that maybe everyone had forgotten who I was. Very wrong. My absence has everyone clamoring for face time.

"Yo, T-Dog, long time, man!" Greg is a muscular, thick-necked cretin who, like Denny, is planning on studying law enforcement at Lake Land. Like just about everyone I know who wants to be a cop (other than Denny), he drinks far more than he should, is quick to start a fight, and always seems to have something illegal on him. He claps me on the back harder than he should. Without thinking, I twist his arm around him and pretend to put him in a headlock. Being a Temples, this is a natural reflex.

Denny is right behind him. "Glad to see you could drop by," he says. "Old lady gave you a night off?" I don't say anything and instead motion for Shad to throw me a beer. He does, and I see Lieutenant Grierson, who's parked on the other side of Hardee's, talking to some blond sophomores, give me a little salute. I nod back at him, and he returns to his conversation, surely about how dangerous the job of a policeman can be on the mean streets of Mattoon.

I open my beer and click cans with Denny. I look to my right, and there are Jessica and Jeff, talking intently to each other—looking deeply into each other's eyes. Denny notices my muted grimace. "Better get used to it, man," he says. "She's been draped over him all month."

I look at Jeff, so skinny and squirrelly and sketchy. Then I look at Jessica, so unaware of what Jeff is really like. I want to be protective of her, but hey, it's none of my business. *You want to take care of yourself? Go to it, Jessica.*

Besides, the last thing I should be doing right now is advising anyone about the opposite sex.

Jessica walks over, with Jeff trailing her. "Hey, Tim, how

213

you doing?" she says. "I was just telling Jeff how much fun we had on our college visit, wasn't I?" Jessica appears to have, disturbingly, already adopted that thing couples do, the way they feign talking to someone else when they're really just talking to each other. People do this with children too. Anytime I talk to my neighbor Lori, she's always directing questions to me at her infant daughter, Kaylee: "Why don't you ask Tim how his classes are going?"

Jeff has that familiar smirk. "Yeah, heard you were hanging out with Herb and Harvey Finkelstein and a sand Negro," he says.

"That's terrible!" Jessica makes a pouty face and mocks like she's upset. Even though she probably is, she's more than likely telling herself that Jeff is just kidding. After all, he's so *funny*.

Yeah. Real funny.

"Something like that," I say, trying to do the John Wayne stoic thing that my dad effortlessly pulls off. "They were nice guys. The day was fine."

Jessica looks at me like she knows I want to say more but am just being "cool" for my friends. She's probably right, but the last thing I'm going to give her—or Jeff—right now is that satisfaction.

"We were thinking of visiting you guys when you're up there," Jeff says, eyes narrowing, lips smacking. "We thought we might drop by that Chester Street club and have a little fun with some of the locals."

Chester Street is the only gay bar any of us have heard of. It's in downtown Champaign, just off campus.

Eric might end up going there, I realize. Then I shudder. The thought of Eric and Jeff in a room together turns my blood to ice.

Jessica doesn't catch on to what Jeff is saying. Instead she grabs a beer from Andy, who has come by with Shad.

"Thanks, Andrew," Jessica says, and Andy blushes. He hunches his shoulders until his neck disappears, trying to suppress a giggle. "So hey, I hope you're still planning on coming over sometime before we leave," she says. "The university says it's always smarter to order your books online before you show up on campus, so that you don't have to wait in line."

I shoot her a glare. "You know how I hate computers." I do. I hate them. They make my head hurt. Besides, they're like a drug. People get so addicted to their computers and their e-mail accounts and their instant messaging that they nearly shake when they're away from them too long. They have to plug in, get their fix. Plus, I can never find the *p* on the keyboard.

"I'd rather wait in line."

"I'll walk you through it; it'll be real easy," she says, and I notice Jeff wobbling back and forth on his feet, like he's impatient about the brief lapse in his status as Center of Attention. This conversation has nothing to do with him. I find myself transfixed by his annoyance. It actually makes me *happy*. I'm feeling pretty good about that until my cell phone rings. I grab it *way* too quickly—*itsheritsheritsheritsheritsher.*

I look at the screen: *Mom Dad. 217-258-8463.* Shit. I angrily flip the phone open.

"What?"

"Don't 'what' me, jerkweed." It's Doug. I can't imagine why he's calling. "You need to bring home some beer."

"I'm out. I can't get you beer."

"Not now, dipshit. When you leave. Grab a case of Natural."

I'm annoyed. The first time Doug has called me in the two months he's been home and it's because he wants beer. *And* he's being an ass about it. "Are your legs broke? You have a car. Go get your own beer."

"For you information, *smart guy*, I dropped a pipe on my foot at work, and I'm not supposed to move it."

I can't resist. "You sure that didn't happen two months ago?" I say. "Because I ain't seen you move much since then."

"Fuck off," he says, with no trace of humor. "I'm not even going to work tomorrow. Dad's freaking out. Says they're a man down with just a week to go till Bagelfest. I think if he had his way, he'd cart me out there in a wheelchair."

I find this conversation more disturbing than I let on. I don't remember my brother *ever* hurting himself. He has always seemed indestructible. "Fine," I say. "I'll get your cripple ass some beer. I wouldn't wait up for it, though."

"I won't." He hangs up.

Without realizing it, I walked away from the group while I was on the phone, and I am now standing under a tree, next to the creek that runs between Hardee's and the U.S. Grant hotel, where everybody went after prom. I am standing here alone, drinking my beer, watching Jessica put her hand in Jeff's back pocket, seeing everyone I have

known for the last eighteen years of my life, and I don't
know them at all, and they don't know me. I dial Helena
and go straight into her voice mail again. I start to speak,
ahh, then stop and hang up.

8.

The next two hours:

Greg tries to start a fight with me. Twice.

Andy shotguns a beer, and Shad trumps him by shot-
gunning one while standing on his head, with Jeff holding
one leg and Denny holding the other. When he's done,
they push his legs apart, and he falls face-first in the
grass, cutting his nose on the smashed can.

Lieutenant Grierson comes over and halfheartedly tells
us to cool it, asks me about my dad, and then goes back to
his sophomores.

Jessica and Jeff disappear for about fifteen minutes.

Denny and Kristen disappear for about five.

A kid named Dan, with a fat face scarred by countless
losing battles with acne, tells me how he's heading off to
boot camp in three weeks. He signed up a few months
ago—just like his dad did before graduating high school.
He thought it would be a good idea, but now Dan's not so
sure about the whole endeavor. "They're gonna send me
to Buttfuck freaking Egypt for all I know," he says, sound-
ing scared, looking scared.

I stand next to my car with Andy and Shad, listening
to the radio. The DJ comes on and introduces "the new

song from noted songstress Liz Phair." My body stiffens, but I lean over and turn up the dial.

I realize that Helena was right. Liz Phair has changed. She doesn't sound unhappy at all. In fact, she sounds like everyone else on the radio. And that's fine. I wonder if Helena would do the same, shedding a bit of herself and her past for the promise of the future. I wonder if she would have, if only I had given her the opportunity.

"Why'd you turn that up, dude?" Andy says. "Who is this chick?"

"It's Liz Phair," I say. "Her old stuff was better, but this is nice too, don't you think?"

Shad looks at me like I just poured gasoline all over myself. "Uh, what the hell are you talking about, man? We should check you for, uh, a, um, Uranus, right, Jeff?" Jeff is a few feet away with Jessica, mercifully not listening. I sigh and change the station.

Two guys who were in my shop class, Matt and Mark, take turns kicking each other in the groin to see who can show less pain. Neither of them does a very good job.

What the hell am I doing here? I wonder. *I don't belong here.*

For the first time, it occurs to me—I belong in Champaign. I belong with *her*.

Helena has opened my eyes to so much, has taught me what it means to want more. University of Illinois is the chance for both of us to have more. I want to tell her that. I want to show her how I've changed.

Still, my phone does not ring.

9.

Denny and I are sitting in a booth, both eating something called the Ultimate Burger, which has four beef patties, six slices of cheese, ten slices of bacon, and four buns. It is smothered in barbecue sauce. Denny picks at his while I take my palm and squish mine into a manageable shape and size. A paper boat of onion rings sits in between us. Most everyone else has gone home. Jeff's car is still here, but I don't know where he and Jessica are.

Denny's eyelids are drooping. "Where's Kristen?" I ask. Denny shrugs. "No idea," he says. "She's fine."

We sift through the onion rings. Because this is the late-night shift, half of them are burned black. It would be easier to eat the chair. The only other person is an elderly woman who looks like she's about to go to church. She's wearing too much makeup and a frumpy old lady's summer dress, blue, dotted with white flowers. She eats her food quickly, like she's running late. She has four large shopping bags with her. She seems entirely unaware that it's one thirty in the morning.

"So, were you really as into this whole college thing as Jessica made it sound?" Denny says.

"What, did she talk to you?" I say.

"Naw, but she talked to Kristen," he says. "Pretty much the same thing."

My brain is so caught up in everything that's happening with Helena that all I can come up with is the standard answer—exactly what I know he wants to hear. "Well, it was cool, yeah," I say. "Beer specials are nice.

Real cool guy was our guide, just took us to a bar, didn't have to deal with any of that 'tour' bullshit. Some hot girls, too."

"Hot girls?" Denny looks at me cockeyed. "Well, obviously, that doesn't matter to you, right?"

I straighten up. "Of course not," I say. "Just commenting, really."

As I'm speaking, Denny grabs an onion ring without looking. He bites in, and there is a loud crunch. His face crinkles, and for a moment neither of us is sure if the crunch was the onion ring or his tooth. He spits it onto his plate, and it looks like a petrified cat turd. He flicks it onto the floor with his napkin and gags, wiping his mouth with a napkin he doesn't realize is covered in ketchup until it's all over himself. "Jesus," he says. "Be right back." He grabs a handful of napkins and makes his way to the bathroom.

The door swings closed. I whip out my phone. I have to check it again. *You have no new messages. Six saved messages. First saved message. From. 2.1.7.2.3.4.8.9.2.7.* All six saved messages are from Helena. The first was one of the first messages she ever left for me. It was nothing much; she just tells me how she's running late to her cousin's, I'll meet you there, don't start without me. The second is one she left in the middle of the night, when I was sleeping in the other room. She had just remembered a joke, and she wanted to tell it to me before she forgot it but didn't want to wake me up. The third message, she's speaking in a deliberately raspy voice, pretending she's a phone sex operator. She makes it to *and then I'll undo your belt . . . right after you give me your credit card number* before she busts into laughter.

I'm just about to hear the fourth message when Denny returns, trying to scrape something from the back of his teeth. "This is what happens when you let retards prepare your food," he says. "I think that thing might have been a finger."

He sips from a mammoth plastic Diet Coke cup with a picture of Dale Earnhardt, Jr. leaning on his car. "So," he says, shaking the cup like it's a pair of dice at a craps table, "seriously, man. Are you *still* planning on being serious with Helena while you're up in Champaign? Like, how's that gonna work exactly?"

I had been too tired to lie earlier, but now I'm too tired to tell the truth. "Oh, I got it all figured out," I say. "It's totally gonna work."

"Really?" he says. "And she's down with this? She doesn't have a problem with you being up there while she's down here?"

"Definitely," I say. I think I sound convincing. Sure.

Denny looks like he wants to say something but changes his mind. "Well, whatever works, man," he says. "If you guys have a plan, more power to you."

A *plan*. For some reason, I hadn't thought of it like that. Needing a *plan*. A course of action. Maybe *that's* the main reason Helena was mad. I didn't have a *plan*.

Oh my God. How could I have been so stupid? How could I not even have looked past the stupid nose on my stupid face? She wanted a *plan*. She wanted me to tell her how it was going to happen, how this was going to work out. Sure, I had a few ideas, but I didn't form them into anything solid or concrete. I guess I didn't feel like I needed to. I like her. She likes me. That's all we need, right? Wrong! I see that now. I want to call her right away. *A plan! That's what I did wrong! I can come up with a plan, I really can! I'm sorry, baby! I'll come up with a plan right now!*

"Yep," I say, trying to will myself into a cocky, "I'm on top of it, dude" smile. "You can't do something like this without a plan. Of course not."

Denny's head is starting to fall onto his shoulder now. He snaps his head up, and his eyes grow real wide. He looked like this when I helped him study for the ACT last year the night before the test. We pulled an all-nighter. I didn't see what the big deal was—*it's just a stupid test*—but Denny was panicked about it, convinced that the ACT meant the difference between being a millionaire and being homeless. I ended up scoring a 31, a meaningless number to me; he notched a 25 and was smiling like an idiot for a month.

"Hey, guys," a voice chimes from behind me. "Good, you're still here." It's Jessica and Kristen. Kristen has a glassy look, her eyes all red and splotchy. She has her key chain, a tiny glass orb with the St. Louis skyline being littered with snow, in front of her face and is staring at it like it holds the secrets of man. It occurs to me: they smell of marijuana.

I make an overexaggerated sniffing noise and dramatically

wave my hand in front of my nose. Jessica gives me an exasperated frown. "We were just having a little fun on one of our last nights together." She lowers her voice to a whisper and leans closer to me. I smell alcohol on her breath but no weed. This floods me with a temporary sense of relief.

"I didn't smoke any anyway. I *like* my lungs." She leans in even closer and lowers her voice even more. "But Kristen and Jeff . . . *yikes*. They probably can't find their feet right now." She puts her fingertips over her lips and fights off a giggle.

I look at Denny, tending to Kristen with a bemused smile. He catches my glance and rolls his eyes. "Well, I think it's time for us to go home, don't you, Tim?"

We head out the glass doors into the parking lot, where Jeff is standing next to his car. I turn to Jessica. "So, hey, you need a ride home or anything?"

She pauses for a moment and looks at Jeff. "Ah, no, I'm fine."

I look at her with as serious an expression as I can muster. "You *sure*?"

Her body stiffens, and she juts her jaw out. She looks just like she did when we were kids, when she would firmly declare that she was not going to play Mom today, she was going to play *lawyer*. "Don't worry about me," she says, resolute.

"All right," I say, putting my hands in the air.

She goes to check on Kristen—who is telling Denny that she never realized how *crazy* stars were—and I walk over to Jeff.

"Dude, you gonna be okay driving?" I ask.

His eyes meet mine. His face narrows and that fucking smirk returns. "What's wrong, Tim?" he says. "Not used to being the only one not going home with a girl?"

I'd like to smack him right now, but I know that I can't. I just grit my teeth and tell him, "No, I'm just making sure you're normal enough to drive. And by the sounds of that statement, you seem the same as you always are. Be careful, all right?"

He straightens and says, "We'll be fine. Worry about yourself."

And as I fidget with my keys, I can't help thinking: I *am* worried about myself. I am worried about coming up with a plan. I am worried that it might be too late. I am worried that I've missed my window—that I've lost Helena forever.

I am worrying so much that it's not until the next morning, when I read the nasty note that Doug has slipped under my bedroom door, that I realize I forgot the beer.

10.

It's around lunch that I decide that enough is enough. Helena's stuff is still sitting in Chuck's office—"left her four messages now," Chuck says, "and I'm about ready to throw the crap out"—and she still hasn't called me back. I spent all morning racking my brain to come up with a plan and found nothing, but no matter: this is ridiculous now. If she's not going to call me back, I'm gonna have to, as Coach Jackley used to say, take the game to her. I know where she lives. I have to go there. If she just sees me, if she just sees how sorry I am, if she sees that I'm trying to come up with a plan, she'll understand. She'll *have* to forgive me. She'll remember what we have, and she'll hug me, and I'll hug her, and it will all make sense, and it will all work out. I have to go see her.

As I'm carrying that afternoon's stash of boxes back and forth from plant to truck, I psych myself up for it. I'm gonna have to go after work. Directly after work. I'll just drive over there, and I'll knock on her front door, and she'll have to talk to me.

What should I bring? *Flowers.* And real ones this time. I'll drop by Jewel-Osco, and I'll ask the florist what's a good bouquet to get for a girl who you want to forgive you, and he'll know exactly the right arrangement. Maybe I should wash my truck. I congratulate myself on having a change of clothes in the backseat; I surely can't show up there all sweaty and gross. I'm ready. I'm ready. I have to go over there. I'm ready.

Here I come, Helena. I just need another chance. I won't screw up this time. I promise.

11.

Time constraints make it impossible to wash the truck *and* make it all the way out to Jewel-Osco while still arriving at Helena's before it's too dark, so the truck's gonna have to be a little dirty. When I get to Jewel-Osco, the florist has already left for the day, so I have the pimply sophomore with the trainee name tag just grab me the first set of flowers he sees, an arrangement of daffodils, which is fine, right?

I drive down Western Avenue toward her house, fixing my hair in the rearview mirror and listening to sports talk radio. One of the Cardinals was arrested after a domestic violence incident last night. I hope they don't suspend him. They've got a huge series with the Cubs coming up. I turn right. And then, just before turning in front of Helena's, I stop the car in the middle of the street and put it into park. I glance up at the mirror. Everything looks good: no boogers in my nose, no zits on my lip, nothing weird in my hair.

You ready? Let's do this. Take the game to her.

I turn left and pull up in front of her house. With a deep breath, I open the Blazer's door and step out.

Helena is walking out the front door with her mother. Helena looks gorgeous, of course, but also ragged and tired, just beaten, really, but that's nothing compared to her mother. Her mom, whom I've never met, is wearing a blue nightgown, almost a muumuu. She is ghastly pale, almost yellow. The nightgown is hanging off her, and she has red scratches on her shoulders. Her eyes are what scare me the most: her face has sunken and they're bulging out of her head, darting around at nothing, completely, utterly lost and frightened. Helena is walking alongside her, slowly, with a hand on her back to guide her, when she sees me.

226

I had many ideas of what Helena's face would look like when she saw me for the first time since that night, ranging from rapture to murderous rage, but I'm not prepared for this. She looks the way someone would if they were trying to untie a damsel from the tracks as a train barreled toward them when, out of nowhere, a tax collector tapped them on the shoulder and reminded them that April 15 was just around the corner. Her look says: *No. Not now. There will time for you, and us, and this. But not now. Please. Not now.*

I stand there, slack. Helena shifts her focus back to her mom, linking her arm through hers and leading her toward the garage. I have no idea what to do. On the one hand, Helena is clearly in the middle of something, and it looks serious. On the other . . . well, I've been waiting to talk to her for days, and she is right here, and I don't know when I'll have this chance again.

I walk toward them. Helena's mom has either not seen me or thinks I'm a tree. I approach slowly to allow Helena to put her mom in the passenger seat and shut the door. She then comes toward me.

"Tim," she says, looking at something behind me. "What are you doing here?"

I hadn't considered the possibility of this question. I would have thought the answer would be self-evident. I stare at her dumbly.

"Tim, I can't talk right now," she says. "My mom's sick. I need to take her to the hospital."

This snaps me out of it. "Oh my God," I say. "Is she okay?"

"I don't know," she says. "I think so, but I just want to make sure. She might be in insulin shock. She might just need to crap. I don't know!" Helena suddenly has a wild-eyed look. She looks like she might burst into flames at any second. I want to hug her.

"Listen," I say. "I'm sorry. I didn't mean to come by so suddenly. Do you need any help?"

Helena shakes her head like she's trying to avoid a bee. "No, I'm fine," she says. "I just need to go." She turns around to the car, but I take her arm gently.

My face goes numb, and my mouth hangs there agape. *Pull it together*, I think. *This could be the last time you see her.*

"Helena," I say. "I'm sorry. I'm really sorry. I screwed up, and I'm sorry. This is all my fault. I forgot to call you, and then, well, then I don't know what happened. But I don't care. I miss you. And I'm so sorry."

Something about my apology loosens Helena's jaw. Her left hand rises, and I have a sense that she wants to touch my face. Her head angles to where it's almost directly perpendicular to mine. Her eyes are filled with something like sympathy. I feel like a sick dog. "Oh, Tim," she says.

I take this as my in. "Meet me tomorrow."

"I don't know if I can—"

"Tomorrow," I interrupt, deepening my voice until it sounds serious, almost grave. "We'll meet at the Embassy. Eight o'clock."

Helena looks at her mother in the car, then back at me.

She exhales. "Fine," she says. "I'll meet you there tomorrow. Eight."

I touch her face now, and she flinches. "Good luck with your mom."

"Thank you," she says, like she's had all the life squeezed out of her.

12.

Ladies and gentlemen—I have a plan.

Not only is this all going to be all right, it's going to be *great*. I've done the research—I even went to a realtor, for crying out loud—and this will totally work.

Here's how it will go: I'll head up to the U of I. That's a given at this point. It's too late to back out now, and besides, I really do want to go. And besides that, *Helena* wants me to go.

I won't half-ass it, either. None of this five-days-in-Champaign, two-days-in-Mattoon business. That's one foot in one world and one foot in the other, and that's destined to be a failed attempt to serve two masters. Does no one any good.

No, if we're gonna do this, Helena's going to have to be a part of *both* worlds. And honestly, what's holding her here? She quit her job. She doesn't have a lot of friends. Her mom, if she turns out to be healthy, desperately needs a change of pace, and the hospitals in Champaign are infinitely better equipped to treat her than the Mattoon hospital. Helena can live with her—at first.

It might be easier for Helena and her mom, as a transition, to move somewhere closer to Champaign for a year or so, while they're adjusting. Maybe she could scoot up Route 57 for the first year, try Tuscola, or Rantoul, or even, if they're feeling frisky, Savoy.

Helena would need a short-term job. I've thought of that too. There's a Pickle's restaurant and bar just off campus; she could waitress there for a few months, pick up some solid tips, certainly make more money than she was dealing with Chuck's shit. Or maybe she could work at one of the *real* fancy restaurants in downtown Champaign, the ones with a wine list that's longer than the menu. She would meet so many interesting people there! I went to one of those restaurants before prom once, and the waitress was a graduate student, with black hair and blond streaks and a butterfly tattoo on her shoulder, and she knew every wine on the menu, she knew where they had come from, what year they were harvested, what dessert they went best with. She wore all white and placed napkins in our laps and talked about how she was going to move to San Francisco after she got her degree, to the Napa Valley, where she would stomp grapes and wear thick protective gloves when she went out to the fields to pick the ripest fruits.

Helena would do great with people like that. She would charm them with her sarcastic humor, she would impress them with her work ethic, she would bowl them over with that irresistible laugh of hers. They would work long hours, late nights, and then when everything settled down, when they were ready to finally close up for the night, they would smoke cigarettes outside, making fun of the customers, raving about the woman in the business suit who gave the 30 percent tip. They would go to the bar, Helena and her butterfly-tattooed, wine-expert friends, and I would meet them there when I was done studying for my finals. We would drink imported beers with names like Grolsch and Newcastle, beers I wouldn't drink back home but am giddy to be introduced to here. We would play darts and shoot pool; when she aims, I will stand behind Helena and touch her hips, pretending to help her shoot but really just touching her hips. The wine friends from the restaurant will look at us and smile, wondering how, someday, they can find someone who makes them as happy as we make each other.

13.

After the first year, once I have myself acclimated to how the campus works and which classes I actually have to work at and which ones I can coast through, it'll be time to start thinking about living together. Under University of Illinois rules, you have to spend your first year in the dorms, and once that's out of the way, we'll be able to do our own thing.

Helena will likely want to be close to her mother, and I understand that and am supportive. After I leave the Blazer back in Mattoon for my freshman year, I'll bring it to campus so we'll have another car, so she can get to work and I can get to school. But that's a temporary arrangement, because here's the master plan: Helena will make enough money her first year to be able to take some part-time classes by my sophomore year. And then we'll be able to drive to campus together! What will she study? Who knows? I don't know what *I'm* gonna be studying yet, so there's no reason for her to rush. If there's any kind of money crunch, I can take on a part-time job after I get out of class too.

The four years will pass before we realize it. (It seems like just last week that I started my freshman year of high school, all cowlicks and braces and zits on my chin. Four years with Helena will zip by even faster.) And then? Well, then we have infinite options. We can stay in Champaign. We can return to Mattoon. We move to Chicago, or St. Louis, or Indianapolis. We can go *anywhere*. Maybe even one of those places she's seen on the Discovery Channel.

Who knows what will happen? There are a million different possibilities. The details of the money and the time frame and everything else aren't what's important; what's important is that we do all this *together*. The slate can be cleared, and we can start a whole new life—just like Helena's always wanted.

And when we have this life, we will look back and we will laugh because it was inevitable that it was going to turn out like this and we can't believe that anything else could have stood in our way. We can't believe one forgotten phone call almost derailed all this, almost sent us off

track. It will seem funny then—like it was a thousand life-
times ago.

It's a *plan*. We can make it happen. She just has to give
me another chance.

14.

The bowling alley at the Embassy is more crowded than I
would like it to be. It occurs to me that we've never been
here on a weekend before. At 8 p.m., Helena isn't here yet,
so I find myself shuttling from one table to another, trying to find the right one, the one with the perfect lighting,
the one that doesn't have a bunch of chattering teenagers
babbling on about Orlando Bloom. I move three or four
times, hauling my flowers and bottles of wine and tinkly
glasses behind me, before I find the only place that's even
slightly isolated. It's right next to the jukebox, which is
playing Bruce Springsteen's "Thunder Road," which is an
odd song for a bowling alley, I think.

During the half hour I'm waiting for Helena, I contem-
plate opening the wine but decide against it. It should be a
dramatic moment, a clear celebration that we have over-
come this difficult period and are ready to start anew. I
lean over in my chair to look at the jukebox window:
hair's in place, nothing in my teeth, collar straight, no
beads of sweat pouring down my neck—yet. I check my
cell phone; *no new messages*. I check it again and am surprised only two minutes have passed.

After repeating this process to the point that it reminds

me of carrying the boxes at work, I see Helena come in. She looks different. Her hair is pulled back, evaporating her round face and pulling her skin back so that her cheekbones are sharp, harsh, and she is wearing a long black jacket that somehow hugs her body tightly yet makes her perfect figure almost vanish. She's wearing oval sunglasses with dark yellow rims. She appears taller, thinner . . . *older*.

"Hi," I say. My facade of cool dissolving immediately, I leap out of my chair and pull the one across from me out for her. She sits down slowly, deliberately, holding her jacket to her knees as she settles, like she doesn't want to wrinkle it. She sits across from me, with her sunglasses still on, and stares forward dispassionately. I find it difficult to return her stare; my eyes are hopping from every possible view in range that doesn't have Helena in it.

My mouth goes dry, and it feels like my lips are covered in cold sores. When I was a kid, I once had to get up in class and give a speech about my summer vacation. I wasn't nervous about it, hadn't even thought about it, until I stood up there and saw everyone looking at me. My tongue rolled back in my mouth, and I started hopping anxiously until it looked like I was jumping rope. Before I realized it, a thin thread of warm pee dripped down my leg and leaked out my left pant leg. No one even laughed or pointed. They just watched in shock. I didn't cry or look for the teacher for help. I just folded my piece of notebook paper, put it under my arm, and sat back down at my desk.

I am desperate not to pee right now.

Somehow, I creak out a sentence. "Do you want to take your coat off?"

Helena does not move, just says, "No thank you. This is fine."

I sit there, with the second set of flowers in as many days, two bottles of Boone's Farm wine, her slender black purse, and a glacier the size of Cleveland between us. I feel like I'm looking at her from behind a large rock, peeking my head over the top like a kid trying to catch a glimpse at a crowded parade. *Hello? I'm right here! Anybody up there?*

"Um, do you want a glass of wine?" I say. I reach below the table and grab the two wineglasses. I had planned this as a dramatic maneuver, a *ta-da!* magic trick. But now it's the closest thing I have to a last-minute reprieve from the governor.

"No thank you, Tim," she says, at least acknowledging I'm in the room. "I'm not thirsty."

The ridiculousness of this statement—the sheer audacity of it—releases me from my foggy torpor. Whatever kind of cold, removed, "You're lucky I even showed up" game she's trying to play has gone on long enough. "Helena, come on," I say. "Take your sunglasses off. Jeez. Pretend you're sitting at a table across from me, at least." Helena pauses for a moment, still motionless, and then slowly, using both hands, as if carrying a plate of something hot, lifts the glasses off her face. I'm half expecting her to have a black eye or something, but she doesn't; she just has the same dark eyeliner she always wears. But her eyes themselves are cold; whatever's behind them is someplace other than here.

She is setting the sunglasses down on the table carefully when, without any warning, a junior high girl, with a Mattoon Middle School Wildcats jacket that's covered in cheerleading letters and pendants, plows into the back of her chair. Helena juts forward, pushing into the table between us and sending the two wineglasses crashing onto the floor. I reflexively catch the sunglasses before they hit the ground.

The girl's mouth makes an O that would be exaggerated on anyone but a thirteen-year-old girl. "Ohmigosh, I'm *so* sorry!" she squeaks. "I just wanted to put a song on the jukebox. I wasn't watching where I was going. Ohmigosh, are you okay?"

Helena turns her head warily. "It's okay," she says in a voice that makes it clear it's definitely not okay. "Just be more careful, would you?"

The girl scurries away with a chorus of *sorrysorrysorrys*, skipping the jukebox altogether. I hear her and her friends giggling when she returns to them. It was only a couple of years ago that I would have sauntered over to them and asked them, *Hey, what are you girls up to tonight?* But instead I'm holding Helena Westfall's sunglasses. Real, passionate, amazing Helena.

With a tiny flip, I bring her sunglasses up from beneath the table and place them in front of her. Without emotion, she says, "Nice catch."

"Thank you," I say.

A staffer from the bowling alley comes over with a broom and dustpan to sweep up the broken glass, and we sit there and watch him ponderously. He looks up at us absently and his eyes widen as he sees us staring at him. We both realize we're scaring him and glance away. He finishes picking up the glass and goes away.

A few more beats of silence. Then: "Okay, fine," she says. "I could probably use some wine."

15.

She returns from the station where they sell carbon-dated pretzels carrying two large plastic foam cups. She doesn't appear particularly happy or anything, but at least she's not on Neptune or wherever the hell she was when she first got here. She sits down, opens the wine bottle with her key chain, and pours us each a glass. Without a word, she lifts her glass to mine, and we do a sad, silent version of a cheer.

It's time. "Helena . . . listen, I'm sorry," I say. "I just wanted to say that first."

Helena looks at her cup for an eternity. "You don't have to apologize, Tim."

"But I do!" I interrupt. "I totally said I was going to call you, and then I didn't. Who knows what you must have been thinking? I mean, I just got so caught up in everything, and it just slipped past me, and I'm sorry. It's just that—"

"Stop," she says. "Please. Stop."

I do, though I don't know why. Maybe it's because I've said sorry so many times, to her, to her voice mail, to the ceiling in my bedroom, that it doesn't mean anything anymore. Not to her, not to me, not to anyone. I look at her and try not to blink. I fail.

"I need to apologize to you, Tim," she says. She folds her hands like she's praying and puts them over her nose. "I've been a pretty reckless person, and Saturday was just another example."

"Helena, I—"

"Let me finish, okay? Can you do that for me?" She's speaking to me like a third-grade teacher. I nod. "I don't know what I was thinking here. It was completely irresponsible of me to let this go on as long as it has. I like you, and you're sweet and smart, and I didn't expect that. But I really didn't want this to happen. It just kind of did."

It feels like I'm sliding down an incline made of ice, grasping for any kind of crevice to latch onto.

"Saturday night was not something different for me. This is who I am. I screw things up. I drink too much and I do stupid things. I hurt the people who care about me." She pauses, choosing each word carefully. "I do believe that you care for me. And I care for you. That's why we have to end this now. It will be easier for me, easier for you, easier for everybody."

"But—"

"This isn't right," she says. "This can't work. You know that, right?"

"Of course it can!" I wail. My voice is high-pitched and cracking. And then I find my footing.

"Helena, I don't care what you did Saturday or about any of that stuff," I say, my hands waving in all directions. "None of that matters. What matters is that we're together, that we work this out. What you did before me doesn't mean anything."

I didn't realize this until I said it, but it's true. I don't care about her past at all. "I mean, I could go to college and you could come with me! You'd love it up there! We could be together *and* I could go to college."

She frowns. For some reason, I'm not conveying *the plan* the way I wanted to. Desperately, I continue, "I have a plan, Helena! I have a way for this to work. We just have to commit to the *plan*!" Christ, I sound like a crazy person.

Helena looks at me for a long time. Her face could be showing me a million things right now. I have no idea what any of them are. She opens her mouth to speak. I'm an Oscar nominee waiting to see if he won.

"I had sex with your brother."

16.

The only position I ever knew how to play in baseball was catcher. I had a strange quirk as a catcher: I refused to wear a protective cup. I know that sounds strange—suicidal even. But I had the fundamentals of catching on my side. I didn't have a strong arm, but my best attribute as a catcher was that I never let balls in the dirt get past me. Pitchers could feel comfortable throwing that 0–2 splitter outside without worrying about a wild pitch or passed ball. What was my secret? The best way to make sure a ball doesn't get behind you as a catcher is to smack your glove to the ground and throw your body in front of it. The next time you watch a game, look at how many lazy catchers just try to backhand balls in the dirt, like they're a shortstop or something. A real catcher puts his mitt in the dirt and propels himself before the ball. This is an unnatural instinct; it's against human nature to *purposely* toss yourself in front of a moving object. This is why I never wore a cup; I let instinct work for me rather than against me. When I realized a ball was in the dirt, what was my first instinct? *Protect my nuts.* My mitt would involuntarily drop between my legs. The beauty of this is, *that's where it's supposed to go.* After that, jumping in front of the ball was easy. I was fearless because my instincts were to protect, not to lunge. I never once missed a passed ball, and I never once got hit in the groin. While catching.

We played a doubleheader against Stephen Decatur last year, late in the season, a meaningless game before the regional play-offs started. On a lark, Coach Jackley put me at third base for the nightcap, a position I had never played. The first batter, on the first pitch, whistled a line drive straight to me. I have no idea how to actually *field* ground balls, and I never even saw it. It took one sizzling hop and deposited itself directly in my lap.

240

There is a moment after you've taken a shot like that, before the world goes to hell, when you feel no pain. It's only a second, if that. You are aware that you are about to experience such excruciating pain that you will be lucky not to spontaneously vomit. But you don't feel anything, not yet. The moment is fleeting, but it's long enough that you can look at everyone and see their faces, their open mouths, their sympathy, their collective recognition of your gruesome plight. In this moment, there is clarity. There is some sort of peace.

And then everything explodes.

17.

I don't know how long I've been sitting here, not saying anything. I don't know how long my eyes have been closed. I don't know how long I have been in flames.

Helena is talking like I'm not here, like she hopes I'm not. "We slept together all through high school and even while he was up at college," she says. "Almost every time he'd come home. The last time was a year ago. In high school, it wasn't just him. There were others on the team. But Doug kept coming back. He would just show up at my door, and I'd drive off with him. One time you were even with him, years ago. He came inside and you waited in the car. You must have been twelve or thirteen."

It occurs to me that I remember this. It was cold, and Doug left his car running and the heat on. I must have been out there for more than an hour. I didn't care; the

Cardinals game was on the radio and I had a Game Boy with me. I was playing Tetris. I am very good at Tetris.

"This is who I am, Tim," she says. "I am irresponsible and promiscuous and a drunk. I am a complete fucking disaster area. And I am the last thing you need at the beginning of your shiny, happy life." She lights her first cigarette of the evening. It surprises me she has waited this long.

"I knew you were there Saturday," she says. "I doubted the neighbors would put the car in the garage and clean up the mess on the lawn. God, what they must think. I couldn't bear to face you. I knew that I had done it again. And when I woke up Sunday morning, I knew I couldn't live like this anymore. I knew I couldn't go back to that job and continue this vicious goddamn circle. I had to start over. I'm sorry you got swept up in this. But you don't want someone like me. I can't just start over with *you*. And you know what? I don't want you to want me."

I don't know who to be furious at. Helena? Doug? Myself? I find myself so confused that I end up furious at no one. I take Helena's lit cigarette, smoldering in the ash-tray, and take a long, deep drag. I—of course—start gagging and hacking. It feels like smoke is coming out my ears. The pain in my lungs is excellent.

Helena hands me my wine and I slug it like it's air. "That wasn't a good idea," she says, and she would be smiling if we were anywhere else on the planet, discussing anything else. I cough up my colon, and I'm finally done.

My head is suddenly clear. I look at her and realize I

don't want to scream at her, or humiliate her, or hit her. I just want her to be happy.

"Helena, you can have a clean slate," I say. "You can start over. We can start over together."

She is quiet for about four seconds, and then it happens. Her face sharpens into a point, and it's the same look Emily had when I didn't call her back after we slept together for the last time. She walked up to me and threw a beer can at my head. It bounced off my chest dumbly, and Emily stomped off. The next time I saw her, she apologized to me. Something about Helena's look tells me I won't be so fortunate this time. She's a cobra about to strike.

"I don't know how I can make this any clearer to you. It's *not happening*. I tried to be nice, but this ends here. We've both caused enough trouble. I mean, did you really think I was going to go to Champaign with you? Did you really think this had a *future*? Do you know what I thought when I brought you to my room that first night? I thought I'd screw with your head a bit. Maybe I was getting back at Doug. I don't know, and I really don't care. I never felt anything for you. I just picked you up—like I picked up that guy Saturday. I thought I'd play with you, then spit you out and go on with my life. And you know what? That's what I'm doing. Right now."

She stands up and puts on her jacket. She takes the sunglasses, fumbles with them, then places them in her purse.

Her glare is ice cold. There is no sympathy in those

eyes, no remorse, no understanding. I do not know who this person standing in front of me is. "Go away. Leave me alone. Get out of my life. I *don't want you.*"

I sit there alone and watch her walk out the door. She walks with ideal posture, how they'd teach it in an etiquette book. I look at my cup of wine, and my flowers, and a few stray shards of broken glass on the floor. She has walked out of my life. And I wonder if she was ever there in the first place.

18.

No. This is not how this is supposed to end.

19.

I jump out of my chair and sprint out the front door. I catch her as she's putting the key in her car door. For some reason, I expect her to be crying. But she's not. She's just opening her car door like she's on her way to grab groceries and a DVD.

"You can't go," I say. "I love you."

I have never said that. Ever.

"Do you hear me? I love you."

Helena no longer looks angry. She just looks tired. "Tim, you're a little boy. Why would I want to be with a little boy?"

And then she slips herself into her car and drives off, to get milk, to get eggs, to rent the new Adam Sandler comedy.

I sit down on the ground. It is cool and soft, much softer than I would have thought.

20.

When I was real young, my parents would fight a lot. Recently, I asked my mom about it; I don't know why I did. She told me that she and my father were very poor, and whenever people are really poor, they get angry quicker than they should. This didn't satisfactorily answer my question, mainly because Mom was talking to me like I was a four-year-old.

When they would fight, Doug would go in his room and shut his door. This was a highly ineffective technique because our house wasn't big enough to mask any of the sounds. I couldn't handle all the yelling, all the conflict, so I would sneak outside and ride my bike to the dam about a half mile from our house. My parents made me ride a big brown banana seat bike with a huge orange flag on the back. It was very uncool, but I loved riding it. I was escaping. I felt free.

The dam doesn't have a name, which I always thought was a shame: dams should have names. It rested in the one overflowing section of Lake Paradise, but the dam was entirely dry save for the most torrential rainstorms. If I had been a more adventurous sort, I might have ridden a skateboard down it. I liked that it never had any water in it. It made it silent, and I had come there for silence. I have always considered it a sacred place; I've never let anyone come there with me. I never even parked near here. I would just go there and sit with my legs hanging over the side, looking at the stars, throwing rocks off the concrete. It is my fortress of solitude.

I am there now, for the first time since I've been able to drive.

21.

I am feeling:

Sad. I cannot believe that this is over. It feels like someone has surgically removed all my internal organs and sewn me back up in my sleep. I have never felt this before.

Duped. She said she never felt anything. How could she *say* that? I'm the kid who has been stuffed in his locker. I'm the kid who was depantsed on the playground. I'm the kid who gives up a quarter for three nickels.

Young. I have always enjoyed being the youngest. Your parents leave you alone more. You don't have any pressure. You just get to go on and live your life as you want, while everyone's paying attention to your older brother. But I hate it now. She called me a little boy. Big man, Tim Temples: she called me a little boy.

Angry. I want to *throttle* Helena. I want to take her and just *shake* her, shake some sense into her, shake her until her brain is straight. I want to take Doug's head to the curb and stomp on it. I want to take everyone who has ever felt anything for anyone and I want to scream in their face. I want them to know that it is madness. I want them to know that their heart will be pulled out of their chest and ground into dust. I want to hurt them. I want to crush them all.

Tired. I want to crawl into bed and sleep until everything goes away.

Guilty. I wonder if I have made anyone else feel like this. I wonder if someone's guts rose into their chest when I kissed them, I wonder if they felt that I was their one, I wonder if my apathy sent them to their own dams. I want to tell them I am sorry. I want to tell them I didn't know, I didn't know how this felt. If I did, I would have been less careless, I would have been a better person, I would have thought more about them instead of, well, instead of about nothing. To Amy. To Staci. To Kim. To Joan. To Angela. To Aileen. To Sue. To Beth. To Julie. To Emily. To Jami. To Carrie. To Erin. To Cindy. To any that I might have missed, because I am an asshole. To all of you: I am so sorry. Because I didn't know. I just didn't know.

Alone. I am feeling very alone.

22.

I drive home from the dam, pulling into the driveway with my lights off so I don't wake up anyone. I don't want to speak to Doug. I don't want to speak to anyone. I just want to go to bed.

I shut off the truck and close the door behind me as silently as possible. I tiptoe to the back patio and place my hand on the sliding door. I hear a voice behind me. "Hey, you're home early, you hot stud."

Doug. *Fuck.*

I pretend I didn't hear him. I start to slide the door open, but Doug yells. "Surprised you're home at all," he says. "You get tired of helping your old lady rock the cradle? She too much woman for you?" I stand there, motionless. *Not now, man. Honestly. Not now.*

He sounds like he's been drinking all night. I turn toward him and put my finger over my lips. "Shhhhh," I say. I turn back toward the door. But Doug isn't letting up.

"Oh, what's wrong, she just don't do it for you anymore?"

It starts with a rumbling in my stomach, a steady tremor, and then it just multiplies, exploding into the most massive of earthquakes. Everything about me is shaking. My nostrils are shooting flames, and my hair is electric wires. I want to take his face and shove it into a meat grinder. I turn and stalk toward him. My rage is overpowering. I want to crush his skull into powder. I'm shouting before I realize I'm speaking.

Before the explosion, I see his face, and it's hesitant. He takes a step back. He just lit a dangerous fuse and understands, too late, that he wishes he hadn't. The expression is quickly replaced by the usual defiance.

"Dude, what the *fuck*?" I am shrieking. "What is your fucking deal?" I am standing a foot away from him, a manager arguing with an umpire. "Seriously. Why are you even *here*? You sit there in your garage, doing who the hell knows what, and you rip on me, and you rip on Mom and Dad, and you just rip on everything. What gives you the right? What are you doing that's so great?"

I am a million flying daggers, soaring through the air, eager to meet their target.

"You realize that you're a fuckup, right?" I yell. "You walk around here like you own the place, like everybody owes you something, like you're King Tut. But you're nothing. You've screwed up every opportunity."

Doug tries to speak. "*I've* screwed up every opportunity?"

"Of course you have!" I scream. I don't care who hears me. I want to wake up God tonight. "You were the best pitcher I've ever seen, and you got to college and you just pissed it away because you were stubborn, because you thought you knew everything. You could have been in the majors. You could have played pro ball—"

"That was Mom's fault!" he says, in a voice that sounds like a child's. This would disturb me if I weren't so interested in taking a sledgehammer to his trachea. "I wanted to sign with the Cards, but she insisted I go to college. Even Dad was on my side on that one!"

I have never cared for Doug and my father's subtle shift of blame toward my mother for this, and I'm certainly not standing for it now. "Don't you think the same crap that happened in college would have happened in the minors? It would have been worse! You would have embarrassed yourself. All you could do is throw a fastball, and that's all. You never learned anything else, because you didn't *try*. And it's not like you didn't get anything given to you. You got your entire college paid for! And what'd you do with it? Nothing! You didn't even graduate! And now look at you. You're fat, you're sitting in your parents' garage, working for the city, hating everything. You're pathetic. You can't even throw your fastball anymore! You're worse off than you were when you started!"

I'm begging him to punch me. I don't know why I haven't punched him yet. But we haven't. Both of us stand there, breathing heavy, glaring at each other.

Doug starts to speak, quietly, like he's about to say something that he knows he won't be able to take back. And then he stops. He takes a step backward. He looks at my feet. Then he raises his head. "I can still throw my fastball past anybody."

"Bullshit," I say.

"You couldn't catch it," he says.

"I can catch anything," I say.

"Get your fucking mitt."

23.

Neither of us says a word as we walk to the open field behind our garage and take the same places we have been taking since I was five. Two well-worn patches of dirt, sixty feet, six inches apart, pounded into beaten semicircles by years of practice. He stands in his usual spot. I stand in mine.

"You want your mask?" he says, sneering. "You're going to need it."

"Shut up and throw."

Doug rears back and fires. His heat is better than I remember. He does still have it. It whistles into my mitt,

250

whap, and my palm flares in pain immediately. But I'm not letting him see that. I'm not letting him see anything.

"Nothing on that," I say. "You throw like Mom. Give me the real cheese." I whip the ball back to him.

He blisters another one, and I just barely snag it. My hand is being whacked by gnomes with machetes. "Weakass," I say, and toss the ball back.

He keeps throwing, I keep catching. I hear him grunting and panting, pulling everything he's got up from his shoelaces. Neither of us warmed up. We just started going. One of us is going to break, and then we'll know, definitively, who wins.

We are now silent. Ten pitches, fifteen, twenty. We are staring at each other. Somehow, he's throwing harder with each one. And then he starts moving toward me a few inches after each pitch. He's raising the ante. And I don't care. Bring it.

Harder. *Fwap*. Harder. *Fwap*. Harder, you bitch. *Fwap fwap fwap.*

He is now about twenty feet in front of the worn patch of dirt. And he's still throwing his hardest. And I am missing nothing. *I am going to beat you because I am better than you. I have learned from your mistakes, and I do not intend to repeat them.*

Doug is starting to pant harder now. He is about thirty feet away. Fearing he might lose, I presume, he breaks the silence.

"You want the really good one?" he says. He's so close now, he doesn't have to shout.

251

"You don't have a really good one."

Our rapid pitch-catch stops, and he straightens. He looks in like he's searching for a sign. His chest heaves, and he hoists up his left leg, Bob Gibson style, flings his arm behind him, and just *lunges*. He makes a sound like an animal dying.

I never even see the ball until it nicks off my glove and strikes me on the left side of my mouth. It doesn't hurt, not immediately, but I crumple to the ground and fall into the fetal position. I touch my lip with my finger and see that it is bloody.

Doug runs—runs—up to me. "Jesus Christ, that one got you good. Oh, man." He leans down on his knees and inspects my face. "Shit, that popped you right in the mouth."

I look at him and show him my teeth. "Everything still there?" I say, garbled.

"Somehow, yeah," he says. "Christ. You took that one flush."

And I sit there, on the ground with my brother, the guiding influence in my life and the man who slept with my girlfriend, my Helena. I stare at him, and I no longer feel any hate for him. I no longer want to kill him. I understand now. He looks sad. He looks lost.

I grab his arm and hang on tight. We pull each other up. I am wobbly.

"I'm sorry, man," he says. "I was probably standing too close on that one."

"I should have caught it."

We stand there, with my hand still gripping his arm.

"I'm just all kinds of fucked up right now," he says. "I don't know what the hell my problem is."

"Join the club," I say.

"I'm sorry I used to bang your girlfriend," he says. "It was a long time ago."

This admission bothers me much less than I would have thought. Right now everything seems very far away, like it happened in another lifetime. "She's not my girlfriend anymore."

Doug glances at me out of the corner of his eye. "Well, that sucks," he says. "Probably for the best, though."

I can only hope. "You think this thing's gonna need stitches?"

Doug shakes his head. "Naw, it's not so big," he says. "You're right. Maybe my heat isn't what it used to be."

The bottom half of my head is numb. "Doug," I say, massaging my jaw, "my face and I assure you, you still have it."

I hear the patio door open. It's my mother, wearing a Sarah Bush Lincoln Health Center T-shirt and a pair of sweatpants. She looks very annoyed. "Boys, it's one thirty in the morning," she says. "Get inside and go to bed, for crying out loud." And we look at each other, and then, with a final flicker of recognition, we do.

24.

That night, I dream that I am standing on top of the Mattoon water tower. I can see the entire town, and I am king of all that I survey. I see the bright stars in the night sky. I see my house, just outside of town, and I see Helena's house, nestled safely behind the dip in the road. I see the plant, on Route 45, on the way to Champaign. I look closer and see the Assembly Hall, where the basketball team is always winning, and Memorial Stadium, where the football team is always losing. I see Munesh and the twins standing on another water tower, and they are waving at me. I see the Embassy, in Arcola, almost halfway between Mattoon and Champaign. It is not Helena standing on its roof; it is Jessica. She is dancing a jig and wearing a chicken costume.

And then Godzilla comes and sets a cornfield on fire. I don't know what that part was about.

25.

On the drive home from a kickoff event for Bagelfest— where Dad had to give a speech reassuring everyone that everything was ready—my parents and I are listening to the Cardinals game. Out of nowhere, Dad turns around to me in the backseat. "I know you've hard a hard time this summer," he says. "So the way things have been going lately, you could probably use a cheer." He flips me a baseball, signed by Willie McGee, my favorite Cardinals player of all time.

I smile. "Thanks, Dad."

"No problem," he says. "Your mom's got me using eBay."

Willie McGee has strangely perfect handwriting. I don't know what compelled my father to do this, but I find myself beaming.

"And remember, kiddo, there are a million girls out there," he says. "Believe you me, I *know*." My God, he *does* know? How did he know? Before I have a chance to figure this out, my mom slaps him on the arm, and we all laugh, and it feels good, and it makes me happy and sad all at once.

26.

I am impressed with myself: I have not called Helena all week. I've thought about her, of course. I've thought about what she's doing right now, if her mom is feeling sick, but I'm not sure what to say to her. I don't think any of it would make any difference. So I've put her out of my mind, stashed her in that little corner with all the strike-outs in the ninth inning. I feel blessed: there wasn't that much stuff clicking around in that corner.

This also makes me feel insane. It makes me feel cold. It makes me feel like I am doing her wrong, like she's chalk easily erased from the board. I find myself wondering if I can remember what she looks like when she's sleeping, what her snores sound like, what her lips do when she's inhaling a cigarette. Can I remember? Has it really just been a week and a half? Was she ever there? Did I imagine her?

27.

The work for Thursday, the last day, is done. No more boxes to stack. No more trucks to fill. Just me sitting in Larry's lawn chair, drinking a Coke. It seems odd that it just ends like this. I imagined one final box, a big dramatic moment, *this is the last one.* But that didn't happen. I just did my job for eight hours, and before I realized it, all the boxes were in the truck. It drove off, and all that was left was me.

I look at the clock. It says 4:45, but it seems like it has said that for half an hour. An empty Dunkin' Donuts box lies on the ground. The doughnuts were bought by me—from Mayor McKenzie—before I came into work that morning, as is plant tradition for people on their last day. Larry is inside somewhere, who knows where, probably telling some unsuspecting soul how Lee Harvey Oswald was actually a mob operative working under Frank Sinatra and Charles Nelson Reilly. I sit in the chair and ponder whether this job taught me anything or if it was just exercise. Did it need to teach me anything? Will anyone here remember me? Will they think of me as a hard worker? Or just the Temples boy loafing around, cashing in on his name? What did this *mean*?

Still. It was just a summer job. Maybe I've been thinking about things too much lately.

I look back at the clock. *Still* 4:45. A pickup truck comes rolling up behind me, where we usually load the cargo truck. I realize it's Larry. And I realize there are about fifteen people from around the plant in the back of the pickup. The Horsemen, Chuck, even Otis, who is wearing a little party hat and has a kazoo dangling from his lips.

"Surprise, kid," Larry says as he pulls in. "The rest of the folks and Larry thought they might want to celebrate your last day and see you off to the whole land of academia. Larry thinks the best way to handle this here thing is to get your ass drunk. So get in."

When I hop into the bed of Larry's truck, I have a smile the size of the water tower.

28.

"Larry thought you might like that little clock trick," Larry says, passing out shots to everyone at the Tumble Inn. "Damn thing said 4:45 all day." Gus, looking unhappy as always, dutifully dumps Southern Comfort into everyone's shot glass. Denny is to my left, with Kristen on his hip. Jeff is behind him, with Jessica standing apart from the group. They're the only two who don't look like they're in a festive mood.

Larry raises his glass in the air. "Larry's seen all kinds of kids come to the plant for the summer and sit there twiddling their thumbs," he says. "Kid, you worked your ass off, and we'll miss having you around here. And you know what? *I'll* miss having you around here."

I raise an eyebrow at him. *I'll* miss you? Not *Larry* will miss you?

He leans over to me. "It's tough keepin' the pronouns straight all the time, you know?" He cheers, and we all

257

drink. The secretary who works behind the front desk starts gagging and runs to the bathroom.

We file into four booths in the back. Being the impromptu guest of honor, I sit at none of them, dancing from table to table, accepting congratulations, shaking hands, answering questions about college, explaining where I'm going to be living, listening to suggestions on how to improve the Illini football team. I feel like my dad, glad-handing and backslapping. I kind of like it, and I wonder, once I get to Champaign, if I'll ever have the opportunity to do it again.

Maybe not. And maybe that's not such a bad thing. Jessica hands me another beer. "So, books tomorrow?" she asks. "I already checked out the online store, and it should be really easy."

"Oh, I don't know, I've got a lot going on," I say, accepting a high five from some guy in accounting I don't recognize but I suspect really wants to be friends with my dad.

"Come on!" she says. "We're leaving for school in three days! Bagelfest is Saturday, and we're not going to have time to do it then. If we wait before we leave Sunday, they probably won't have our order by Monday. We *have* to do it tomorrow. You really don't want to wait in those lines, you know."

I nod halfheartedly. Chuck drunkenly waddles over. The Horsemen stiffen. "Hanging out with your boys, I see," he says. "And you boys have even brought your fine ladies." Chuck puts me in a pretend headlock. I wiggle out quickly so as to avoid Chuck's pit stains.

29.

Otis from the night shift walks up to me and places a beer in my hand. He then salutes me and walks out the front door, into the night.

30.

"I bet you're wondering if I've nailed her yet," Jeff says in the urinal next to me. He is smoking a cigarette with one hand and drinking a beer with the other.

I zip up and head to the sink. "Actually, I wasn't wondering that," I say, lying. "I honestly don't care, and I don't want to know either way."

"Bullshit," Jeff says, cigarette still in his mouth. "She needs some real man meat before she heads up to live with all those lesbos up north. That means I'm going to have to act fast. . . ." I ignore him and walk out the door.

The party is thinning. It's Larry, Chuck (currently trying to convince Gus that he hasn't had enough), the Horsemen, Jessica, Kristen, and a couple of co-workers from the plant discussing NASCAR. I am pleased by this. I have an urge for some air.

I step outside and feel the tug of Helena. She should be here. It seems wrong that she wouldn't be. Did anybody tell her? She wouldn't have shown up anyway. Would have been a scene. She hates those.

I miss her.

I don't want her to come to Champaign with me anymore. (She wouldn't want it, and, honestly, it would have

259

never worked.) But it seems wrong for her to just *vanish*. Is she really gone, just like that? What does she think of me? Does she really believe all those things she said about me? Does she really think I'm just a little boy? Does she think I'd be like Doug and just use her? I hope not. I hope she knows me better than that. I hope she knows how she changed me.

Larry comes outside and lights his cigar.

"Nice party you got here," he says. "Larry's been here for twenty-five years, and he won't get half this bash when he leaves."

"Don't say that, Larry," I say. "People here love you."

"Larry don't want 'em to, you know?" he says. "Larry should have left this place a long time ago. Folks get stuck here, Tim. *You* got a chance to do somethin' different."

I remember something. "Hey, Larry, when you seeing your kids again?"

Larry takes a long puff off his cigar. "The ex-wife took 'em to South Dakota," he says. "Just left last week. She met some guy on the Internet, and they're gonna live out there with him."

"Larry," I say, stunned. "I'm so sorry. Why didn't you say anything?"

"Oh, you had enough on your mind, kid," he says. "Besides, Larry's okay with it. He sounds like a good fella. It's beautiful country. They'll love it. Larry'll see 'em over Christmas. Besides, Larry's been getting on e-mail, and he's gettin' pretty good at it. Hell, he'll probably talk to them kids more now over e-mail than he ever has." He takes another puff.

We stand there as the air becomes crisper. I shiver.

"You thinkin' about Helena?" he says.

"Yeah," I say. "I am."

"Larry figgered," he says. "She's a good woman. Had a hard life. You were good to her, you know. First time Larry ever saw her smile in the four years she'd worked there."

"Larry?" I begin.

"Don't worry, kid," he says. "Larry'll keep a good eye on 'er for ya."

"Thanks."

31.

An hour or so later, everyone is milling around outside, waiting for the signal that it's okay to leave now. It's me, Larry, Chuck, Andy and Shad, Denny and Kristen. Larry is listening impatiently to Chuck's long-winded exercise in self-righteousness when, out of nowhere, Jessica comes thrashing through the front door, with Jeff trailing behind her.

They hurry far enough away that I can't hear them, but they're obviously having a furious fight. Well, that's not quite accurate. Jeff is fired up about *something*, but Jessica is looking at him like he's a specimen in a petri dish. Her head is cocked, like she's watching a lab rat, as he stomps and yells and kicks his feet. The commotion has stirred our crowd at the front door. Denny and Kristen stand next to me, stunned.

From afar, Jeff puts a hand on his hip and says some-thing that makes Jessica's lips purse. She gets a contem-plative look on her face for a second, and then she flashes comprehension. Then, without a moment's more thought, she deposits her right fist in his stomach. He doubles over and keels to the ground. I look down at him as he gasps for air, and then I look up at Jessica. She gives a self-satisfied grin, then hops in her car, spins out, and drives off, kicking up rocks behind her.

Jeff stumbles over to where we all stand. "Jeez, man, that hurt."

"What did you say to her?" I ask.

He winces. "If I told you, you'd probably hit me too."

Chuck wobbles over to him and puts his arm around him. "Don't let those chicks get you down, kid," he says. "Come inside, have a drink with me. I've had my eye on ya, and I want to talk to you about your position at the plant. You've got good instincts. You think like I do. I like that." They walk into the bar.

I look over at Kristen and Denny, and their smiles are like sunshine.

32.

The next morning, I walk across the poorly clipped front lawn of Professor Charles Danner, stepping over a torn-up Hefty bag and some broken pieces of wood. The Danner yard used to get so sloppy that my dad would go over and clean it up for them, but these days, everyone's too busy to help Charles out. I knock on the front door—I hate doorbells; they seem too intrusive—and Professor Danner opens the door and lets me in.

"Yes, Jessica's in her room. She'll be out in a minute," Professor Danner says, disheveled as always. He is wearing a sweater with a plaid jacket over it, even though it's about eighty degrees outside and he hasn't turned on the air conditioner. "Ah, you can have a seat if you'd like. Would you like, I don't know, a glass of water or anything?"

"I'm fine, sir, thank you." I always call Professor Danner "sir." I bet I'm the only person in town who calls him that, which is why I do.

Professor Danner shuffles around the room aimlessly, picking up paperweights and setting them down, looking for something to occupy his attention in the silence. Having exhausted all possible permutations, he sits down on the couch across from me.

"So, Tim, are you ready for the big day?" he says. "It's astounding that it has finally arrived, don't you think?"

"Yeah, two days," I say. "Seems like it snuck up on me."

"It's true," he says. "When you knocked on the door just now I thought, it wasn't long ago that you were knocking to see if Jessica could come out and play." He puts his glasses down and taps his foot for a second. He then looks up at me.

"You will make sure my girl's going to be all right up there?" he says, with a more serious, lucid look than I have ever seen on him.

"Of course, sir," I say.

"I will miss her very much," he says, scratching the back of his head. "This house will be awfully quiet without her around." He eyes a spot in the distance somewhere, and his face goes slack. He suddenly looks very old.

I wonder if he will make it. I wonder how he will get along. I wonder who will come pick him up when he runs out of gas.

Jessica bounds out of her room with her hair in a towel. She takes it off. "Surprise!"

I notice, with a start, that Jessica's hair is bright blond, rather than the sandy brown she's had since birth. Both her father and I do double takes.

"Do you like it?" she says. "I thought it might be kind of fun, you know, to try something different before we left."

"Well, I, uh, er," Mr. Danner stutters. "It's, well, it's certainly different."

Jessica frowns. "Do you not like it, Daddy?"

He straightens up in his chair. "No, love, it looks great," he says, smiling. "You're beautiful."

She comes over and pecks him on the cheek, then motions me to join her in the computer room. "Let's get you wired."

33.

The *p* key is around here somewhere.

It has to be. *P* is a rather common letter. It should be easily accessible. But I can't find it anywhere. Jessica, who made me sit here and therefore should be more patient, is tapping her fingers on the desk and whistling. "Keep looking," she says, smiling. "I swear it's on there. Honest."

There it is. I want to press it a thousand times. *Gotcha.*

I am on the Web site for Follett's bookstore, where I am trying to find *Introduction to Clinical Psychology*, the main textbook for Psychology 105, one of my five classes. The others, according to this sheet of paper sitting on my lap: Economics 102, Rhetoric 104, Algebra 110, and Kinesiology 115 (which, I'm proud to report, is *bowling*). These classes seem almost fictional to me now, and impossibly hard, especially since now I can't find the *l*.

"Bah!" I say, pushing my chair back from the computer. "I hate this crap."

"Well, you're going to have to get used to it, because you're going to be sitting in front of one for the next four years," she says.

"Great," I say. "I'm gonna fail out in a week." But I won't. Somehow, I know I won't.

I click around a few places, making a few jokes about porn sites along the way, and then find the correct textbook. I take out my mom's credit card and punch in the numbers, and then *wham*, I'm an official college student, with classes and a book and everything. I raise my arms in the air. "Woo!" I yell. "Success!"

Jessica laughs and takes a paper out of my lap. "Okay, now we have to find your rhet book."

I turn to her. "You know, you really popped Jeff last night. I think he ended up puking later."

265

Jessica tries to hide a grin and fails. "Well, he deserved it." Then she leans in closer.

"Can you keep a secret?"

I nod, eager. "I had a rock in my hand. I kind of just shoved it into him. Please don't tell anyone. I like the idea of people thinking I'm a badass."

"You *are* a badass," I say. "Rock or not. Most of us have been wanting to do that for a long time. So what did he say?"

Jessica avoids answering the question directly. "I tell you, kiss one boy a couple of times, and they act like they own you or something." She smiles, and I pity the Champaign fool who fails to take Jessica seriously.

Her dad walks in with a plate of grilled cheese sandwiches. "I, ah, I thought you two might want some lunch," he says. The sandwiches are burnt jet black and are melted to the paper plate. He also seems to have forgotten to take the wrapper off one of the slices of cheese. Jessica is unfazed. She kisses him on the cheek and says, "Thanks, Daddy." He leaves, and she leans over to me. "I'll order a pizza later," she whispers.

I search for the rhetoric textbook, accidentally shutting down the computer twice. While we're waiting for it to start up again—*reboot*, Jessica calls it—I ask if her dad's going to drive his own car to Champaign Sunday or if we're all going to jam into the same moving truck.

"Actually, he's not coming," she says, frowning.

"Wow, really? That's kind of surprising," I say. "It's a big day."

"He's overwhelmed by this whole thing," she says. "He's gonna be all by himself in this house. He'll get so lonely."

"My parents will keep an eye on him," I say. "They'll make sure he doesn't set the house on fire or anything. And even if you weren't leaving, Dad would probably want to take care of the lawn anyway. Drives him nuts how little your dad mows."

Jessica takes in a little air, and her lips tighten together. She turns to me. "Are you sure about all this?" she says. "I mean, aren't you worried? Because I'm a little scared. I could totally get lost up there. And Dad will be back here, and who knows what will happen."

I find it sweet that Jessica is now—two days from school starting—starting to get cold feet. I look at her, and I see who she will be. She will flourish in Champaign. She will earn straight A's, and she'll be the envy of everyone who knows her. She's going to absolutely *rule* that campus.

I also see who she'll be if she stays. How she'll slowly stop dreaming, stop hoping for more, and start watching home renovation shows for comfort. I'm glad that will never happen to her.

I get a pang in my heart; I hope by our senior year, she still remembers me.

"Life will go on just fine here without us," I say.

Jessica laughs and sighs. "Yeah, it's just scary to leave everything behind, to completely wipe the slate clean."

It's so scary, Jessica, that it absolutely must be done.

"Sometimes the people we leave behind need to make

their own choices with their lives," I say. "Sometimes they need their own slates wiped clean." And I'm talking about Mr. Danner, and Helena, and Doug, and everything, and everyone.

"Why, Tim," Jessica says with mock surprise. "that's very profound of you."

"Thanks. Now . . . where's that damn *p* again?"

34.

The day of Bagelfest has finally arrived. I follow the signs to the Delta terminal and pull into short-term parking. I take a piece of notebook paper and write *Kuhns* on the back of it so everybody's favorite *CSI* corpse knows I'm there to pick him up. I cross the street to baggage claim, just avoiding the car of an old lady who can't see over the dashboard. And there I stand. My phone rings. It's Dad again.

"You there?" he says.

"Waiting in baggage claim," I say. "Indianapolis is a shithole."

"No kidding," he says. "Listen, they just told me he has a friend with him. So you should drive him back here too."

"You mean I shouldn't just leave him here and make him find his own ride?"

"Don't get smart," he says. "They're staying at the Holiday Inn downtown. You know where that is?"

"Of course I know where that is." Junior-year prom. "Anything else?"

"Did you clean your truck?"

I see two darkly tanned men waiting at carousel four. One of them sees me and my sign and starts waving like a grandmother watching her grandson pass by her in the graduation line. I certainly *hope* that's them.

I walk over to them as their bags arrive. "Hey, is one of you guys Jacob?"

"You mean you don't recognize the world-famous Jacob Kuhns?" says the shorter, Italian-looking one. "Honey, I would have thought everybody from Mattoon had your picture on their wall."

Jacob is tall, handsome, and muscular, with smooth, blandly perfect skin. He's wearing a skintight light brown shirt and blue jeans he must have been airlifted into. He looks like one of the people who are always dancing behind Madonna at her concerts.

"Hi, I'm Jacob," he says, shaking my hand. "You wouldn't happen to be related to Doug Temples, would you?"

I've never thought Doug and I look like each other, but every other human on the planet apparently disagrees. "Yep, I'm his brother, Tim," I say. "You know him?"

"Oh, yes, I graduated a year before him," he says, and he whispers, thinking I can't hear, the words, "Total asshole jock," in his friend's ear. His friend is wearing a pink shirt with the word *Slut* spelled in what seems to be glitter. "This is my friend A. J."

A. J. takes my hand in his right hand and touches my wrist with his left. "It's a pleasure to meet you."

Jacob shoots him a cold glare and says, "You promised you wouldn't embarrass me." A. J. grins impishly.

Moving right along. "So, yeah, I'm your ride back to Mattoon," I say. "You guys have all your bags?"

I haul their stuff back to the Blazer and dump it in the backseat. We leave the airport and pull onto I-70 back toward Mattoon. Jacob sits in the front seat while A. J. rustles through all their luggage in the back.

"What are you doing back there?" Jacob says.

"I'm sure I forgot something," A. J. says. "I'm looking through everything to see if I can find out what it was." Jacob looks at me with an "I know he's an idiot, but he's my idiot" smirk, and I nod, smiling.

We cruise down the highway. Jacob pops in a CD by a band he says is called the Scissor Sisters, even though the lead singer of the band is a guy. He turns to me. "So, are you one of the guys who helped set up the Bagelfest parade? Because I'm curious as to how this is all going to work."

"Not really," I say. "My dad and my brother know a lot more than I do. But you're the grand marshal of the parade. I think all you have to do is sit in a car and wave."

"Like Miss America!" says A. J. in the backseat, excitedly.

Jacob frowns. "Something like that."

I'm trying to remember anything I saw Jacob in. I missed the infamous *CSI* episode. There was that Gap commercial, but I have a feeling Jacob isn't that proud of that. Then I remember.

"Hey, didn't I see you on *Blind Date* one time?"

Jacob sighs. "Yes, you did," he says. "My agent said it

270

would be a good idea. I told him I was an actor, not a reality TV show goon, but he absolutely insisted. It's the only thing anyone ever remembers."

"That girl on that show with you was a *whoo-arrr*," A. J. whistles from the backseat. "She's just like the stuck-up Philly girls I grew up with. Gimme gimme gimme!"

I turn behind me to A. J. "Are you an actor too?"

"Please," he says. "I'm no *the*spian, if that's what you're asking. I'm more of a hanger-on of the rich and famous, like your star, Jacob, here." Jacob playfully throws a quarter at him.

It occurs to me that Jacob is gay and that A. J. is his boyfriend. This ridiculously late realization must be painted on my face, because Jacob turns back to me.

"You know, I don't care what everybody says about it because A. J.'s going to ride with me in the parade," he says. "If they can't handle it, it's their problem."

I laugh, hoping he doesn't think I'm making fun of him. "I don't think it'll be a problem," I say. "You know how people are in Mattoon. They'll talk themselves into thinking you're cousins or something."

Jacob chuckles and asks if he can smoke, and I nod. He rolls down the window. I realize something—after going my whole life without meeting one gay guy, I've met three in the last two weeks. I feel like I have a million questions for him. But what will he find offensive? Maybe I should try some common ground first. I strain my brain to come up with anything. Then I remember Eric's trivia.

"So, you know, the high five?" I say. "That was invented by a gay man."

Jacob looks at me, and he and A. J. bust immediately into gales of laughter. And I join them.

35.

I just pegged some little kid in the face with a Jolly Rancher. I really popped him good.

The kid was sitting there with his mom, watching me drive the Camaro down Broadway in the twentieth annual Bagelfest parade. He had that excited, hopeful look kids have at parades, *Here comes the candy man!* So I chucked a bunch of candies from the bag next to me, and one of them drilled him on the head. He started bawling, of course, and his mom went to console him. I was too much of a coward to do anything but look straight ahead and inch along.

I'm following the grand marshal car, the convertible with the mayor, Jacob Kuhns, and A. J. from Philadelphia, and they are waving and teenage girls are swooning as they crawl by. My father is in the seat next to me, tossing candy himself, wearing his high school letterman jacket. There's a big poster of him in his minor-league jersey taped to the side of the car; we bring it out for all the parades. Mom's walking behind us, with Daisy and hundreds of other golden retrievers. It's one of the conceits of the Bagelfest parade: every year, everyone in town who has a golden retriever walks it through the parade. They look so cute. It's the biggest hit every year.

And I have never seen a parade this big in Mattoon. The sidewalks are filled with people, rows and rows of them, six deep at least. Some have banners with slogans like, MATTOON IS BAGEL-RIFFIC! and, 20 YEARS OF BAGEL EXCITEMENT! One guy is wearing a mock football helmet that's in the shape of a bagel; it even has a layer of spackle impersonating cream cheese spread around it. Some woman has an inner tube painted brown and has wrapped it around her dog, who looks awfully unhappy. And atop the movie theater is the kicker: the World's Largest Bagel, all five hundred pounds of it. It looms over the city, casting a shadow larger than the water tower's. It is also already covered in bird droppings. A stray cat that somehow got up there nibbles at one of its edges.

And we inch along. My dad leans over to me. "The mayor keeps asking me who Jacob's 'friend' is," he says. "I told him he was his personal escort. All the stars have them." He laughs. My dad loves parades.

36.

The parade ends at the Cross County Mall, whose parking lot is filled with tables and chairs. A head table, on a stage built by the parks department and the Temples family, has spots for Jacob Kuhns, A. J. (put together at the last minute), the mayor, my father, and a representative from the Lender's company, a tiny man with a stutter.

I pull up in front of the Alamo, the old-people bar

right by the mall, and Dad tells me I can pick any table I want or not eat a bagel at all, he doesn't really care. "Oh, and try to find your brother," he says. "Your mother has been looking all over for him." He leaves, and I call Doug's cell phone.

"Yo," he answers.

"Hey, where the hell you been?" I say. "No one knows where you are."

"I'm at the Alamo, having a beer with a friend," he says.

"Really?" I say. "I just pulled into their parking lot."

"Well, get in here, then," he says. "I probably owe you one."

I walk in the front door and can't seem to find Doug anywhere, even though there's hardly anyone here. Lynyrd Skynryd is playing on the jukebox. I walk up to the bartender. "Hey, have you seen—"

"Hey, dipshit," he says.

I turn to my left. Doug is sitting with a redheaded woman whom I recognize vaguely. But she's not the one I'm staring at. Doug has shaved his beard. He is wearing a button-up shirt and a pair of pressed khakis. He even combed his hair. He looks about ten years younger.

"You shaved your beard," I say.

"What beard?" the woman says. Doug shoots an "Ixnay on the eardbay" glare at me and introduces me to Erika. "We went to high school together," he says. "She came all the way back from Chicago to attend today's festivities." I shake Erika's hand, but I can't stop looking at

274

Doug. He looks like the Doug I remember. He looks like my big brother again.

"How'd the parade go?" he asks.

"I think I might have killed a small child with a Jolly Rancher," I say.

Doug nods. "Good work!"

He asks me if I want a beer, but I tell him that I don't have time, that I'm supposed to meet Mom at the table just beneath the stage. "The whole thing is supposed to start in about ten minutes, as soon as they finish the Little Miss Bagelfest contest," I say.

Erika finishes the rest of her beer. "Well, then what are we waiting for?" she says. She's pretty. She has cool slender black-rimmed glasses and is wearing a summer business suit. "It's not every day you get to see ten thousand people eat a bagel at the same time."

She walks ahead of us as we leave the Alamo. Doug leans over to me. "She's hot, right?" She is. "Yeah, this lady is in *law school*," he says. "And when she gets into town, she calls *me*. Can you believe that shit?"

"You look a lot better without the beard," I say.

"Well," he says, grinning, "it was getting pretty itchy."

37.

The seating arrangement on stage looks like this: A. J., Jacob, the mayor, my father, and the Lender's representative, whose name is Jose, even though he's obviously not Mexican. Each has a plateful of bagels in front of him.

Almost the entire town is in their seats. My table has Doug, Erika, Jessica, her father, and my mother. We each have one bagel in front of us. Next to my right leg, Daisy is panting; she has a bagel in front of her too.

"Thanks, everyone, for coming and making this the best Bagelfest *ever!*" the mayor screams into the microphone, causing feedback that makes everyone cover their ears. "Before we begin, I'd like to introduce everyone. Obviously, Bryan Temples, as everyone knows, has been the driving force behind this whole enterprise." Dad stands, and he receives a rousing ovation.

"But we also have some very special guests with us for this very special day," the mayor continues. "First, with us from Kraft's Lender's division, is Jose Rooney, associate vice president of corporate communications." Jose stands up, looking bewildered, to a smattering of polite applause.

"And finally," Mayor McKenzie says, as the electricity in the crowd grows, "we have the grand marshal for our event. You've seen him in television commercials, you've seen him on *CSI*, and—and we just found out about this, this is breaking news—this Christmas you'll see him as Angel Number Four in the CBS television production of the Mitch Albom book *Lessons My Nana Taught Me*. This guy is so famous," he blares, pointing at A. J., "that he has a personal assistant who traveled all the way from Los Angeles just to watch over him today. Ladies and gentlemen, Mattoon's native son, our very own Hollywood star, Jacob Kuhns, and his assistant, A. J.!"

The citizens of Mattoon let loose a roar I've never

heard outside a football stadium. Jacob looks slightly embarrassed, but A. J. is eating it up, waving manically to the crowd, bowing dramatically, and striking beefcake poses for photos. When the crowd settles, everyone sits but the mayor. "All right, so if our timekeeper is here," he says, "I think we are about ready."

The mayor's wife stands off to the side of the stage with a starter pistol in her left hand. "On your marks," she says, sans microphone, "get set . . . *go!*"

At once, four of the five people onstage start stuffing bagels into their mouths. Only Jose, who can't quite grasp what's happening here, sits there dumbly. The crowd is screaming. My mother is jumping up and down, yelling, "Go, Bryan, go!" Erika and Jessica are cracking up, and Doug is sitting there with a satisfied look of bemusement. He notices me looking at him, and he winks.

"And . . . *time!*"

Jose nibbled half of one bagel. Jacob only finished three. The mayor put down six. My father, bless him, ate nine. But none even came close to A. J., who scarfed down fifteen in five minutes. The mayor, mouth still full of cardboard bagel, takes the microphone. "Our winner is A. J. the assistant!" he yells. "Congratulations!" A. J. jumps up in the air, his arms and legs flailing wildly, like one of those people who won both showplace showdowns on *The Price Is Right*. He blows kisses to the crowd. Jacob is giving mock bows of praise to A. J. as my father, ever competitive, tries to be a good sport but claps limply.

A. J. grabs the microphone. "Thank you, thank you,

everyone!" A. J. yells. "I can't believe that a little assistant from Philadelphia could come so far and make it so big! Thank you!"

And then we all eat our own bagels, ten thousand Mattoonians strong, united. There is plenty, plenty of butter. I think of Eric and Gabe as I note, no lox.

38.

Nighttime has come, and most of our town has gone home to deal with their inevitable digestive problems. Doug is helping Dad clear out some tables, and I walk out to Jessica's car with her, her father, and Mom.

"So, we have everything straight for tomorrow?" I ask Professor Danner.

"We should just come by your house at 9 a.m., yes?" he says. I nod.

He looks very sad. Jessica puts her arm around his waist. "Oh, Daddy, it'll be fine," she says. Jessica opens the passenger side door for him, and she gives me an impish "I can't believe we're actually doing this" grin as she drives off.

My mom is rubbing my back again. "So don't stay out too late tonight," she says. "We've got a big day tomorrow."

"Don't worry, Mom," I say. "I kind of just want to go for a drive, be by myself tonight anyway."

Mom's eyes moisten. "Oh, Tim, don't be sad," she says. "I think your dad and I are sad enough for all of us." She

278

gives me a long hug, and she walks toward the stage to meet Dad and Doug.

And then it's just me. That *is* what I want to do tonight. I just want to drive. It seems kind of silly—it's not like everything's going to vanish just because I've left town—but I feel like I want to take everything in one last time. I hop in my car.

I drive to the high school. It looks enormous to me, but I know that as the years go by, it will shrink and shrink.

I drive to Peterson Park, where I dropped the ball during that last play at the plate, the one that cost us sectionals. Will I ever play baseball again? Real *baseball*? I doubt it. I'm not good enough to play for the college team, but I loved the process of putting on the chest protector and the shin guards and the mask, loved when they had to wait until I was geared up to start the inning. I miss the way it felt already. I know I will only miss it more and more, until I just forget.

I drive to Denny's house. I don't go in. I just look at it, that front yard where I broke my nose playing football. When Dad would come to pick me up, I always whined, "But we just started having *fun!*" I wanted to play in that yard all night. I'll see Denny when I come home for holidays or weekends, but his life and mine will separate, and we'll know a little bit less about each other every time, until finally we're just giving each other bland updates that are easy to explain in the short time we have together.

I drive to Hardee's, but I don't pull in. It's crawling with people, but I don't want to talk to anybody. Hardee's—the

279

one place that would stay open for us all night. Will I find this quaint eventually? Will I chuckle about the crappy fast-food restaurant with the retarded servers? With the cop who tried to pick up high school kids? With the ditch out back where I saw so many fights? I know that every time I come by here, from now on, I will feel a little bit older, a little bit more displaced, a little more like I don't belong. And eventually I won't come by at all.

I drive to my secret parking spot. How many girls did I bring here? Five? Ten? A dozen? I have a hard time remembering all of them, and this makes me feel horrible, so much that I just drive right by, leaving it behind me, where I hope it stays.

I drive by the plant. I don't stay here long. From the outside, it's just dark and depressing, a labyrinth of cold detachment. The plant will always be the same, no matter who comes in, no matter who comes out.

I drive home. All the lights are off. Everyone has gone to bed. Everything I've ever done, I did here first. My first steps, my first words, my first game of catch, my first kiss, my first masturbation session, my first everything. New places are out there, somewhere, for all the rest of my firsts. I just don't know where they are.

I have one more stop, but for this, I'm gonna need a bike.

I pull the old brown seater with the huge flag out of the shed. It was once way too big for me; now I'm afraid I'll crush it. I haven't brought it out in years. Looking carefully for cars, I pull out of our subdivision and pedal as fast as I can. The wind whips through my hair, and I feel free, I feel like I can ride forever, I feel like I am pedaling for my life, for my past, for my future, for everything that has happened that I can't change, for everything that is coming that I don't know about. It starts to rain, slowly at first, then harder.

On instinct, I jut out my right arm to signal a turn, and I pedal down the lane toward the dam. I struggle up the steep hill, as always, and I arrive. I flip the kickstand on my bike and walk to the fence that protects, poorly, passersby from falling into the nonexistent rapids below.

And it's then that I see—like a mirage or a figure from a dream—*her* sitting there, on a blanket, with a bottle of wine, wind flapping through her hair, smoking a cigarette, shivering slightly. I rub my eyes. When I open them again, somehow, she's still there.

"Hey, assface," Helena says. "I knew I'd see you here tonight. What took you so long?"

39.

Without realizing it, I'm sitting next to her.

I'd forgotten I'd told her about this place. I am without words. So is she. We sit there and watch Lake Paradise shimmer in silence. After about five minutes, I take off my jacket and put it over her shoulders.

"Thank you," she says.

"You're welcome," I say.

The night is flawless. We hear crickets in the distance, big rigs flying by on the road behind us, a fish occasionally leaping out of the water and heading back down again, life going on, whether we're here or not.

Helena is sitting right next to me. Helena is sitting right next to me.

"Helena," I say, and she turns her head slowly toward me, knowing that someone had to speak eventually but disappointed anyway that the silent reverie had to end.

"Yes?" she says.

"Did you really mean what you said? Did you really never care for me?"

Helena stifles a laugh. "What, are you kidding?" she says. "Of course not. I was just trying to make you go away."

"Good," I say. "Because I really liked you."

"I know. I really liked you too."

We hear a moo from a farm nearby. It starts to rain again, but neither of us moves.

"Are you ready to go tomorrow?" she asks.

"I think so," I say. "Dad packed the truck up for me and Jessica on Friday. Neither of us has much, and the dorms are really small anyway, so it didn't take very long."

"That's not what I meant," she says.

"I know," I say. "But I don't really know the answer to your question. I mean, I *guess* I'm ready. But I feel like the person I am tomorrow is going to be an incredibly different person from who I am right now, and I don't really like that feeling."

Helena lights a cigarette. "I don't think that's true, Tim," she says. "You are always you. You could put you in China, and you'd still be a dumb jock."

"And you'd still snore."

"Yeah." She laughs. "But you know what I mean. This isn't that big of a deal, you know. People do this all the time. It's just your turn."

Just my turn. Something about that makes me feel better. Everyone goes through heartbreak. And separation, and displacement, and confusion, and the aching suspicion that they have no idea what they're doing—at all. *It's just my turn.*

A mosquito buzzes around Helena's head, and she tries unsuccessfully to swat it away. I start to help her and eventually catch it in my fist. I open my palm and look at it, already sucking blood from my hand. When I was a kid, I used to squeeze the flesh around where a mosquito was feeding until it overdosed on blood and exploded. It's a neat trick. But now I just watch him.

"What's gonna happen to you?" I say.

Helena takes a sip of her wine. The bottle is already empty, and I realize she really has been here for a while. "I don't know," she says. "Stay here with my mom, try to find another job. My mom's friend says there's an opening for a secretary at her law firm, and I think that would be good for me. I look good in business suits. And I'm thinking of maybe taking some classes at Lake Land. It's cheap, and Mom said she'd help out. I could be, I dunno, a paralegal or something."

I don't know what a paralegal is, but I like the idea of Helena in a law firm. I know somehow she'll be the smartest person there. I know she'll be running the place in five years.

And I know she'll be okay.

"I missed you," I say.

"I missed you too," she says. She takes my hand in hers. We don't look at each other. We just look at the calm lake.

She stands up. I start to stand with her, but she puts her hand on my shoulder. "No. I just wanted to see you before you left. You stay. It's time for me to go."

I find myself welling up, something I promised myself I'd never do. I fight it off. And she's right. It's time to go. This is how it has to happen.

She bends down and kisses me on the forehead. "Be safe, Tim," she says.

I start to say something; I start to tell her that she's wonderful, that my life is different somehow for having had her in it. I start to tell her that I think she's amazing. I start to tell her that I'll never forget her. I start to tell her something, anything. But she's already down the hill, to her car, to whatever awaits her.

And I sit there. I look at the dam. Water is starting to spill over the edge. The rain has finally allowed it to serve its purpose. I watch the flow of water slide down the concrete and form tiny pools below. It is gorgeous.

40.

Jessica's dad has a cold. He looked perfectly fine yesterday, but now he's hacking up a lung. My mother, forever the nurse, tries to help him, give him a Kleenex or an Advil or something, but he shakes his head and says he's fine, yes, yes, he's fine, just the changing of the seasons.

Denny came out to the house for takeoff, and he is sitting on the roof of the moving truck, his legs swaying left to right, fidgeting with his hands. Doug is smoking a cigarette next to the truck. Erika is with him. She looks poised and strangely comfortable here. She even helped us carry some final boxes.

Dad closes the back door of the truck, claps the latch, and locks it. "All right," he says. "Looks like we're all set here. We better hit the road. That place is gonna be nuts tonight."

As if on cue, my mom starts crying. Dad tells her to knock it off, save it for later, you're coming *with* us, for crying out loud. Jessica's dad walks over to me. "You have my number," he says. He takes my hand and shakes it, with a firm grip and eye contact. He then turns to Jessica, who bursts into tears.

"Oh, Daddy," she says. "I'm gonna be home all the time, okay?" He nods, and she buries her head in his shoulder. He is attempting to be stoic, but his bottom lip is vibrating. Jessica wails.

I walk over to Doug. "When I come back here, I want that gut gone, okay?" I say, and he mock-punches me in the stomach.

"You're lucky I don't give you another fat lip," he says. He also takes my hand and shakes it, but that's not enough for me right now, and I pull him into one of those uncomfortable hugs that brothers have done for generations. I look at Erika and tell her to keep an eye on this punk, and even though I meant it as a joke, she nods and says, "I will. Good luck to you, Tim." Denny comes over and reminds me he'll be in Champaign in a couple of weeks, so make sure the beer's cold. I shake his hand, and he smiles.

Jessica won't let go of her father, so he wiggles out of her embrace and takes her head in his hands and looks her in the eye.

"Everything's going to be fine here, all right?" he says. "You just worry about what you have to do up there." She nods through the tears, then turns to me and wipes her eyes with her palms. "Okay," she says. "I'm ready."

"Me too," I say. My mom pulls herself up into the passenger seat of the truck, and Dad starts to walk toward the driver's side. Then he stops and looks at me.

"How about you drive?" he says. He tosses me the keys, and I catch them because, as I've said time and time again, I can catch anything you throw at me.

ACKNOWLEDGMENTS

Whenever I've read acknowledgments pages, I've always been surprised how the book's editor is the first person thanked, before parents, wives, or even angry creditors. Now that I've gone through this whole process, anyone who doesn't thank their editor first deserves to be shot. Kristen Pettit at Razorbill is the *lone* reason you're holding this book in your hand (or your feet, or whatever). Her faith in this project exceeded my own every step of the way; she picked me up when I lost hope, steered me back on track when I inexplicably wrote dozens of pages about Albert Pujols—and even gave me restaurant recommendations. It would be impossible for an editor to do more unless they somehow grew a second head. Thanks are also due to my agent, Kate Lee, at ICM, who supported me even though I didn't know how to blog.

My fellow editors at The Black Table (blacktable.com)—A. J. Daulerio, Aileen Gallagher, and Eric Gillin—graciously picked up the slack at our site while I was busy typing this whole thing up. It has been a difficult year for the Leitch family, but we have stuck together and are stronger for the experience (my sister, Jill, gets bonus points for reminding me of the rules of euchre). And of course my Shari Goldhagen: I am honored beyond comprehension to be your teammate. (Go. Team.)

The following people were much helpful in helping me hammer out the final manuscript of this thing; their kind words and suggestions talked me down off the ledge several times: Amy Blair, Mandie DeVincentis, Denny Dooley, Matt Dorfman, Jason Fry, David Gaffen, Tim Grierson, Jen Hubley, Andy Kuhns, Greg Lindsay, the Registered Rep crew, Patrick Cadigan, Matt Pitzer, Sue Rosenstock, Erin Schulte, and R. A. Miller.

And to my beloved cat Wu-Tang, who went to that litter box in the sky while this book was being written. (All told, it was the dangling participles that did him in.)